Grimm Aut

Danielle Ackley-McPhail	Gail Z Martin
Diana Bastine	*Larry N. Martin* (signature) Larry N. Martin
Danny Birt	Bernie Mojzes
Dustin Blottenberger	Christine Norris
James Chambers	Jody Lynn Nye
Elaine Corvidae	David Lee Summers
Kelly A. Harmon	Jean Marie Ward
Jonah Knight	Jeff Young

Gaslight & Grimm: Steampunk Faerie Tales

edited by
Danielle Ackley-McPhail
and Diana Bastine

eBooks
Stratford, NJ

PUBLISHED BY
eSpec Books LLC
Danielle McPhail, Publisher
PO Box 493,
Stratford, New Jersey 08084
www.especbooks.com

ISBN (trade paper): 978-1-942990-31-4
ISBN (ebook): 978-1-942990-32-1

Art Direction: Mike McPhail, McP Digital Graphics

Copyeditor: Greg Schauer
Interior Design: Sidhe na Daire Multimedia
                www.sidhenadaire.com

Dedication

To Sadie Rae Remchuk
my tough little faerie tale princess

Contents

In Wolf's Clothing

based on Little Red Riding Hood

JAMES CHAMBERS

"I APPRECIATE YOUR INDULGENCE. TRADITION MUST BE OBSERVED WHEN dealing with my grandmother." Despite all the time Madame Marceline Rene spent in New Alexandria, her Parisian accent remained strong.

"I have no quarrel with tradition," Morris Garvey said, "only with cold mornings on rough seas."

"You think a coach would've been faster, smoother, and warmer," Marceline said. "But a journey across water clears the mind and cleanses the soul."

"I suppose there are worse places to be than on Paumanok Sound in January."

Morris shivered and rubbed his gloved hands together. He eyed the whitecaps biting the Sound like gnashing teeth on which the modest ship heaved and rocked. Far beyond the craft's wake stood the New Alexandria skyline and the Middle Borough Bridge slowly resolving into clarity as the rising sun burned away the morning fog. Seagulls hung aloft on the wind. A whistle blew. The ship jolted against the edge of a dock, and then the engines in its belly grumbled and hissed, working to steady it while two crewmembers leapt off with ropes to tie it in place. Once the ship was secure, Morris offered Marceline his hand as she stood; it was a gesture of etiquette rather than necessity because Morris could not think of a time he had ever seen her even a hair off-balance.

"Was the journey so bad you would prefer to have shortened our time together?" she said.

"Spending less time with you is never my preference. But if you want time together we could've simply spent the day in my labs."

"Leaving my poor, sick grandmother all alone in the woods." Marceline shifted the satchel slung from her shoulder; she had not removed it all morning.

"If by 'all alone' you mean tended by a staff of thirty-five and by 'woods' you mean her twenty-six room summer mansion, well, then, yes, I guess that's true."

All mirth fled Marceline's expression. "There will be plenty of time in the lab on other days, but I'm afraid time is no longer bountiful for my grandmother." She descended a gangplank dropped in place by the crew and stepped onto the dock.

Chagrined, Morris hesitated, watching the crew unload crates of supplies bound for the estate and then joined Marceline. "I'm so sorry. I shouldn't make jibes when your grandmother is ill. I'm completely at your service. Anything I can do to help you and your family, all you have to do is ask. I have all the time in the world for you."

"Do you really mean that?" Marceline asked.

"Of course I do." In light of all he and Marceline had done for each other over the last few years, the question surprised Morris. Marceline's expression hinted, though, that there was something deeper in the asking than a need for mere reassurance.

"Thank you," Marceline said. "My grandmother must meet you under the proper circumstances. Lifting her spirits will help her condition. Perhaps even buy her a few more days or weeks. Our family's ways may be odd, but I won't be the one to cast them aside."

"What ways are those?"

"Some things must be experienced rather than explained." Marceline smiled and held Morris's arm. "You and I don't know how things might one day work out between us, but I wouldn't want us to wind up together without my grandmother's blessing, and she won't give that unless we show her it's deserved."

Morris raised an eyebrow. "Ah, that sounds perhaps a bit... *premature*."

"Don't be frightened," Marceline said. "I know all too well I've got competition for your heart. But losing Michel taught me there are things in this world you must not wait to do if you're ever to do them. Michel and I put off far too much in the life we were to have together—and when he died, it all perished unrealized. During the other night's incident at the opera, we both brushed with death—and I won't learn that lesson twice. I'm not asking you for a commitment, but if we are to have a future together, it must be with my grandmother's approval and so I must do this now. If one day we go our separate ways then this will have been only time spent between lovers. Besides, it's good for you to get out of that witch-infested enclave of a city once in awhile."

"That's *my* city you're perjorating," Morris said.

"Oh, yes, forgive me, I know." In a taunting singsong voice, Marceline said, "Morris Garvey, inventor of steampowered chimney sweeps, founder of Machinations Sundry, technological genius, and New Alexandria's favorite son. The man is the city, the city is the man."

"Don't believe the hype. I don't," Morris said. "Besides, only downtown is infested with witches. Really it's only one neighborhood — and they're not all bad once you get to know them."

"As you've come to know their queen?"

Morris tensed. He was tempted to tell Marceline that Anna Rigel, the Queen of New Alexandria's witches, had not spoken to him for three weeks after his latest failure to live up to her expectations, but he knew no reply was best whenever it came to women Marceline perceived as her rivals. Awkward silence hung between them until one of the attendants, Mr. Bucheron — a mute, hulking man nearly seven feet tall — brought their overnight bags and ushered them along the dock.

"In Paris, at least, people once knew that the best way to deal with witches was at the stake," Marceline said.

"If I didn't know you well enough to recognize your sarcasm I'd be horrified," Morris said.

Marceline cast Morris a simmering look over her shoulder. "Perhaps you overestimate how well you know me."

Morris laughed, but his voice transformed into a cry of alarm as Marceline took the first step down from the dock and the plank twisted beneath her foot. She stumbled and thrust out a hand to steady herself. Morris latched onto it, stopping her fall and tugging her back onto solid wood. In the process, though, she yanked him off balance and forced him to jump from the side of the dock to avoid falling off face first. He landed up to his chest in frigid water, stumbled on slippery rocks, and went under. The cold shocked him. He gasped by reflex, and the taste of sea salt flooded his mouth. He burst to the surface, coughing and pushing water from his face. A pounding wave broke against his back and shoved him under a second time as the powerful undertow clutched his feet from beneath him. He stayed under for several seconds before he regained his footing and surfaced. The wind howled around him, and his ears rang. Marceline shouted orders. Mr. Bucheron and the crew scrambled down from the dock to help Morris onto the rocky beach.

He knelt there, arms wrapped across his chest, a trembling and icy mass of needling aches.

"Listen...to that...my teeth...are actually...chattering...," he managed to say.

"Take him to the huntsman's shack. Hurry!" said Marceline.

Mr. Bucheron tugged Morris to his feet. With the help of the crew and Marceline at his side, Morris followed a winding, uphill path through the woods to a little building on a bluff overlooking the Sound. The men rushed Morris inside and deposited him on a day bed in the main room. The place stood dark and quiet, unused for some time. Morris hoped it had a fireplace, but he did not see one. Marceline dismissed the crew, shutting the door after them to block out the wind. She stepped to a brass-and-steel console on the wall and ran her fingers over a series of knobs and dials, working them with practiced efficiency. Morris tried to grasp the purpose of the mechanism, but the cold numbed his mind as much as his senses. Dark spots dappled the edges of his sight. Somewhere below him an unseen beast roared, and then Marceline whirled from the console, rushed across the room, and peeled Morris out of his dripping wet coat. She stripped off the rest of his sodden clothes and piled them on the floor.

"What...are you doing?" Morris asked.

"Trying to stop hypothermia. You won't get warm in wet clothes."

"Must...get warm...of course..."

Morris lay back on the day bed, and the world misted out of focus for a moment—or several moments, Morris could not tell. When it came clear again, he found himself awash in a soothing blast of hot air. It poured down from an array of brass vents that resembled showerheads mounted in the ceiling. Morris heard the dim *thump-pum, thump-pum, thump-pum* of a steam engine working somewhere in the building and realized the roar he had heard had been a furnace firing to life. One by one, his senses awakened. Late-morning sun flowed in through dusty windows. Softness and warmth suffused him. He was snugged under an animal skin with Marceline's naked body pressed firm on top of his, her arms and legs embracing him. Her cinnamon-scented breath drifted across his nose.

"Show me your hand," she said.

"...what?" Morris asked.

"Your *hand*." Marceline grabbed Morris's right hand and drew it from under the skin. "Your fingertips were blue. Your lips too." She paused and brushed his mouth with a kiss; her lips felt like hot embers. "They look fine now. Can you feel anything?"

Morris lifted the edge of the skin and glanced at Marceline's pale flesh.

"I can feel everything," he said.

Marceline blushed. She slid out from under the skin, let it fall back onto Morris, and scurried out of the room. "Then you're warm enough you don't need me."

Marceline returned wrapped in a vibrant red hooded cloak clutched tight around her. Her high cheeks glowed deep pink from windburn, her dark hair hung in wild curls, and her eyes flickered with intensity. Morris could not look away from her. The heat in his body was her heat, shared to preserve his life. He had saved her, and she had saved him. It was not the first time; he knew instinctively it would not be the last. *Perhaps Marceline is right and we do belong together*, Morris thought. He sat up, drawing the skin around his torso. Marceline flopped into a wing-backed chair covered with fabric in an ornate *fleur-de-lis* pattern. She adjusted the satchel, again slung from her shoulder, and exhaled.

"It was clumsy of me to trip like that on the dock," Marceline said.

"You've never had a clumsy day in your life," Morris said.

Marceline's expression sharpened; by chance, Morris had struck a nerve.

Hoping to soften her irritation, he said, "It was only a loose board. If you weren't so distracted worrying about your grandmother, I'm sure you would've seen it."

"Well, you looked quite dashing pulling me back from the brink."

"Not so much pulling myself back though." The shack, dark and cold when they arrived, now brimmed with light and heat. Delicate pipes and vents spider-webbed the floors and walls, all cleverly placed to be unobtrusive, yet, from what Morris saw, masterfully designed for efficient distribution of energy. "What is this place?"

"The huntsman's shack from back when my family kept game and hosted hunts. I took it over and made it livable. It's quiet, warm, and you can see the water. It's my refuge when I come here. I've made it almost entirely self-sufficient."

"You did it all?"

"Planned and built it myself."

"I'd say I'm impressed, but then I expect no less from you."

"I should hope so," Marceline said. "Which in itself is high praise coming from the brilliant Morris Garvey."

Seeing Marceline was not teasing him, Morris smiled and rubbed the animal skin between his thumb and forefinger. "What is it?"

"Wolf."

"Damn big wolf." The skin reached from his shoulders to his ankles, its gray hair streaked with black and white. "Haven't been any wolves around here for a century or more."

"It came from France. It's very old, part of history. It's been in my family for many generations."

Tingling warmth gathered inside Morris, replacing the cold vacating his body.

"You've heard the tales of the *loup garou*?" Marceline asked.

Morris nodded. "Lycanthropy."

"Would you believe me if I told you that wolf skin was taken from one?"

"I might if I believed in fairy tales. The *loup garou* is a legend," Morris said.

"There's a kernel of truth at the core of every legend. It's the thing that makes them immortal, isn't it? What makes us pass them on to our children and grandchildren. It's as if the characters in the stories urge themselves upon us so they can live as long as we remember their tales."

"Facts suit me better than stories," Morris said.

"In stories, the *loup garou* is a monster because he is a man who becomes a wild animal, but humans and animals are not so different—except that few animals are capable of true evil. They are only animals, after all. They do what they must to survive and to protect their young. There's great honor in the life of a wolf, like the path of honor my family has followed for generations. The *bad* wolf—the lone wolf in the stories—that wolf is a true monster; that wolf lives only for himself and his hunger, and has no idea of his sin until he hurts or destroys the thing he loves."

"Are you trying to tell me your family is a family of…werewolves?"

The tingling sensation of returning warmth became a burning heat Morris relished at first but which soon distracted him. To his raw senses every smell intensified, every sound amplified. The scent of Marceline's skin and breath nearly overwhelmed him, and he ached to touch her hot flesh again. Yet at the same time, he felt dizzy and sleepy as if coming down with the flu.

Marceline laughed. "No. But magic exists in the world, does it not? So why not the *loup garou*? Or at least some sense of it?"

She stood and paced around the room. Her cloak opened and closed, revealing then hiding her nude figure beneath it. Morris stalked her with his eyes. Desire surged inside him; a primal and ferocious wanting rose from a place deep in the ancient foundations of his being, in the parts of his soul that echoed with inchoate memories of savagery. He perceived Marceline as the only woman in the world, and his existence depended on possessing her.

He resisted the urge to take her in his arms. "A man cannot become a wolf."

"Perhaps not in body, not anymore in this age of reason, at least. But what of the spirit? Shamans of the native peoples of this land believe that men may take on the attributes of their totems — of eagles, crows, and coyotes. Couldn't magic do that? Transform us to take on aspects of an animal?"

"I don't know...." Morris said.

He hated feeling confused and disoriented. He was usually three steps ahead of everyone else in the room, but Marceline, at least his equal in intellect, often surprised him. She knew how to knock him off kilter and keep him there. *In more ways than one*, he thought as he watched the edge of the red cloak flap and fall, exposing flashes of her long, bare legs. A bead of sweat trickled down his brow. He felt feverish, yet a chill ran through him. He pulled the wolf skin closer. Marceline entered a patch of shadow across the room — and she emerged from it altered. Thinner, more limber, her movements quicker — her face softer, smoother.

Younger. She looks younger, Morris thought.

It was a dizzying alteration: Marceline, ten years older than Morris, now looked almost childlike, standing in a shaft of sunlight. The cloak swirled around her supple, confident body, and yet she looked as pure and fresh as a maiden. Morris struggled to make sense of what he saw. He wondered if all this sprang from the last dream of a drowning man — but he burned far too hot to still be in the water.

His eyes fixed on Marceline's satchel, which she had not let out of her sight once.

He pointed at it. "What's in there?"

Marceline knelt and opened the flap. Her hands trembled.

She seemed apprehensive coming so close to him — as if he frightened her — but Morris did not understand why. Only a few minutes ago she had placed her entire body against his. *But that was before she changed, before she put on the red cloak.* He looked into the satchel, full of little foil-wrapped boxes and bundles wrapped in silk and tied with ribbons, as well as crystal bottles, their stoppers sealed with wax, their bodies sheathed in velvet swatches. The scent of spices wafted out.

"Delicacies and medicines for my grandmother. My mother sent them from Paris and entrusted me to deliver them. She warned me not to stray from the path."

"What path?"

"The path to Grandmother's house."

Marceline snapped the satchel closed, straightened, and left the room.

Morris waited on the daybed, uncertain what to do or think. His body shook with growing heat, and he felt like he was floating out of himself. He wished he was back in the city, surrounded by its rush and tumult, deep in one of his labs, his employees snapping to carry out his orders, and his equipment responding to all his manipulations with precision and predictability. His situation improved little when Marceline returned wearing a red velvet winter dress, high boots, a scarf, and gloves beneath her cloak; the satchel remained strapped from her shoulder. She carried Morris's freshly dried clothes to the daybed and dumped them beside him, everything except his hat, coat, and gloves.

"Get dressed. They're dry. I have a drying device in the other room."

"What about my coat?"

"Wear the wolf skin." Marceline took a bronze clasp from a pocket in her cloak and tossed it atop the pile of Morris's clothes. "It's time I was on my way to Grandmother's."

Morris dressed without letting the wolf skin break contact with his body, afraid to slip out of its warmth. The door clicked and bumped and in rushed a cold gust of wind. He looked up from buttoning his pants to find Marceline gone. Her absence stirred in him a ferocious need to hunt her. He rushed into the rest of his clothes and secured the wolf skin with the clasp. His belt and the leather kit of tools he carried with him lay on the bed. He almost left them, thinking they would be useless for hunting, but a deeper, suddenly irritating part of himself insisted he pick them up and fasten them around his waist. He did so, and then he dashed out the door.

He sniffed Marceline's scent from the wind and raced into the woods.

Morris ignored the path, feeling more at ease moving among the bare trees and the brittle winter remains of the brush. The sun and the wolf skin warmed him until the old pines that populated part of the woods cut off the sun's rays. In the shadows, he relaxed; the gloom favored his

hunt. He inhaled a deep breath through his nostrils. He smelled Marceline, heard her not far away. He could cut across the woods and head her off. He ran until he reached a good hiding place along the path, and there he listened to her approach. Her aroma set his mouth watering, his pulse throbbing. She would never see him coming. He could rip the cloak from her body, tear through her dress, and feed the hunger grinding inside him.

Morris stepped back from his hiding place.

What am I doing? I don't want to hurt Marceline.

He touched the clasp holding the wolf skin around his shoulders.

It felt hot, and its touch alarmed him, but he could not decipher why, except that somehow it and the skin were avatars of the animal instincts that had taken over his mind. He remind himself that he was not a wolf but a man—one of reason and intelligence, one in control of himself—but he could not recall his name or where he came from. *The woods have always been my home.* But he knew that was not true. He sifted through hazy memories of a place filled with shining metal and glass, with light, and the noise of work and electricity, with voices and power, a place where the world made sense, but it did not expel the repulsive urges rising inside him, nor suppress the lure of the wild existence that called to him. The struggling, questioning part of him wanted to undo the clasp and shrug free of the wolf skin, but then Marceline appeared on the path, and the sight of her ended all Morris's uncertainty.

The red hood covered Marceline's head, its fabric a splash of blood against the gray winter light. Every step closer Marceline took electrified Morris. She looked so vulnerable, so young and untouched by the world. He relished her tenderness even as a faint voice deep inside his consciousness warned him this too was wrong. Marceline was neither weak nor fragile, nor was she an innocent child; she was strong, forceful, intelligent, and wise. She was a woman of the world, not the girl approaching him—and yet, at the same time, she *was* that girl. A girl Morris found irresistible. Then Marceline reached his hiding place, and he had no more time to think.

Morris stepped onto the path and blocked her way. Only his caution at taking her in plain sight on the path held him back from attacking.

Ignoring an urge to growl, Morris said, "Where might you be going, young lady?"

The words sprang from Morris's lips as if on cue; he had no choice but to speak them.

Marceline halted and jumped back. "Great wolf, you startled me!"

"I'm so sorry," Morris said. "Please accept my sincere apology. I saw you from the woods and only wondered if you realized how dangerous this path is for a child to walk alone. If you tell me where you're going, perhaps I can help you get there safely."

"Thank you for the kind offer. I'll be safe enough if I stay on the path. I've walked it many times. I'm only going to my grandmother's cottage at the edge of the woods. Maybe you know it?"

Morris inched closer to her. "Why, yes, I do. Along my way here, I happened by it, and I noticed that your grandmother's woodpile is down to sticks and twigs. You'd be a very fine granddaughter if you brought her some firewood. There's plenty around here to be gathered."

Marceline scanned the woods on either side of the path. "What a wonderful idea! It will please Grandmother so much to have a warm fire." She stepped from the trodden dirt to the brush and snatched up a piece of a deadfall, saying, "Thank you, great wolf."

Morris heard her only from a distance.

The moment she had strayed from the path he dashed into the woods, running hard. He had lied about passing the girl's grandmother's house and its dwindling firewood supply, but if he could reach the end of the trail before her, he could take advantage of Marceline's delay to devour anyone he found in the house and then lie in wait for her.

Why do I want to do that?

Morris darted among the pines — the wolf skin flapping — without answer to the question, acting by instinct. *Not instincts but compulsions, driven by something.*

He skidded to a stop on fallen pine needles. It occurred to him that he had a device that could help him, and he stuck his hand into his belt pack. Inside was a jumble of knobs and edges, none of which felt right. He knew the device must be there; he had built it to — what? To protect him from magic? No, not to protect, not precisely. To warn him? It didn't matter. He had no idea anymore what the tools and gadgets in his kit did. Wolves needed no tools to hunt. He wanted only one thing.

He resumed running and soon reached the edge of the woods, where he found no ordinary dwelling. If indeed its builder intended to construct a cottage, he had constructed the cottage of a king. Scaly with latticed windows and brick and stone flourishes, it rose three stories from the manicured grounds.

That's not right. That's not how the story goes.

Story.

The word clung in his mind. *What story?* Marceline's words echoed in his faltering memory: *There's a kernel of truth at the core of every legend and fairy tale.* Important words but the animal part of him resisted his efforts to figure out why. The wash of input his heightened senses brought drowned reason from his mind. It was simplest to ignore his doubts, trust his instincts.

But they aren't my *instincts, are they?*

He found a door and entered the house. It was silent inside.

Another thing wrong. People should be here, servants.

He smelled only one person: a woman — a scent like Marceline's but different. He followed it up a wide staircase to the second floor, trying to suppress the snarls curling his lips, a passenger in his own body. At the top of the stairs an open door issued the woman's scent. Morris entered the room. With the curtains, a murky gloom clung to the bed chamber. His senses picked up the heat and sound of a woman in the bed.

"Who's there?" she said. "Marceline, is that you? Your mother wrote that you would come. What did you bring me, sweetheart?"

Afraid any attempt to speak would produce a growl, Morris did not answer.

He approached the bed, unable to stay away. The woman in the bed was old, yet her aroma tantalized Morris. Across his mind flashed visions of her skin rent apart, her blood spilled out, his face slicked red with it, and his teeth dripping with gore as he swallowed bits of her flesh — but in the visions, he possessed a wolf's face. He reached out a hand and gripped the old woman's wrist.

"Your hand," the woman said. "It's burning."

Morris snuffled and panted.

The woman sat forward, pushing off her bedclothes. Her eyes widened, and her mouth quivered as she stared into Morris's face. "Are you…still in there? It's easy to get lost. Even the best and purest of men can fall to the temptation. It's happened before — when Marceline was young, before she met Michel. That time it wasn't meant to be. The boy she chose had a good heart but a weak mind, and the woodsman did his duty — as he did it for Marceline's sisters when they chose poorly. Is that how it is for you? Or are you worthy of my granddaughter? Are you a wolf or a man?"

Morris tightened his grip. The woman winced.

Her pained expression startled him. He felt a rush of guilt for hurting her, but he did not let go.

He shoved his other hand into the kit strapped at his waist and rooted around among the tools. They had a use if only he could remember. His fingers scrabbled among them until finally they touched familiar contours. He withdrew the item: a compass. He watched the dial bob and turn until it found north then showed it to the woman before he set it on the bed. Reaching back into his kit, he removed a pocket watch, which he opened and placed beside the compass. Next he found a small wrench, a screwdriver, and a pair of wire snips; he lined each up on the comforter until finally he took out a device slightly larger than the watch, its fine gears visible through a glass face. It glowed with a deep blue light—and then Morris remembered its purpose, how he had conceived of it and built it, and how the first one had been much larger.

He leaned close to the old woman, drank in her scent. In his mind images of animalistic violence clashed with those of blueprints and tools. He left the glowing device on the bed in front of the woman and then released her wrist.

"I'm a man," he said, with a hint of a snarl. "That is a magic detector I invented. We are all under a spell."

"Then do what you must," the woman said with excitement. "Finish the story."

Morris growled. His body tensed. The wolf inside him wanted him to howl, leap onto the bed, and tear into the woman. Instead, he seized her, hoisted her over a shoulder, and carried her to a massive wardrobe in the darkest corner of the room. The woman gasped as Morris lifted her and again when he kicked open the wardrobe doors and stuffed her inside. Pressed among the dresses and gowns hanging in the wardrobe, she looked frail and ghostly, but her eyes flickered with the same intensity as her granddaughter's. Morris closed the door and secured it by tying the handles together with a cord he yanked loose from the window drapes. He slunk back across the room and slipped into the old woman's bed, following the demands of the spell that drove him. His nostrils filled with the woman's scent rising from the sheets, a scent so much like Marceline's it maddened him. His skin seemed to burn with the touch of the fabric and the coarse warmth of the wolf hair. His ears picked up every sound. The old woman's heartbeat. Marceline's footsteps as she approached the front door. He saw into the murky room as if it were daylight.

Marceline's footsteps tapped on the stairs.

She called out, "Good morning, Grandmother! Are you awake? I've brought you some good things to eat and drink, and I've stacked some wood for your fire. Are you there?"

The hallway floor creaked, and then the door opened. Marceline entered the room.

"Grandmother?" she said.

"Over here, dear." Morris tried to disguise his voice in a whisper, but it did not hide the low growl that crept into it. "In bed."

"You don't sound well, Grandmother. Do you have a cough?" Marceline crossed the room. "Why is it so dark in here?"

"Dark?" Morris whispered. "I can see you fine, dear."

"Mother sent you medicine and goodies to eat and drink."

"Eat, yes..." Morris whispered.

"Grandmother?"

Marceline reached the bed.

Morris threw back the bed clothes and grabbed her. He pulled her off her feet, swept her onto the bed, and pinned her against the mattress. The red hood fell from her face, the cloak spread beneath her like a wilting flower, and Morris snarled. He brought his face close to hers and sniffed. Then he ran his nose along her cheek and dared to touch her lips with the tip of his tongue as he inhaled her breath. He stayed there for a time that seemed much longer than it could have been, Marceline staring into his eyes, her expression animated with fear, hope, and anticipation. Then Morris withdrew, slid off the bed, and stood. The story exhausted, he would go no further. He undid the clasp and let the wolf skin fall to the floor. The heat inside him cooled. At the same moment, Marceline slipped free of the cloak and left it on the bed as she rose. She embraced Morris and kissed his cheek. When they separated, she had resumed her normal appearance, her beauty once again etched in the lines and flaws of her true age.

Morris turned his back to her and gathered his tools. "Your grandmother is in the wardrobe."

"Mr. Bucheron, please, if you would," Marceline said.

The enormous man emerged from a darkened alcove clutching a long and weathered axe, which he propped against the wall before he went to untie the cord and let the old woman out of the wardrobe.

Morris glanced at Marceline. "An axe?"

"In case you proved more wolf than man," she said.

Morris raised an eyebrow.

"Don't worry," Marceline said. "He would only yank the cloak from you to break the spell. But the axe is part of the story. It masks his presence from the wolf."

With Mr. Bucheron's help, the old woman got back into bed and pulled the covers to her chest. She looked brighter and stronger, her color heartier, and her breaths came deeper and less forced. She gestured for Marceline to hand her the satchel.

"Show me what gifts my daughter sent me."

Marceline set the satchel on the bed and undid the flap. Her grandmother plucked out one of the little wrapped boxes, tore it open, and then took a bite of one of the petits fours inside.

"Delicious! I haven't had any appetite for three weeks, but now I'm starved." She swallowed the rest of the little cake then gobbled down another. "So, this is Mr. Morris Garvey."

"Yes. Morris, please meet my grandmother, Madame Rose Artel."

"Madame Artel, I'd like to say it's a pleasure, but I'm still trying to sort out how I feel about all this—whatever *this* was."

"The cloak and the wolf skin are magic. When used together by a man and a woman who share a sense of true intimacy, they bring a fairy tale to life. Those who play a part in the story then share a little of its immortality."

"We discovered this when I was younger," said Marceline. "For generations, my family has used the magic to test the intentions of suitors. By chance, my older sister used it once when grandmother was gravely ill, and the magic healed her—an unexpected side effect."

"So you brought me here to heal your grandmother," Morris said.

"Don't be thickheaded, Mr. Garvey," Madame Artel said. "I may feel better for awhile, but at my age there's only so much time even magic can buy. Marceline brought you here because she loves you. And you're in love with her, at least a little, or the magic wouldn't have worked."

"You staged all this? The accident? Sent the servants away?"

Marceline nodded. "It was supposed to be me who plunged into the water and you who warmed me back to health. The water really does cleanse the soul, and sharing our body heat to warm you helped to—how do I put this—*catalyze* our intimacy."

"What if I'd attacked you on the path?"

Marceline reached into the satchel and produced a small revolver. "Mother thinks of everything."

Morris sighed. "No axe, but I might've been shot."

"I'm a good shot. I'd only have wounded you."

"I appreciate that. So, Red Riding Hood, the Big Bad Wolf—you mean all that really happened a long time ago, and these items are what's left? I don't know if I can believe that."

"You don't have to. It doesn't matter if it's real. It works. My family has used it for centuries to test the honor of our suitors."

"You, Mr. Garvey, are a most honorable wolf," Madame Artel said. "I should be most pleased to welcome you into our family should I happen to still be breathing when you and my granddaughter decide to stop wasting time and get on with your lives together. And if I am not, then you have my blessing posthumously."

Morris said nothing. His gaze fell to the wolf skin piled on the floor.

"Are you upset with me?" Marceline asked.

Morris shook his head. "I told you I'd do anything to help your grandmother and your family, and I meant it even if I didn't understand what I was doing. It's only that—well, you put your life as well as your grandmother's and mine in my hands. You put an awful lot of faith in me."

Marceline smiled and shook her head. "It was not faith. I knew you would not disappoint me."

"You've been wrong before," Morris said.

Marceline's smile flattened and she nodded. "True."

"Then I wonder, after all, who is really the wolf in this tale?"

𝔚𝔥𝔢𝔫 𝔓𝔦𝔤𝔰 𝔉𝔩𝔶

Based on The Three Little Pigs

CHRISTINE NORRIS

"GET THIS BLOODY THING MOVING, LIEUTENANT NELSON. *NOW!*"

The captain's furious tone caused the pilot's face to turn white, his hand shaking only slightly as he raised it in a salute.

"The *Athena* has left. We were supposed to be beside her. And yet, Mr. Nelson, we are still in port. Why is that, Mr. Nelson?"

Nelson tried not to let the captain see him flinch, but was unable to hide his anxiety. The captain narrowed her eyes—he was a seasoned pilot, and she was not his first commander. *Why is he anxious now? Because, like the rest of them, he has heard the stories. Perhaps it is better that way*, the captain thought. If she was feared she wouldn't have to fight to be respected.

"I am trying, Captain. The balloon is full, but we've only just lit the furnaces, and you know how long it takes for the steam to get to the engi—"

"I did not ask for excuses, Mr. Nelson. I asked for results. Or did you miss this morning's meeting? Were your ears full of wax when the admiral read the intelligence report? "

Nelson swallowed deeply and shook his head.

"I thought not. If we are not underway in precisely five minutes, I will have you removed from duty. Permanently."

The captain did not think it was possible, but Mr. Nelson's face turned even paler. He understood the captain's meaning perfectly, the threat undiminished by either her size or age.

"Yes, ma'am. Five minutes to launch."

Captain Nightingale did not even acknowledge the pilot's assent before she turned on her heel, her anger evident in the set of her shoulders and her determined stride. She knew Nelson was doing his best. Her fury was not due to anything the pilot had or had not done, only her frustration. She had been assigned to this ridiculous vessel, and now, on her first assignment, she was stuck in port, struggling to get this hulk of an antique moving.

The rest of the bridge crew kept their eyes glued to their maps and dials. They must have overhead the captain's verbal assault on the pilot and did not want to be next.

Good. Saves me the trouble of yelling at them. The captain perched on the edge of her seat, but her body was not yet ready to be still. Her foot tapped out a steady beat, her fingers drumming on the armrest of her cushioned, velvet-upholstered chair, the beat of her heart resounded by the hum of the engines below. If sheer will could be used at fuel, this ship would have taken off long ago and flown faster than even the engineers could imagine. Patience had never been her strong suit. This first assignment wasn't much—just a reconnaissance mission—but she had already botched it by not sticking with the *Athena,* her partner vessel.

Not that the commander of that vessel had bothered waiting, ruddy blighter.

"Three minutes to launch." The announcement came over the loudspeaker, echoed by the pilot's voice on the bridge. He glanced at the captain, his face pulled tight with anxiety, which was only slightly relieved by the captain's nod of approval.

"There's an...incoming message, Captain." The wireless operator's voice cracked, and he did not turn to acknowledge her. Nightingale's stomach knotted with dread.

"Who is it, Lieutenant Commander Hemmings?"

"It's..." The operator swallowed. "It's the commodore, ma'am."

"I see." The knot in her belly turned into a stone, dragging her down. Still, she pulled her shoulders back and lifted her chin. "Patch him through to the loudspeaker, please." She balled her hands into fists and jammed them into her thighs, bracing herself. "No, wait. I'll take it personally."

Lieutenant Commander Hemmings nodded. He flipped a switch on the wireless console, and a green light lit up on the ornate wireless receiver, which sat on the arm of the captain's chair. Captain Nightingale lowered herself onto the seat, her spine straight as a bar of steel. She cleared her throat, and then lifted the polished dark wood and brass of the handset to her ear. There was a loud click and a bit of static.

"Captain Nightingale." She tried to announce herself with as much confidence as she could muster, and hoped her nerves did not show.

"Petunia! What are you waiting for, an engraved invitation? Or can't your crew get that beast into the air?"

Captain Nightingale bristled at the sound of her brother's brash voice as it assaulted her eardrum. "We are already underway." She hoped her voice did not betray the small lie. It wasn't the first time she had been less than truthful with him—they were siblings, after all—but now she was also lying to a superior officer. *Superior in his own mind, at least.*

"By the time you get here, the mission will be over. Or is that your plan, little sister? Are you afraid you can't live up to your own reputation? I told Command there was no use in having a woman as a captain."

There was a sly, gloating edge to his words with which Petunia was very familiar. If it had been any other officer, she would have kept her cloak of dignity and professionalism wrapped around her. Of course, if it had been any other officer, they wouldn't have spoken to her in that manner. But her façade of control dissolved like wet paper, anger filling her chest and spilling over into her mouth.

"Not at all, Commodore *Porky*. First of all, you're not going into battle, you're chasing intel." Her voice was low, her mouth very close to the handset's speaker. "Second, you know that or else you wouldn't have flown off on your own. Or maybe you would have, since you barely passed Strategy at the Academy. But don't you worry. As I have done my whole life, I will be there to save your bacon when you get in over your head."

There was a pause on the other end and Petunia could practically hear the blood rushing to her brother's face, his round cheeks turning the color of ripe apples. Using the childhood nickname had been going too far. It had slipped out in anger, but she wouldn't take it back. He would only see it as further proof of her weakness.

Her brother's voice came through in a hiss. "Just you remember, little sister, the only reason for your command of that—vessel—is because—"

She never knew what insult he had been ready to hurl at her. A sudden shout cut her brother's rant short, followed by an alarm that blasted through the handset. Her brother's voice was barely audible, as if he were holding the handset away from his mouth as he shouted the order that made her blood run cold.

"Wolves at the door! Battle stations!"

"Paul?" There was no reply. "Commodore Nightingale! What is happening?" There was a loud *thunk* followed by the muffled sounds of

battle preparations. Paul must have dropped the handset. She pressed her ear closer to the earpiece, trying to make out what was going on.

The thunder of running feet. The unintelligible bellowing of orders. And then an explosion.

Petunia yanked the handset away from her head. Sound blasted from the device—a chorus of alarms, shouts, and blood-curdling screams.

"Porky?" Petunia whispered into the radio receiver. She dropped the receiver as if it had burned her skin and jumped to her feet, terror filling her throat like bile.

"Lieutenant Commander Hemmings, get him back!"

The wireless operator tapped frantically on several buttons, making several attempts to hail the *Athena*.

"It's no use, Captain. I can't make contact. It's like their wireless has been disabled."

Petunia choked back the sob that tried to escape from her throat. "Keep trying." She spun toward the pilot.

"Mr. Nelson, we must be in the air. *Now!* All personnel to the ready." She tried to keep her voice steady and authoritative, but was only barely certain she managed it.

Mr. Nelson's head whipped around, his mouth opening to protest. But when he caught the look on the captain's face, his objections withered like grapes in the sun. His jaw set, he slammed his palm against a button on the console.

"Thirty seconds to launch."

Instantly the bridge's lighting went dim. The alarm sounded, blaring throughout the ship. Under their feet, the floor shook, reverberating in response to the firing of the engines. Crew ran about making final preparations. Captain Nightingale paced across the bridge, her mind whirring, both anticipation and fear crawling inside her like insects inside a dead tree.

The fear was for Paul and his crew.

He is a good commander, despite being a know-it-all pain in the ass and a pompous bore. He will keep that ship in the air until... She shook her head, pushing the thought away. He was a fellow soldier, not only her sibling. *It is a great honor to die in battle. If that happens,* Petunia thought bitterly, *it will be just the way he wanted. Glorious.*

The anticipation was because, if she had heard properly, she was going into her first battle. This was her chance to prove herself, to shut up the critics, of which her brother was only one. There were plenty who thought her appointment had been a huge mistake.

The rumbling beneath her feet changed to a higher pitch as the engines revved to launch speed. Mr. Nelson looked over his shoulder.

"Ready to launch, Captain. On your order."

Petunia sat in her chair, gripping the handles to stop her hands from shaking.

"Launch."

The word nearly caught in her throat, erupting from her mouth as a half-bark. The pilot pulled a large brass lever topped by a shiny oak knob.

The ship dropped as it lurched away from the moorings, iron and gears groaning. She's sluggish, Petunia thought, once again cursing the fact she had been stuck with this white elephant. Sunlight fell through the windshield as the ship backed away. The roofs of the town came into view, nestled against the mountainside above, their peaked roofs red and orange in the sun, the wattle-and-daub like burnished gold held together by beams of ebony. Smoke curled from chimneys, lazily drifting toward the sky. Above and below were other ships, merchant and Alliance, tethered to their berths. Free of the port and mountain, the valley opened up beneath them, the river twisting and writhing three miles below. So peaceful and quiet, with no indications anyone knew anything about the battle raging somewhere on the horizon.

Lieutenant Nelson pushed the lever upward and turned the wheel, made of brass that had been polished to a high shine by the repeated grip of countless hands. The port and the town swung away from view as the great metal beast turned to face the open sky.

Petunia stood and faced the windshield, pulling her shoulders back and lifting her chin, ready to face whatever it was that awaited them. The skies were clear as far as she could see. Where was her brother? He had only left ten minutes ago, but his ship was so light and fast, there was no telling the miles he had put between them.

"Ensign Lukacs, how long until we reach the *Athena*?"

The navigator consulted his charts, carefully measuring with a brass compass. Then he studied a small screen embedded into the dashboard in front of him, flashing green dots indicating other ships in the area. "Twenty minutes, at least, *if* we go with all speed."

Twenty minutes. Time shrank faster than a snail covered in salt. Her stomach churned as she watched the mountainside and the town slip away. Petunia flung herself into her velvet-upholstered chair, her youth showing through the cracks of her commander's veneer.

Damn this slowness! The *Persephone* was never meant for battle. This ship—she could not bear to think of it as *her* ship—had started life as a luxury airship, meant for transporting rich passengers on leisurely vacations to far-flung and exotic lands. It was covered in shiny brass and dark oak, with velvet curtains and crystal chandeliers—or, at least, it had been until its conversion. The war had been long, with many ships lost. The Wolf Brigades made the skies too dangerous for luxury cruises, and so the *Persephone* had been pressed into service.

Much of her finery had been removed, replaced with guns and iron and the machinery of war. But the engines remained the same. The ship was so heavy that the newer, lighter engines would burn out under the stress of her bulk. The wind turbines, like those that made the *Athena* run, had never even been mentioned.

She's a good, sturdy ship, they had told Petunia. *She's enough for you to command, anyway*. When she had graduated from the Academy at the top of her class as the youngest to ever do so and the only woman, Petunia had had high hopes for her future. With the highest possible scores on her command tests, she knew she was destined for great things. But her gender and her age had worked against her, inspiring only jealousy in her fellow cadets and disdain in her superiors. Even the stories of her supposed wild behavior at school—only half of which were true—could not garner her much respect. On the morning she received her official letter informing her of her command, her brother couldn't grant her even a little praise.

"*You* have a command post?" Porky had snatched the letter from her hand across the breakfast table. He skimmed it, his face turning bright red with anger.

"They didn't have a choice. You saw my exam scores. And then there was my practical exam…"

Paul held up a hand. "Please, don't remind me. That little stunt of yours in the flight simulator will hound me until my dying day."

"You? Why you? It was me that did it." She didn't even try to hide her pride.

"Yes, but I am your brother, and it was reckless, therefore I am guilty by association."

Petunia lifted a defiant eyebrow. "It got the job done, didn't it? Here I am, youngest Captain in the Alliance."

Paul *harrumph*ed and skimmed the letter. A smile crept onto his face, and Petunia's stomach dropped like a stone. She knew that look, the smug smile that said he knew something she didn't. He had handed her back the letter and sat back in his chair, still smirking.

"What? What's wrong?" Petunia had scanned the words again, searching for whatever he had seen that she had missed.

"Oh, nothing…" Paul scooped the last three strips of bacon from the serving tray and deposited them on his plate. "I'm sure you'll have great success, *Captain*." He laughed, a haughty sound laced with several snorts, and shoved another strip of bacon into his mouth.

"Leave her alone, Porky." A voice floated into the dining room from the entrance hall, followed by the sound of the front door clicking shut.

Paul spluttered, the bacon nearly choking him. "I told you never to call me that." He wiped his mouth with his napkin, his expression turning dark as storm clouds. "What the hell are *you* doing here?"

The man who appeared in the dining room doorway was tall, with long, lean muscles. His hair was like Petunia's, dark and shiny as raven's feathers. There was scruff all along his chin, and his skin was tanned from being in the sun. Petunia couldn't help but smile at her eldest brother.

"Wilbur!" She raced toward him, arms outstretched, but stopped just before she reached him, her arms falling to her sides and her expression wary and confused. "Why did you come? You know what will happen if they catch you."

Wilbur's blue eyes danced as he wrapped his little sister into one of his patented bear hugs. "Would I miss your big day? You only graduate from the Academy once. And don't worry, I know what would happen. Which is why they won't catch me."

Petunia scrunched her nose in worry. "Yes, but, Wilbur —"

Wilbur!

The thought jarred Captain Nightingale from her memory. *Of course, why didn't I think of it before?* She ran her hands through her hair, leaving the short dark strands swinging around her ears like a curtain. "Mr. Lukacs, are any other ships in the vicinity of the *Athena?*"

The navigator once again consulted his instruments, while Petunia held her breath. "There are no Alliance ships in the area, ma'am."

Petunia ground her teeth together and pushed down her desire to scream. "I did not ask if there were any Alliance ships in the area, Ensign. I asked if there were *any* ships."

Spots of color flushed high on the navigator's cheeks. He licked his lips and hurriedly made a second check.

"Captain, I see…uh…it appears to be a pirate vessel, approximately five minutes south of Commodore Nightingale."

Petunia allowed herself a small smile, hoping she was right. "Can you tell what vessel, Ensign Lukacs?"

He squinted at the console. "*The Sky Dragon,* ma'am."

Captain Nightingale closed her eyes and thanked the Universe. Wilbur was nothing if not predictable. He was always close to home this time of year. "Please open a channel and hail them, Lieutenant Commander Hemmings."

The wireless operator wasn't quite able to stifle the choking sound that erupted from his throat. He recovered quickly, and with a sidelong glance at the navigator that didn't escape the captain's notice, he pressed his headset onto his head and began turning knobs and dials. The wireless sang a scale of electrophonic whining mixed with static. Finally, Hemmings adjusted his microphone and cleared his throat.

"Hail, *Sky Dragon*. This is the Alliance vessel *Persephone*. Do you copy?"

Petunia held her breath, hoping her brother would remember this was her vessel and reply. Seconds ticked by, each excruciating. *C'mon, Wilbur. Answer!* Not only was *The Sky Dragon* closer to Paul's ship, but she was twice as fast as the *Persephone*.

A screech of feedback made Hemmings rip the headset from his skull and drop it on the console. The voice on the other end sounded tinny and small.

"Put it on the intercom, Hemmings, if you please."

It was clear that the lieutenant commander did not please, and if Petunia had to guess she would say that the man also had deep questions about the sanity of his captain. Despite this, he flicked a switch, and the voice turned into a booming tenor that almost made the captain weep with joy.

"I repeat, we copy, *Persephone*. Petunia, is that you?"

The tone of her brother's voice said he knew it was important. She would never have contacted him, certainly never over Alliance channels, otherwise. Her breath, which she hadn't been aware she had been holding, whooshed out.

"It's me, Wilbur."

"What's wrong? Are you all right?"

Petunia inhaled sharply. "I'm fine. It's Por—I mean, Paul. His ship's being attacked by a Wolf Brigade."

"What are you talking about?"

"We had a report, and were dispatched to check on the intel. But it was weak, we didn't expect to find anything. Paul wouldn't wait for me, and flew off on his own. Something's happened, he said something about Wolves just before the radio went dead. We're too far out to reach him anytime soon. Can you go and help him?"

There was no immediate reply, and the pause seemed to weigh a thousand pounds. "He won't want my help, you know."

"I don't *care!* This is our brother, Wilbur! "

A deep sigh ripped through the intercom, echoing around the bridge like a Northern gale. "You're right, as always, little sister. I'm on my way. *Sky Dragon* out."

Petunia opened her mouth to thank him, but the loud click on the other end of the wireless said he was already gone. She closed her eyes and sank back into her chair, the anxiety that had squeezed her chest like a too-tight corset loosening. Wilbur would make it all right, just like he always had. Paul would be furious at her for calling their brother, but if he was still alive, she could live with his anger.

When each of them had turned fourteen, their mother had told them it was time for them to choose their life's path. It had been expected that both sons would choose the military, after family tradition, while Petunia would make her parents proud by becoming a well-respected society wife.

Two of the three had been complete surprises.

Wilbur had run away and become, of all things, a pirate. Their parents hadn't spoken to him since. Petunia's deepest desire had been to go to the Academy. When her mother heard that, she broke into great heaving sobs, calling her, with all her usual drama, the great disappointment of her life. She had tried to disown her only daughter, but Petunia's father had talked her out of it.

Paul, the only one to do as was expected of him, had laughed at his sister's ambition and vowed never to speak to his brother again. Petunia desperately hoped that never was about to arrive sooner than anticipated. She chewed her thumbnail, a childhood worry stone. The waiting was intolerable. She needed to know what was happening!

"Status report, Ensign."

The navigator watched his screen carefully. "We are twelve minutes away from the *Athena*, Captain. *The Sky Dragon* is headed her way. They should reach her in two minutes."

"Any response from Commodore Nightingale on the wireless, Lieutenant Commander Hemmings?"

"Nothing yet, ma'am. I will keep trying."

She looked over at the pilot. "Can we get any more speed out of this piece of...ship?"

"We are at full speed, Captain. If we push her any further, we'll blow the engines."

It wasn't what she wanted to hear. They needed to *move*. She couldn't bear to sit another second, and instead paced across the bridge. The navigator and radio operator hunched their shoulders as she passed, as if preparing for a blow. If Petunia were a betting woman, she would take odds that the crew was wondering if they were about to personally experience the impetuousness that had bestowed her with her reputation. She glued her gaze to the skies outside the expansive front window. A perfect robin's egg blue, traced through with wispy clouds. It mocked her with its serenity.

"We're in periscope range, Captain." The navigator's words had the sharpness required when speaking to a superior officer, but Petunia thought she caught an undercurrent of sympathy. She spun on her heel, barely able to stop herself from running to the periscope platform. The navigator called out the coordinates as she pulled the polished brass tube from the ceiling and flipped up the eyepiece. Slowly she turned, until she caught a flash of movement. She rolled the dial attached to the right side of the scope, and the scene came into focus.

"Holy shit!"

The expletive flew from her mouth, but she could not take it back, as it summed up what she saw through the scope.

Fire. A sea of orange and red flames shot from the bulk of what had once been the *Athena*. The conflagration greedily ate at the hull, and Petunia cursed again. *Stupid, ridiculous construction.* The ship was the newest in airships, designed for speed and built from woven reed-plants soaked in some Alliance-classified compound to make them strong. Nothing more than a giant basket, it was light, propelled by wind turbines attached to the stern. But it had been designed as a gunship, with long-range missiles as her main weapon. It was never intended to go into a dogfight, for the very reason Petunia witnessed now. It was flammable. *And my idiot brother drove right into the middle of it alone. Yet they call me the reckless one...*

The crew ran across the deck, trying to salvage their craft and fend off the enemy. Planes—the Wolf Brigade—buzzed around the *Athena* like flies around fresh carrion. Petunia scanned the boat, hoping to get a glimpse of Paul, but she couldn't make out one crew member from the other. He was probably on the bridge, giving orders. Reluctantly, she turned the scope away from the carnage, looking for *The Sky Dragon*.

There it was. The ship came from the East, plowing ahead, white sails unfurled. The Wolves must have spotted it as well, because the Brigade turned toward it, leaving the battered *Athena* to lick her wounds. Petunia leaned her head against the coolness of the brass, letting the relief wash over her before looking up once more.

Wilbur had an easier time fending off the Wolves than Paul had. His guns were larger, his men pirates who had no trouble using non-Alliance approved fighting tactics. Puffs of smoke rose from *The Sky Dragon's* long guns. Planes went down left and right in brilliant bursts of flame. The pirate ship moved close, hovering above the deck of the *Athena*. Ropes snaked down, spanning the distance between the two vessels. The dark silhouettes of men slid down the ropes. Petunia wondered what Paul's re-action would be when he realized who had come to his rescue. She could just picture his face, and the image made her smile.

The first of Wilbur's pirate crew had just set foot on the deck of the *Athena* when the hull exploded. A cry of alarm and horror ripped from her lungs. She wanted to turn away, but forced herself to look. A huge hole gaped in the side of the ship, low in the hull. Petunia knew the schematics for that ship as well as she knew her own. The munitions store. *Damn.*

On deck, there was no longer any semblance of order as men scattered, trying to escape the flames as the ship's nose pulled toward the green grasses of the valley below. The first time a man threw himself over the side of the burning ship and plummeted toward the ground, it was a shock. After the fourth, it wasn't any easier to watch, but it was no longer surprising. Moisture trapped itself between her face and the eyepiece, and when she wiped it away she found it was her own tears. She was glad her face was hidden from the crew. It wasn't weak to mourn the dead, but in the proper moment.

"How much longer until we're in range to fire, Ensign Lukacs?"

"Three minutes, Captain. Six minutes until we reach them."

Three minutes. The words rang in Petunia's ears, reverberating like a church bell. There was nothing they could do about the Wolf Brigade until they were in range, and this damn ship could not seem to get out of its own way. She watched through the periscope as the battle slid closer at a glacial pace, the whirring of her thoughts making up the speed the engines did not have. What could she do to help them? A world could end in three minutes.

A man appeared on the empty deck of the *Athena*. There was no mistaking that portly physique. *Paul, thank the gods.* He looked hale enough as he made his way to one of the ropes. He made a valiant attempt to haul himself toward Wilbur's ship, but his arms were not up to the monumental task. Petunia gasped as he slipped and slid. He hung in mid-air, twirling like bait in front of the hungry Wolves. Then he started to rise. Petunia adjusted the scope, to focus on her brother's saviors.

Men from both Wilbur's crew and the *Athena* leaned over the side of *The Sky Dragon*, pulling Paul toward them. Her brother looked over his shoulder, and though Petunia couldn't see his face, she knew him well enough she could imagine his expression as he watched his beloved ship burn to ash. She watched him until he clambered over the side of the pirate ship, safe and sound.

Lukacs' voice broke through her thoughts. "It appears the enemy is retreating, Captain."

Petunia turned, her face still plastered to the scope, searching. No offense to the navigator, but she needed to see for herself.

The planes were tiny specks, flying away from the wreckage of the *Athena* as it fell out of the sky. They *did* appear to be retreating, but something felt wrong. Petunia watched them carefully, looking…there it was! The Brigade was regrouping, pulling into the dual-flank attack formation called the Wolf's Bite. She had seen it dozens of times in films they had studied at the Academy. They flew in low, out of sight of the crew. *The Sky Dragon* was a sitting duck.

Petunia's stomach dropped. The pirate ship was well-manned and well-captained, but even it could not hold off a Wolf's Bite.

"Raise *The Sky Dragon*!" Petunia shouted across the bridge. Hemmings set to his task with urgency, his lips tight against the mouthpiece. Seconds ticked by, Petunia holding her breath. The wireless operator turned toward her, his expression grim.

"No reply, ma'am. I'll keep trying."

"Ensign Lukacs, status report."

"One minute until we're in range, four minutes to arrival."

Petunia's heartbeat slammed against her ribs like a trapped bird as she watched the Wolves move in for the kill. She wanted to scream, to warn them to turn around and look behind them. If *The Sky Dragon* could get off a few shots and take down some of the Wolves, it might buy them time.

The hull was hit, several missiles making contact in blooms of orange. *The Sky Dragon* wasn't as delicate as the *Athena*, but it was made of wood. It wouldn't withstand the Wolves' concentrated attack for long.

"Almost in range," Ensign Lukacs announced. "Thirty seconds."

Petunia shook her head. *We will be too late.* Another attack by the Wolves and Wilbur's ship would go down. Fire ran through her veins as she snapped the periscope handles up and marched to the pilot. Without a word to Lieutenant Nelson, she flicked the switch that opened the steam valves as wide as they would go, then grabbed the throttle lever and shoved it up with all her might. The ship jerked, tossing any standing crew onto the floor as it surged forward.

"Captain? What are you doing?" The panic in Nelson's voice did nothing to deter Petunia's actions. "You'll burn up the engines."

"I know what I'm doing, Lieutenant Nelson."

"But Captain Nightingale, I must insist that you—"

"Stand down, Lieutenant. That is an order."

The pilot hesitated, clearly caught between his duty to the ship and his loyalty to his captain. But he took a step back, resignation written across his face. No doubt he mentally composed his testimony for Petunia's court martial. It didn't matter if they discharged her, as long as she saved her brothers. Paul may have gotten himself into trouble, but *she* had sent Wilbur after him. It was up to her to set it right.

She watched the gauges, her eye on the needles and her hand on the throttle. The needle on the airspeed gauge rose, and her heart with it. The ship had finally gotten past its own inertia, cutting through the sky like a blade. Her engines hummed, and she seemed to be saying the same thing that was on Petunia's mind: *Just watch what I can do if you give me a chance.*

She counted in her head—*twenty-eight, twenty-nine, thirty.* The needle on the steam pressure gauge just slipped into the red zone when she slowly pulled back on the throttle. The ship's engines whined as they slowed, and Petunia glanced out the panoramic front window. They were close enough to no longer need the periscope. *The Sky Dragon* drifted only a mile off. The Wolves had bitten her hard. Smoke poured from somewhere in the hull, while fire licked the ship with greedy tongues of flame.

She stepped back from the console. "Lieutenant Nelson, you may return to your post."

"Yes, Captain." Nelson's expression was still troubled, but behind it flickered signs of pride.

"Before I give it back to you, Nelson, I need to know something. We are headed into a fight. Will you be able to follow orders, no matter what they are?"

Nelson pulled his shoulders back, the glimmer in his eye turning into steadfastness. He saluted her. "Yes, ma'am."

"Excellent." She retook her place, but did not sit down. With her feet planted and her arms behind her back, she barked her orders loud and clear.

"Lieutenant Commander Davies."

The tactical officer looked at her, a hungry gleam in his eye. "Yes, ma'am?"

"Fire at will." She turned her attention to the wireless operator. "Mr. Hemmings, any response to our hails?"

"*The Sky Dragon's* put out a distress call, and I have replied. Waiting for a response."

"Keep communications open. Ensign Lukacs, please plot our course to lend aid to the crew of *The Sky Dragon*." The image of the men leaping to their deaths from the *Athena* was etched into her mind like a tintype. She could not bear a repeat occurrence.

One side of Wilbur's ship actively burned. Men leaned over the side with heavy blankets, trying to beat out the flames, but to no avail. The figurehead smoldered, the angel's carved face turning black, her open mouth looking as if she screamed in agony.

The Wolves had swooped in for another attack, their energy focused on the pirate ship. The rat-a-tat of the *Persephone's* machine guns punctuated the air. It was deeply satisfying to see several of the planes explode and spiral toward the earth. Like swatting gnats from the sky.

The Sky Dragon's sails hung in tatters, aflame like the rest of the ship. The ship listed to her port side. Soon she would tip over, or just fall from the sky altogether.

"Get us as close to that vessel as possible, Nelson." She took a breath and continued. "Lieutenant Commander Hemmings, put out the call for all available men to prepare for a rescue operation. Mr. Davies—clear the road, if you please."

The tactical officer leaned close to the flower-shaped end of the speaking tube in front of him and shouted.

"Fire cannons one and three."

There was a small *thwump*, followed by another as the missiles broke free of the long guns mounted two decks below, in what had once been passenger quarters. The Wolves banked hard, but not before half a dozen more had been obliterated.

Outside the window, *The Sky Dragon* loomed large. Petunia didn't need to tell Lieutenant Nelson to keep the *Persephone* high beside the wooden craft. If the balloon caught fire, it would be the end of both ships. Though she couldn't see it, she knew that at this moment her crew opened the side doors, feeding wooden ramps across the empty air between the two vessels. Lieutenant Commander Davies kept his eyes on the enemy. They hadn't bothered to form a Wolf's Bite, flying in loose formation toward the *Persephone,* firing relentlessly. The ship didn't even sway. Their bullets bounced off of the iron hull like a great breath blown at a brick wall.

Petunia smiled as another wave of planes came straight at them, firing bullets that sounded like a heavy rain against the hull.

A voice, muffled, came through the speaking tube beside the wireless operator. He pulled it close to his ear and asked the speaker to repeat.

"Rescue is complete, Captain. All souls safe onboard, and the hatches have been secured."

"Very good. Get us clear, Lieutenant Nelson."

The ship turned to starboard. As the burning *Sky Dragon* slipped from view, *Persephone* turned toward the open sky. They were far from clear — Wolves darted in and out of the clouds, as if taunting them. Or trying to hide.

The door to the bridge burst open, the crystal knob cracking as it banged against the wall. Wilbur and Porky tried to enter at the same time, both getting stuck in the doorway before Wilbur elbowed his way through.

"Petunia! I mean, Captain Nightingale." He stopped and saluted. "How can I thank you for your help?"

Petunia felt her cheeks bloom with blush, and had to stop herself from throwing her arms around her brother. "It's the least I could do, after I asked you to head into danger in the first place. I am so pleased that you and your remaining crew are safe. I am sorry for the loss of your ship, though." She turned to Paul. "And you as well, Commodore. Please accept my condolences on the losses you suffered today."

Paul opened his mouth wide, his face red, then he closed it. He seemed very interested in something on the carpet as he nodded. "Thank you." It was quiet, almost mumbled, but they were words she never thought she'd hear from Paul's mouth.

"You're not angry at me for calling Wilbur?"

He glanced at his brother, then moved closer and spoke low. "I was, but I see now the prudence in it. Good show. I'm sorry, Petunia. Sorry for everything I…said to you. Sorry for not waiting. I put personal pride over protocol. Inexcusable…"

Petunia lifted her eyebrows in shock. She thought hell would be reporting icebergs before she ever heard Porky apologize to her. She took his hand and squeezed it, and that was all that was needed.

"Enemy incoming!"

The tactical officer's pronouncement shattered the peace of the moment. Petunia jumped back into commander mode, every nerve ending tingling. Paul stepped toward the captain's chair, then hesitated and nodded to his sister.

"Your ship, Captain."

The remains of the Wolf Brigade, roughly a third of the planes that had begun the battle, gathered in the distance. They flew in tight formation, their trajectory headed straight for the bow of the *Persephone.*

This was no Wolf's Bite.

It was a suicide mission.

"Lieutenant Commander Davies, aim all of your weapons, every last gun on this ship, at the center of the pack. Do not fire until I give the command."

The tactical officer consulted with the navigator, then muttered instructions and coordinates into the speaking tube. Paul tugged on her shoulder.

"Petunia, you can't win. We've already lost two ships, and you are alone out here. Live to fight another day."

Petunia pulled back and looked him straight in the eye.

"And give them time to gather strength? Not on your life. I will send them back with their tails between their legs, if they get back at all. Lieutenant Nelson, half-speed ahead."

The *Persephone* sailed forward, on a direct course with the Wolves. If the Brigade had any indication they were being challenged, they did not show it, because they continued their charge. The planes loomed closer — they were well within range, and yet Petunia held her order.

"Captain, we need to pull back." Lukacs' voice cracked with fear. "Impact in thirty seconds."

"Wait for my signal, Lieutenant Commander."

The planes closed in. Petunia could clearly see the blood-red mouths, filled with white, sharp teeth that had been painted on the nose of each aircraft. Perhaps the Wolves had been lulled into thinking the *Persephone* would be a slow, easy target. But this former luxury ship was a wolf in sheep's clothing.

"Twenty seconds until impact, Captain."

"Petunia," Wilbur whispered in her ear. "While you have the spirit of a pirate, I have to agree with Paul on this one. This is insane. If you fire at this range, you risk your own ship."

Petunia turned her head and looked her brother in the eye. "Not this ship. She's not wood, or made of reeds. She's iron."

"Fifteen seconds until impact." The tension in the tactical officer's voice vibrated as tight as a plucked violin string.

Petunia, her eyes never leaving her enemy, counted to five. "Fire."

The blast briefly deafened all on board as every weapon on the *Persephone* let loose its ammunition. Thirty yards ahead, the concentrated blast of firepower detonated. A chain reaction of explosions ripped through the Brigade as the crafts caught fire or were thrown by the blast, taking their closest neighbors with them. Some tried to peel off and save themselves, but it was too late. Bits of shrapnel pummeled the *Persephone's* hull, sliding off like water. A single piece hit the windshield, cracking the corner of the thick-paned glass.

"Take us up, Lieutenant Nelson," Petunia shouted. "Full speed ahead."

They sped through the debris field, pushing crippled and destroyed planes aside with their metal bulk. When they were clear, Petunia gave the order to bank starboard, toward home. As they swung around, they witnessed the remainder of their enemies falling to earth. Not a single Wolf was left to tell the tale.

Petunia took a deep breath and unclenched her hands, which she must have balled into fists sometime during the fight.

"Status report, Lieutenant Commander Hemmings."

"Minor damage to the lower hull. One of the guns jammed and injured two men. No major breaches." He stood and saluted. "Well done, Captain."

The entire bridge crew broke out in applause. Paul nodded his approval and joined the crew in their salute. Wilbur, not one for formality, pulled her into a rib-crushing hug.

"A pirate at heart. I knew it."

Petunia laughed. "Maybe. Just a little."

When the excitement died down, Paul walked the deck, his gaze appraising every detail. "She's not such a bad vessel after all. Maybe I should—"

"Don't even think about it, Pork...Commodore." Petunia teased her brother, but her warning was genuine. She stroked the velvety back of her seat. "This is *my* ship, and you can't have her."

Paul's sudden glare frightened Petunia. Had she gone too far, speaking like that in front of her crew? But he seemed to be studying his sister, seeing her in a new light. What was that she saw in his eyes? Could it be respect? He pulled his lower lip over the upper in a thoughtful way.

"You're right. I don't think anyone else could handle her better."

Petunia's smile was as big as the sky as she settled herself into her chair.

"Mr. Nelson, take us home."

From the Horse's Mouth

based on The Goose Girl

BERNIE MOJZES

O
NCE UPON A TIME THERE WAS A GIRL…" THE HORSE HEAD SAYS, before wheezing into silence. It hangs on the soot-stained wall, jaw moving like it's chewing cud, grinding worn molars against yellowed bone and rusted iron, a hideous scraping that hurts just to hear. Then the fire in its eyes goes dead, and even that stops.

There's jeering from a handful of the pub's denizens—old regulars, you suppose—but most folk don't notice, too busy in their drink and their card games, in their boasts and arguments, debates and digressions. In the working girls who flit bright like wanton butterflies through the crowd.

A heap of rags stirs at the corner of the bar; as it moves, its parts become distinct: thin arms, stooped body, wild, grey hair atop a wrinkled, sagging face.

Could she be the one? This broken, toothless hag?

You've heard rumors, followed them to this festering canker of a city, to this street, this pub, hoping against all odds that you've found her. And now, hoping you're wrong.

The hag doesn't look up from her empty cup.

"There'll needs be brandy, if you're wanting to hear more."

Her voice is like factory smoke scraped across a farrier's rasp, harsh yet insubstantial.

The bartender glances over, but the others gathered around the horse head wave their hands in dismissal. They've all heard this tale before.

You reach for your purse.

The bartender takes your money and fetches three drinks: one for you, one for her, and the rest of the bottle for the horse. He doesn't offer you change.

When the old woman turns to bring the horse its brandy, you can't help but gasp. Her face, her throat, the flesh of her hands is a mass of scars: punctures and tears that hatch her skin in fine white lines and pucker her flesh. One bright blue eye regards you with cold disdain; where the other should be is just an empty socket.

She stares at you for a long, uncomfortable moment, then shakes her head and shuffles by to pour the brandy in the horse's mouth. It doesn't run through the holes where the desiccated flesh has peeled away. The old woman flicks a match against the wall and touches it to something deep inside the skull.

The eyes warm. The horse head hisses. Gears turn. It makes a noise that is part fire and part old man clearing his throat. And then it begins:

"There was once an old queen whose husband had died, and who loved her daughter very much, and..."

Princess Gisela stood before her mirror as her maid brushed her long, golden tresses.

"Oh, Jutte," she said, as she said every morning, "I think that perhaps today is the day. Her Grace my mother has been entertaining the suitors' emissaries for months now. Oh! How wonderful it will be when I am at last married!"

"Perhaps, m'lady," said the maid as she braided the princess's hair with gold ribbons.

It was not five minutes before the Queen announced her presence. "Oh, darling Gisela," she said, "I have the most wonderful news!"

"Tell it right!"

The old woman raps the horse head on the nose with the back of her hand.

"Nobody wants to hear *that* story," the horse head says. Its voice crackles like flames, and burbles like water. Its voice cannot be mistaken for human.

"Tell it anyway."

"Nobody will pay for that, but if any here have loose tongues, it may be you who pays, mistress."

The horse head swivels on the wall, its eyes studying the small audience. Gears turn. Steam hisses.

"'I have made a match for you,' the queen said, 'with a handsome, young king of a rich and powerful land—'"

"Tell it right," the old woman says, again. "Dear one, tell it true this time. For me."

The horse head exhales through its nose, twin streams of steam or smoke, you don't know which, in the dim-lit pub.

"That will require a lot more brandy," it says.

You wave for the bartender.

In her dank room in the dungeon beneath the stone ramparts of Festung Vohschlern, Gisela worked. Sometimes, when she remembered, she ate. Sometimes, less often, she slept. She stank like a wet muskrat in a fireplace. The workroom stank of mildew, and soot, and sulphur.

Gisela's workbench was littered with tools, large and small. Half the workroom was devoted to a system of pulleys that supported the skinned carcass of a horse. White bone and polished steel gleamed beneath cables and tendons, red muscle and leather straps.

"I think today's the day, Jutte," Gisela said.

She glanced at her maid, who lay slumped in the cot they shared of late, snoring lightly. Gisela understood only too well. Her own eyes were drooping, but this was not the time to sleep. Not for her.

She measured half a capful of fine, white powder from a vial and rubbed it on her gums. Straightened her shoulders. Ran trembling fingers through her frazzled hair, cropped short after the time it caught in the gears.

Time to test her creation.

She filled the furnace with the purest grain alcohol to be had in this time of war—oil and coal burned too dirty, and fouled the delicate mechanisms—and touched a match to the pilot light. The horse burbled for a time, and then? Then it raised its head.

"Falada? Are you in there? Is there still any of you left after all this time?"

The horse looked at her, and at its body. Its mouth moved, as if it was learning its own workings. And then it spoke.

"My Lady. When I swore I would come back even from the land of the dead itself if you called, I thought it was but to comfort you in your grief. What have you done to me?"

The old woman strokes the horse head's nose, presses her cheek against the horse head's cheek.

"Thank you," she says. "Please don't stop."

"Wake up, Jutte!" the princess cried. "We've done it!"

For an hour, the princess and her maid taught the horse how to use its limbs, and then — the final test — they worked the pulleys and lowered Falada to the floor.

He walked slowly and stiffly at first, but soon enough was able to get around as well as a horse might in a cramped workroom.

Gisela sent Jutte to fetch her mother, the queen.

"Look, Mother!" she said, when Jutte returned with the queen. "Isn't he beautiful?"

The queen regarded the horse, who made an awkward bow.

"Your Grace," he said. "I am ever at your service."

"In a month, we can have a dozen like him," Gisela said, "and two score in two months' time. We can break Hüttesbad's forces and drive them from our lands forever." The war provided no shortage of dead men and horses. No shortage of raw materials.

The queen's face was grave.

"If only we had a month."

"What happened?" the horse asked.

"They have crossed the Elbe and broken our lines."

The princess's shoulders dropped. "I was too slow. After everything father taught me, I still failed."

"We all did what we could," the Queen said. "There is no blame. I have sued for peace. We cannot hope to win, but we can make their victory very painful, and they know this. They are open to bargain."

"What do they want from us?" Jutte asked.

"They have demanded half our treasury, and a yearly tribute," the queen said, "as dowry." She didn't look at her daughter. "I'm sorry, my child."

"No," the horse said, steaming. "Heinrich is a monster. I will not allow it."

"Heinrich will take what he wants, one way or another. He will take my kingdom as he took his father's if he must, through blood and poison. But if he is willing to take it by marriage, and spare our people's lives, then what choice is there?"

Gisela laid a hand on the horse's side. "Dear Falada, I must." Her voice was calm, but her hand trembled against his flank.

"Then take me with you," Falada said.

"I can't. It would take me a week to make you a skin to wear."

"I think," said the queen, "that it will take a week to gather the dowry. That much I can give you."

The guns, for once, were silent.

Gisela and Jutte rode together across their forces' front lines. As per the terms of the betrothal armistice, their men had withdrawn out of sight of the river, while the Hüttesbadians had pulled their troops back to the far bank of the Elbe.

Gisela rode Falada, as magnificent a steed as any had ever seen. Jutte followed on a lesser mount. The lines parted to let them through, and the men gathered in silence around them. Gisela had memorized a speech for the occasion — strength, honor, perseverance — but her voice failed her.

A third of the dowry had been sent ahead. Another third was packed into saddlebags. The final payment was to be delivered on Gisela's safe arrival and marriage.

It was a mile to the river's edge. Gisela was to make the trip un-escorted — unprotected — as a symbol of good faith. Jutte, she reasoned, hardly constituted protection, and regardless, was as unwilling to leave her side as Falada had been. After fording, they would be escorted to Burg Hüttesbad, where the princess would meet for the first time the man responsible for the deaths of so many of her people. Meet him, marry him, and bed him.

And perhaps, if fortune favored her, kill him.

As they rode, they came upon a stream that fed into the Elbe. The water burbled happily in its bed. Jutte stopped her horse. She climbed down into the shallow gully through which the stream flowed.

"Your Grace," Jutte said, "are you thirsty? Would you like some water?"

"That would be nice, Jutte," Gisela said.

"Then come down here and get it yourself."

Something in Jutte's tone gave the princess pause. She slid off Falada's back and climbed down into the gully.

"Quickly," Jutte said. "We can't be seen here. Change clothes with me."

"What?"

"If King Heinrich marries me instead of you, his claim on our kingdom is void. We can send Falada back with the news, and he and your mother can use the respite to rebuild the army and win our freedom."

Both of them knew that it was unlikely that anything would win their freedom. But it might save their kingdom.

When Gisela and Jutte came to the river's bank, it was Jutte who wore the dress of gold and silver thread, and whose long, golden tresses were braided with flowers as befits a bride. She rode the faithful Falada proudly, while Gisela followed on the lesser steed, in a plain, green dress befitting a maid.

The Hüttesbad army was massed on the far bank, stretching as far as the eye could see.

"Is it too late to change my mind?" Jutte asked.

"Yes," said the horse. He plunged into the cold water.

"It was a good plan," the old woman says, into her drink.

"No," the horse hisses, beginning to wind down. You know the signs, by now, and raise a banknote to catch the bartender's eye.

"It was a bad plan," the horse head says, "but all the others were worse."

King Heinrich was watching from his throne in the courtyard, the first third of the dowry in chests around his feet. He was handsome and held himself proudly, as befits a king. He rose as the procession approached.

His men dropped to one knee before him. Gisela and Jutte dismounted. Gisela followed the soldiers' example, while Jutte affected a more regal bow.

"You're not as ugly as I expected," the king said.

An old man, standing in the crowd, giggled loudly.

"Thank you, your Grace," Jutte said.

Gisela glanced sidelong at the old man. He wore stained robes, rich but tattered. His hair and beard had not seen a comb in years. Even so, Gisela recognized his face. King Gustav had been kindly when he visited Vohschlau so many years ago, to pay his respects after her father's death. He had given her a gift, a semi-mechanical creature her father had once built, of mouse bones and watch gears. Her father had given it to Gustav on the birth of his son. Eleven years later, Gustav returned it to Gisela.

"My son would only break it," he had said.

Gisela had dissected it, and then reassembled it. It was the foundation for the work that had culminated ultimately in Falada.

Yet another eleven years later, old King Gustav giggled into his filthy beard and smeared snot and spittle across his face.

"Little mouse!" he said, dancing. "Little mouse! Little, little, mouse, mouse!"

"Just because you're not hideous, don't think too highly of yourself," King Heinrich said to Jutte. "Even *this* old fool can tell your true worth."

Two of the soldiers approached the throne with the bags containing the dowry. They held them open for his inspection. Inside there was gold and silver, fine jewelry and gems. Generations of family heirlooms.

King Heinrich nodded.

"Throw it all in the furnace," he ordered, "and smelt it down to bricks. Kill the horses and the wench. Strip my bride and burn her clothing. When she's been inspected, have her brought to my chambers."

A soldier raised his rifle and shot Gisela's horse in the head.

Falada started. He spun and kicked at the soldier, crushing his chest. Other soldiers shot at him, hitting him twice in the chest and again in the neck.

Falada collapsed, and did not breathe.

Jutte threw herself between Gisela and the soldiers' guns.

"She is my friend, dear husband," she said. "If you slay her, there will be no peace between our kingdoms."

The king stared at her a long while. "You don't expect me to take your little assassin into my home, do you?"

"Nevertheless," Jutte said.

The king shrugged. "It is of no difference to me whether she lives or dies, I suppose, as long as she stays far from me."

He paced, three times to the left, three times to the right, and again, three times to the left.

"Give her to Kürdchen," he pronounced. "No other woman will have him, and she can help with the geese. Deliver the horses to the knacker. Into the furnace with the rest."

"Why would he burn everything?"

The words slip from your mouth before you realize you're speaking aloud. The horse head ignores you.

"Would you hear of Jutte's humiliation?" the horse head asks. Soft, like wind across rusted pipes. He isn't speaking to you. "Stripped in the public square and scrubbed raw? Inspected for needles hidden beneath fingernails, in her hair, in all her hidden places? Would you hear of the queen's marriage bed, locked high in the tower? Or would you perhaps wish to hear of the goose girl's rape?"

The old woman stares into her empty cup, and says nothing.

"'The first time he touched her—'"

"Enough," the old woman says.

"I grow thirsty," the horse head says.

Money passes through the growing audience toward the bar.

They tied a rope around the horses' hind legs and dragged them to the knacker for rendering.

Though he was largely unharmed, Falada was afraid to do anything that would lead to his mistress' discovery. He lay perfectly still as he was hauled through the dust. He had months of experience being dead, so it was not difficult to fool the soldiers.

At the knacker's yard, the two horses were raised up and hung from hooks from their ankles. The knacker set a bucket under Gisela's horse and cut its throat. Blood flowed thick and clotted from it, filling the bucket.

The knacker set another bucket under Falada and raised his knife.

Falada snapped his teeth at the knacker, and kicked.

The knacker was a fat man, filthy and uncouth, who smelled like his work. Even so, his fear made him quick, and he fell away from the horse into the mud with only minor wounds. Gasping, he ran for his ax, and before Falada could thrash free of his ropes, the knacker struck him thrice in the neck.

Falada's head fell into the dirt.

The knacker poked it several times, but it remained lifeless. He lifted the head and brought it into the barn, where he intended to examine it more fully. He set it on a table.

"When I give you to the king," he said, "he will make me a wealthy man."

The horse head opened its eyes. From outside came the sound of splintering wood, of snapping rope. Of horse's hooves, galloping.

"When you give me to the king," Falada said, "I will tell him that you sold my body to his enemies, and he will have you drawn and quartered as a traitor."

The knacker ran out into the yard, but the post on which Falada had hung was broken, and the body was gone.

Spring grew old and fat and turned to summer: the air hot and heavy, and filled with mosquitoes and biting flies. The geese grazed the grass to its roots, and moved to new pastures.

Every morning, now, Kürdchen and Gisela drove their geese past the knacker's barn, where Falada's head was mounted on the wall above the barn door. Every morning, Gisela stopped beneath her faithful Falada's head, and said, "Alas, Falada, hanging there!"

But Falada had hung there for months, and his fuel had burned away. He could but watch in silence as his love was dragged away by her stupid and brutish husband.

"Not husband," the old woman says.

"She cooked his food, and slept in his bed. She did as he bade without argument. She grew heavy with his child. If that does not a husband make, then what?"

"Something else," the woman says. "Something worse."

Steam — you *think* it's steam — issues from the horse head's nose.

"Worse than what befell Jutte, the new queen, whose union was blessed by God and the Bishop? Whose husband loved her so thoroughly that she bore the bruises of it on her flesh for all to see?"

The old woman turns away, and is silent.

"What of Falada?" you ask, to break the impasse. This is the story you came to seek, and if some parts must be sacrificed to reach the end, so be it.

"Falada was a fool," the horse head snorts.

"Falada was noble and brave," the old woman says. "And above all, kind. The princess was an idiot not to have taken him as her husband, no matter that he was a shoemaker's son. No matter what the cost. Instead, they fumbled with each other's bodies in back rooms and hay lofts while Jutte kept watch."

"'Kept watch,'" the horse head snorts again, and the old woman, whom you might have suspected to be beyond all this, blushes.

"Is it any wonder," it continues, "that poor Falada fled to the army? Better to face the enemy's guns than to choose between two women."

"Did he truly love them both?" you ask.

The old woman's breath catches, and she looks down, away from you, and from the horse head, at the filthy bar. At her empty cup.

"Yes," says the horse head. "Truly."

It was not difficult for Gisela to convince the knacker to let her visit Falada in private. Though she had no coin to pay, he was a lonely man, and gentle enough. She learned to rub grease infused with sweet mint under her nose to overcome the smell of him, and to wash before returning to the goose boy's house. And in return, he gave to her each night a flask of plum brandy, and time alone with Falada.

In truth, had she asked, he would have done far more for her, for all that she carried another man's child. Once, drunk on brandy, he confessed his love of her to Falada.

"You should tell her," Falada said.

He did not, of course. But he began feeding Falada regularly himself, and never questioned the goose girl's comings and goings, so that he could pretend to himself that when she came to his bed, it was something other than a business arrangement.

And thus summer came and went, and autumn also, and the nights grew long and cold.

It was on the shortest day of the year that the midwife was called to the palace, and in the midst of the longest night of the year, Jutte brought forth a child into this cruel world. When the infant was cleaned and put to breast, the midwife rushed to the goose boy's hovel, where Gisela labored until nearly daybreak.

The knacker brought the news to Falada, and the two drowned their sorrows and their jealousy that day in plum brandy, and long into the night.

The old woman's lips are set in as straight a line as her scars allow.

"You have never said this before."

"*Tell it true*, you said."

"Had... Had Gisela known, she might have done things differently. Jutte was truly trapped, but Giselle could still make a choice. It didn't have to end this way. Falada should have told her."

"He should have betrayed the confidence of his only friend?"

"He was not your friend!"

"No?"

They glare at each other long enough that most of the audience tires of this private, silent drama, and wanders away to find other pleasures.

"Heinrich is still king," you say, softly enough that you hope only the woman and the horse head can hear. "What went wrong?"

Gisela's labor had been hard, and she had not come through unscathed. The child would not come, and the midwife feared that both might die. She used a knife to ease the passage, but though she sewed the wound closed afterward, the healing was slow.

Kürdchen was easily the stupidest man Gisela had ever met, and though he was not cruel in his nature, neither was he kind. He was simply incapable of understanding that others were any different from the geese he drove—to be cared for so that they could be used. With the King's gift of Gisela, Kürdchen had learned the use of women, and made use of Gisela as soon as the midwife left.

That night, while he slept, Gisela fled, taking the child with her.

Kürdchen woke to find her gone. He waited all morning for her return, and then he took the geese out, expecting her to be home when he returned.

Each morning for three times three days he waited for the goose girl, and each evening he expected her home, and he was always surprised to find she was not there. On the tenth day, he went to complain to the king.

King Heinrich sat in his court, dandling his baby on his knee. His queen sat beside him. So pleased was the king that he had a child that Jutte's bruises had almost healed.

Kürdchen burst into the chamber.

"I won't tend geese with that girl any longer. She won't do as I say, and is of no use!"

King Heinrich turned his child toward the goose boy.

"Look at the idiot boy, child," he said. "Some day, all these idiots will be yours."

He handed the child to his queen.

"Five lashes for the idiot," he said. "Get him out of my sight."

"That must have been gratifying," you say.
"Shut up," the horse head explains.

The king's father, Gustav, came across the goose boy as he sat by the river, weeping.

"It is a beautiful day, young Kürdchen," the old king said. "The sun is warm and the snow is soft and the geese are fat and ready for the axe. Why do you weep?"

The goose boy told him of his unjust treatment at the hands of the king and the goose girl. The old king laughed through the telling, and when it was done, thanked the goose boy for the splendid joke.

The goose boy laughed as well, because that is what one does when a joke is told, even when — *especially* when — one doesn't understand it. And the goose boy had never understood a joke in his life.

"Where is she now, this goose girl of yours?" the old king asked.

"I don't know. She should be home, with me."

"Ah, but dear Kürdchen, *you* aren't home. So it stands to reason that she cannot be. But she must be someplace, just as you are someplace, so where might she be?"

The old king questioned him further, and then stood abruptly. He placed a nettle behind his ear and skipped off down the road, whistling a bawdy tune, as was his habit.

"A nettle?"

The horse head glances at you.

"King Heinrich was very protective of his father's reputation after the sudden illness that took his wits, and very nearly his life. Gustav had been a good ally and friend to his neighbors. His affliction left him a drooling fool, and though he gradually regained his speech, he never again showed the keen intellect of his youth. There are those who say Gustav was poisoned, for which King Heinrich blamed his neighbors, and went to war in retaliation. There are others who say Gustav was poisoned, but only pretended his feeblemindedness from fear of his son. But they do not say it very loudly."

"Poison!" You shake your head. "I cannot imagine any man would stoop so low, especially to his own father."

"Those who sin are always first to suspect sin of another," the horse head says. "What other reason to burn the dowry than to purify it by fire of any poisons?"

"Finish the story," the old woman says. "I think there is not much time."

"Time for what?" But you already know.

"Before you have to leave, child," says the old woman.

Most would have dismissed Kürdchen's stories of talking horses as the construction of a feeble mind, but old King Gustav was well acquainted with the ways of broken minds. He went straight to the knacker's barn, skipping and whistling his aimless tune, but when he arrived, he crept carefully into the yard. But there was no horse head above the barn door where the goose boy had said.

Gustav crept closer and pressed his ear to the barn door.

Inside, he heard voices; a woman spoke in hushed tones to something that responded with a thick, harsh tongue that whistled softly. He listened long enough to determine to his satisfaction that the woman's voice belonged to the missing goose girl, and that she was, indeed, the true Princess Gisela.

He seized Gisela and dragged her from the barn.

"I have been a fool too long," he said. "Now it is my son's turn. Let us see how well he can rule when the truth comes out."

He brought her into the dining hall, where the king and his bride sat among the lords and ladies of the court.

"Behold!" he said, "I bring you Gisela, Crown Princess of Vohschlau."

The king laughed. "That? A princess? Your madness grows, old man. Where is your nurse?"

"I am not mad!" Gustav cried, though he was likely somewhat mad to think this might work. "I heard it from the horse head's mouth."

"Come, father," King Heinrich said. "Take your place at the table and we shall bring you some nice soup to drool in. How could you think that ragged thing could possibly match my exquisite bride?"

He lifted his queen's chin with a crooked finger, and felt her tremble. He looked in her eye, and could see the truth upon her face. For a moment his smile failed. But only for a moment. He would not be made fool in front of his subjects.

"Go back to your geese, girl," the king said to Gisela. "And father, you had best take your rest tonight. Perhaps you will feel recovered tomorrow."

He bent his head to cut a piece of meat for himself, and Jutte stabbed him in the neck.

"Surely you know the rest of the story," the horse head rasps.

"Not this version," the old woman says. "Tell the child."

The horse head clears its throat with a small belch that spits viscous, black oil on the floor.

"The king lived through the night. His father did not. The knacker took the horse head and fled into the forest, and was never found. Gisela and Jutte were thrown into the dungeon until the king was recovered enough to witness their punishment. A barrel was built to hold them, and three times three hundred nails driven through it. They were closed into the barrel and rolled behind a team of horses three times around the castle, and then the barrel was let loose to roll down the hill to break against the rocks in the river."

You open your mouth to speak, but the words won't come. Finally, they do.

"And the children? What of them?"

"The king said it would be cruel to separate a mother from her child," the old woman says.

There are shouts in the street. This is the moment of truth. And yet, the question comes obliquely.

"There are some who say one of the women survived, floating down the river impaled upon a hundred nails, scarred beyond recognition."

The old woman assesses you with her one eye. "There are also some who say that only one of the children's bodies was ever found, smothered between the women's bodies."

Heavy boots ring on the cobbled street. The bar is emptying quickly. The bartender is nowhere to be seen.

The horse head wheezes. "Bring me a drink, child."

As you do, the old woman breaks open first one, then a second cask of brandy and pours it over the bar. The liquid spreads across the old oak and across the floor. The horse head drinks from the bottle.

"You have her eyes," it says.

Which 'her'? But time has run out. And really, does it matter?

There is a shout, and the door comes off its hinges with a bang. Uniformed men stream into the room. The old woman flicks a match against the bar, and flames engulf the brandy-soaked wood.

"Run," the horse head says.

And you do.

The (Steamy) Tale of Cinderella

based on Cinderella

DANNY BIRT

"ANNE, WHERE ARE YOUR LACE GLOVES? BETH, DO SOMETHING ABOUT your bustle at once!"

Sara-Bella rolled her eyes as she came up on deck. Lady Mary would probably continue chivvying her two daughters until they were on the royal yacht having their tea, and might not even stop then. *And all to 'catch a man.' Ridiculous.*

The prince's yacht, though? Now *that* was worth going over to see, even if it did mean that she had to wade through this entire port-of-call's list of eligible who's who to get to it. Being the daughter of a shipbuilder gave Sara-Bella a keen eye for oceangoing vessels, and if this one's design belied the secret she thought it might...

Beth paused in her primping and cast an aghast look behind Lady Mary toward the hatchway. "You *must* be joking!"

Anne and Lady Mary turned and displayed similar reactions.

"What?" Sara-Bella asked, hands spread wide.

"You can't visit the Crown Prince's royal yacht looking like *that*!" her stepmother said emphatically.

"Like what?"

"Wearing sooty trousers, and those ridiculous glass shoes? Hair all full of cinders? Why, it's unconscionable!" Lady Mary declaimed. "If you don't know how to dress properly, at least get back to your engine room before someone sees you, Sara-Bella."

"Yeah, Sooty Sara," Anne snickered.

"Cinder-Bella," Beth chimed in.

Sara-Bella gritted her teeth. *Here we go again.* "Trousers aren't unconscionable, they're practical."

Lady Mary waved the comment away. "Princes have servants to be practical for them. Ladies are to be beautiful, and refined, and...and everything you are not."

"Only if they're trying to ensnare a man." Sara-Bella snorted. "It's not like I—"

"*Sara-Bella!*" Lady Mary snapped, furious.

Sara-Bella bit her tongue as her stepsisters looked at her curiously. "Look, all I'm saying is I'll stay out of Anne and Beth's way while they're hunting potential husbands, alright? You know I will. They can bring home as many men as they can fit between their legs for all I care!"

"Yuck!" Anne shrilled.

"You're disgusting," Beth spat.

Lady Mary bristled like an affronted hedgehog. "That will be the last time you so much as *hint* that one of *my* daughters would engage in polygamy. Do you understand me?"

Drat. I should have bit my tongue harder. "Yes, stepmother."

Giving a nod after she was sure her remonstration had sunk in, Lady Mary turned to fuss with the pleats in Beth's dress. "This is not an engineering conference we're attending, this is a social visit — one that will help your sisters climb in society if we can catch the right man for them. Your appearance would repel all the eligible bachelors from your sisters' sides, which is unacceptable. You shall remain here."

A bell sounded from the royal yacht's gig, indicating they were ready to ferry passengers.

"I'll keep my mouth shut," Sara-Bella said, desperate. "Please? I just want to see the ship!"

Lady Mary gave her a hard stare. "You've made it quite clear that you are not fit to be in society. It's as much for your own good as for everyone else's. Now stay out of sight while we're gone." Lady Mary loaded her blood offspring over the gangplank and onto the gig without a backward glance.

Another teardrop fell from Sara-Bella's cheek into the ocean. She had stared out the porthole throughout the sunset and watched the lighting come to life aboard the glass-bottomed yacht. It was even more beautiful at night, in her opinion, with the illumination enhancing the graceful lines the ship's designer, Prince Henrique, had so thoughtfully added.

"There's enough salt and water in the ocean without your adding to it, you know."

The voice from below startled Sara-Bella so badly that she almost fell out of the porthole. Once she steadied herself, she looked down to behold an elderly woman floating in the water. It took her befuddled mind a moment to recognize exactly what she was looking at: long white-and-gray hair floating every which way like seaweed; shoulders, breasts, and tummy unencumbered by clothing; a powerful gray tail where legs should be... One of the Mer-folk had come to see her.

"Madam," Sara-Bella greeted her. Her father had raised her to always be polite to the Mer-folk, but it had been years since she had last been visited. She had thought maybe the Mer-folk only cared for her father and not her.

The Mer-matron reached up with a finger, wiped a tear from Sara-Bella's cheek, and brought it to her own lips. "Now, then. What's so wrong with the world, minnow?"

"Oh, nothing," Sara-Bella sulked. "So long as you don't mind never being allowed to go anywhere alone, but not being allowed to go anywhere *with* anyone, either."

"Tough times indeed, little one," the matron consoled.

"I mean, I can't even be myself in my own home! My stepmother thinks that all my tastes are wrong for a woman to have."

"Nonsense. I know several sharks who would say you taste wonderful!" She lazily flopped her wrist at Sara-Bella's backward jolt. "Now, now, I'm trying to lighten the mood, minnow; no need to look at me that way."

"I just hate being tied down like this," Sara-Bella muttered, settling back down. "Not coming, not going, just...."

"Well, I'm not a fan of nets myself," the matron said. "So, what's your wish, little fish? Where would you go if you *could* go?"

Sara-Bella's gaze hungrily gravitated to the prince's ship. "There." The largest glass-bottomed hull in the world was an engineering marvel all on its own, but it was the engine room she really longed to see.

The Mer-matron shrugged. "Done. Hop on."

"What?" Sara-Bella asked, taken aback.

"I'll swim you over. Won't take but a trice, my guppy."

"But they'd see us!"

"No problem, we'll just duck under, then."

"I'm afraid I can't hold my breath that long," Sara-Bella said sadly.

"Hm, no, that won't work, then. Let me see... Ah!" The matron's expression brightened. "What you need is to be dressed properly."

Sara-Bella groaned. "Not you, too!" she wailed.

"Be back in a whale's hiccup."

The matron disappeared under the waves, leaving Sara-Bella blinking in mental whiplash. *Mer-Women don't wear a stitch of clothing! What would she know about fashion?*

...Nothing. She knows nothing about fashion. So why would she go get me a dress?

She wouldn't. There must be more to this than frippery.

Sara-Bella had no sooner chosen to trust her patroness than the matron returned.

"Here we are!" she said, popping her torso out of the water with a powerful thrust of her tail and tossing what looked like a fur coat around Sara-Bella's shoulders.

She took it back off to look at it at arm's length. "What is this?"

"It's a coat that a selkie friend of mine doesn't need any more, now that she's gone froggy," the matron said.

"Froggy?"

"Living on the land, poor daft dear. Go ahead, hop in and try it on!"

Sara-Bella felt nervous. "I'm still not sure I should..."

"Why not?"

"Because...because..." Sara-Bella thought, and the more she thought, the more her rebellious side took over. "Why not, indeed?" She squeezed out the porthole, held her breath, and jumped in the water with a splash. With the matron's help she slipped her slippered feet into the coat, then her arms, and finally her head.

Only then did she notice the strange feeling — as if her hands and arms weren't inside a fur coat, but were actually the flippers.

"I'm a *seal*?!" she said. Of course, it came out as "Or, or, *or*?"

"Only temporarily, dear," the matron said, understanding perfectly. "You'd have to stay in that coat past sunrise to become a selkie yourself — just be back on your ship before then and you'll be as you always were. Leave the coat in the porthole there and I'll drop by to pick it up later.

"Of course," the matron added, "if you decide that living like you have been isn't the life for you, you *could* keep the coat... But that's up to you. For now, go enjoy yourself, dearie," she said, tapping the seal's nose with her finger.

"Thank you," Sara-Bella said in her strange seal dialect. "You've been a godsend, good mother."

Without wasting another moment, Sara-Bella took off swimming. What a feeling! The water simply *whoosh*ed by her. Had she more time she might have done a bit of cavorting for the joy and the freedom of...well, freedom, but there was an engine to inspect. Maybe if there was time on the way back she could have some fun, but until then magic would just have to wait its turn.

First she circled the ship underwater, staring through the glass bottom of the boat at the tea-goers as they stared back at her — even daring to wave a flipper at them. She spent a bit of time looking at the paddle wheel, then the hull. Finally, she located a ladder built into the side of the hull, took the selkie's skin off, and hung it over the lowest rung that was out of the water.

She clambered up the ladder, but paused before she reached the deck because of a familiar sound: steam hissing through a pipe. Sara-Bella looked through one of the open portholes to behold the engine room. Perfect! And since the yacht was at anchor, there was no one around: even better! She wriggled her way in and stood up. Suddenly aware of how conspicuous she would be if anyone did come in, she donned one of the long, thick leather coats used by the engineers to keep errant sparks and coals from burning holes in their clothes.

What a marvel the gleaming engine room was to Sara-Bella's eyes. It was obvious that a great deal of thought had gone into its design. A few innovations were so unusual but well-considered that Sara-Bella thought she might just have to try them out in her own ship—If she could convince the funds out of her stepmother, that is. The portholes showed excellent craftsmanship, particularly in the thick glass. The size of the crankshaft was downright astonishing, as befit the royal yacht. Through the boiler ran more pipes than seemed necessary... possibly backing up her hypothesis about the ship's design in the first place.

"Oh, Papa, how I wish you could see this!" she whispered, running her hand along some of the gauges. Being sonless, her father had lovingly shared his interest in ships and mechanisms with the only child he had.

The quiet sound of steam rushing through pipes suddenly grew far more shrill as it escaped a pipe somewhere to her left.

"Blast!" a masculine voice yelled. "Somebody give me a hand here!"

Aware of the danger an out-of-control steam engine posed to passengers, Sara-Bella heeded the call for help. Working quickly, the man and Sara-Bella got the steam shunted through a different set of pipes.

"Well, there goes that idea," the man said in obvious disgust, wiping the accumulated droplets from his engineer's coat and flicking them to the deck.

"What were you trying?" she asked, mimicking his motions.

"A new alloy for the pipe fittings. Evidently doesn't stand up to pressure. Or heat. Or maybe both. Eh, either way, it doesn't work." He shrugged the problem away. "You'd think after all the testing the royal shipyard put her through that this sort of thing wouldn't happen, but it *keeps* happening, over and over and over. Might as well melt the whole ship down and start anew." He gently kicked the pipe.

"How could you say that? It's beautiful!" Sara-Bella protested.

"It's fair enough, but it's not *good* enough," the man sighed.

"Good enough for what?"

He turned away and as he did, under his breath, he muttered, "Doesn't matter anyway."

"For submerging?"

Had Sara-Bella not been watching closely, she may have missed the hitch in her companion's smooth movements. "What makes you say that?"

"Overall design. Water-tight everything beyond normal building specs; reinforced portholes with thrice-thick glass; angled prow with no figurehead; glass bottom to make sure you don't hit the ocean floor."

The man appeared to be wrestling with some concept in his mind. "And what do you think of her design? Overall, I mean."

"I told you: she's beautiful." Sara-Bella gently laid a hand on the hull. "I doubt that she'll function as the Prince would like her to, but with a few modifications to the design, her daughter might."

"Modifications like what?" the man said, his body turning more fully toward her.

"The royal shipyards might want to try copper instead of bronze on the next model, for one thing," Sara-Bella mused.

"Why?"

"It's lighter. I'm quite sure the Prince would be able to submerge his vessel, but getting it to come back up—now, that would be the trick."

Excited, the man replied, "That's where the power of steam comes in!"

"Yes, I thought as much," Sara-Bella mused. "The engine is powerful enough, but the side paddle wheel simply won't do. Add a rotary propeller at the prow and stern of the ship, figure out a way to point the prow toward the surface, and pour on the steam. My, this would be such an exhilarating project!"

"Hold those thoughts. Don't go anywhere." The man tore open his engineer's coat and patted at his pockets. "Paper, paper, where's the—ah. Pencil, pencil...Ready! What else should I consider?" he asked eagerly.

Sara-Bella's train of thought had already stopped short at seeing the out-of-place fine cut of a tuxedo under the sturdy engineer's coat. Suddenly, she recognized who she was talking to. With a gasp, she backed away from him. "You're the—" The toe of her slipper caught in between two pipes where they met the deck, and her ankle twisted. She fell with a cry, clutching at her leg.

Initially moving to arrest his erstwhile companion's fall, the prince faltered at the high-pitched utterance, looked at her more closely, and said in an almost accusing tone of voice, "You're a woman!"

Despite her pain, Sara-Bella burst into laughter and upturned a hand. "Should I say I'm sorry?"

"No, I didn't mean that as a...That is, I... Oh, bother." Smiling in both sympathy and embarrassment, he knelt next to her. "Come, my lady, I will help you to a cabin to lie down. Who should I call to aid you in your convalescence?"

Her heart skipped a beat. "No one. I came alone."

"No escort?" His eyebrows raised.

She avoided his gaze. "No."

"Well, which ship should I notify?"

"None! I must return on my own. At once, in fact. Help me up, will you?"

He stood and extended his hand, and was almost yanked off his feet as she made liberal use of it. "My lady, this is nonsense. You shouldn't be going anywhere with an ankle that badly injured. Look at it—It's already swelling!"

Sara-Bella hobbled toward the porthole which had allowed her entry. "I mustn't stay. My stepmother would be furious."

He pursued her. "Calm down, I'll have a talk with her. What's her name?"

"I'm sorry, Prince Henrique, I really must decline to answer that." She clambered through the porthole and back into the ocean.

"Heavens!" The prince's head followed her out the porthole. "What is *your* name, then? Please!"

"I cannot give it to you, sir. I am sorry," she said wistfully, donning the selkie's suit under the water where he could not see it.

"Was our conversation that meaningless to you?" he cried out. "My God, you're the first person I've told about my plans who hasn't all but laughed at me!"

At that, her heart broke. "The best name I can give you is... Cinderella." Her head ducked under the little ocean waves. The prince waited for her to return to the surface, but instead, after a moment, the surface of the ocean became turbulent as something moved away at great speed.

The prince's butler, Ajax, found him there, unmoved, a few minutes later. "Something out there, Your Highness?" the man asked as he strode up.

"A girl," he replied absently.

Knowing how absentminded his prince could be when he got around his steam machines, Ajax sneaked a peek out the porthole for himself to make sure there wasn't actually a woman out there in distress while the prince was trying to design some marvelous machine to help her. Seeing no one, he chuckled.

"Alright, my Prince, if you're seeing mermaids, no more drink for tonight, hm?"

Henrique looked up at his butler. "She wasn't a mermaid, Ajax, she had legs. Two of them. I counted."

"And how would you go about counting a lady's legs?"

"It was quite simple, actually. She was wearing trousers."

The prince's butler heaved a fond sigh. "As you say, my Prince. Incidentally, Captain Osgood has requested your presence on deck. Many of our guests are refusing to leave the ship until they've made your acquaintance at least once, and things are getting rather crowded up top."

Henrique's shoulders slumped at the idea of more girls throwing themselves at him. "Yes, of course. Lead on."

They walked toward the hatchway leading toward the deck, but only a few paces away, Ajax found he had lost his prince again. When he turned around, though, he found to his surprise that the prince was liberating a glass slipper from behind a pipe.

"My word!" the butler said. "There really was a lady down here with you!"

"Yes, Ajax."

"And she jumped in the water? Through a porthole?"

"Yes, Ajax."

The man scratched his head. "She was really wearing trousers?"

"Yes, Ajax."

"How... uncommon. That's a right uncommon piece of footwear, too," the butler said, peering at it. He laughed once. "Are you sure it wasn't an angel come down to visit you?"

Henrique had a perplexed smile. "No, I'm not."

Ajax's jaw dropped, but his expression gradually turned into a mirroring smile. He knew what that look meant. At last, his master had made his choice! "Shall I have the Captain end the tea for the evening, then, Your Highness?"

"Yes, that would be—No, wait." Henrique grabbed Ajax's arm. "Before you do, inquire among the locals as to which of them have stepdaughters of marriageable age. There can't be that many in the fleet."

"Gladly, Your Highness."

"Honestly, the nerve!" Lady Mary fumed. "Not showing up to your own tea, and cutting it short besides? Is this what passes for manners at the royal palace?"

"We did meet some nice boys," Beth said meekly.

"Unsuitable," Lady Mary dismissed the lot. "Beneath our station. The big fish had yet to make an appearance. Oh, for heavens' sake, what is the meaning of that hullabaloo? Go see what's going on, Anne."

"Why me?" the elder daughter whined.

"Because I am quite tired, and you are younger and spryer and *a dutiful daughter does what she's told*, is why."

Anne huffed, but got up and went to the rail. When she got there, all tiredness was immediately driven away by what she saw. "Mother! Mother!" Anne squealed. "The prince's gig! It's trimmed in courting lace! And it's coming this way! And everyone's cheering! And they're looking at us!"

"Impossible," Lady Mary scoffed. "Why, he didn't even see either of you last night!"

"Maybe he was watching in secret?" Beth hypothesized. "I hear the royal yacht is full of secret rooms for watching people do things!"

Lady Mary's eyes widened. "You're right, my darling. The prince may have been... browsing!" She and Beth rushed to join Anne at the railing and, sure as fire is hot, there was the gig headed straight at them, bypassing all the other ships surrounding the royal yacht.

Breathlessly, the lady set to chivvying her daughters again: "Go make yourselves presentable. No, not the same thing you wore last night, something fresh! And put on new perfume, you both stink!" As the two girls scurried down through the hatch, Lady Mary glanced back one more time. Yes, the gig was coming directly for them. "Royalty, as I live and breathe. Living in a palace the rest of my days with servants at hand and foot!"

She hurried below, then jolted to a halt. "Sara-Bella," she gasped. "Good God, what if the prince sees her in those abominable trousers? *Sara-Bella*!" she shrieked. "Get a dress on!"

"I don't have a stupid dress," came the terse reply from the engine room.

"You can fit into one of Anne's!"

"Why does she have to wear one of *my* dresses?" Anne whined loudly from her cabin. "Why can't she wear one of Beth's old rags?"

"This is no time to argue!"

In what seemed no time at all, the bell from the gig sounded. Lady Mary, despite not looking particularly well-kempt, went to answer it to give her daughters more time to prepare. She graciously welcomed the prince and his manservant aboard. "Would you care to come with me to the parlor for refreshment, Your Highness?" she asked.

"I would be delighted," Prince Henrique said.

They made their way to the parlor and Ajax barely had time to set the tea to steeping before Anne and Beth made their grand appearances, each dropping a low curtsy

"Now, sir, to what do we owe the pleasure of the royal presence on our humble little ship?" Lady Mary asked. Of course it was obvious what he wanted, given the pomp of his arrival, but there were proprieties to be observed.

Equally formal, Prince Henrique said, "Madam, I have come to ask for the hand of one of your daughters in marriage."

Lady Mary stood and curtsied low. "Your Highness, you are welcome to whichever of my daughters has most pleased your eye."

"With respect to the lovely ladies in front of me," he sketched a seated bow, "the daughter of whom I speak is not within eyesight."

Taken aback, Lady Mary posited, "Perhaps you are simply unable to recognize her in daylight?"

"She was... differently-attired," Henrique admitted. He motioned Ajax forward with a box in his hands. "The daughter in question was wearing this rather remarkable slipper; I had hoped to slip it back on the foot from whence it came."

"You'll need to come back in a few days if that's all you came for, Prince Henrique," Sara-Bella said as she hobbled into the room, doubly encumbered by managing her foreign skirt. "My ankle's swollen a trick and no mistake."

Her stepfamily recovered from their shock all at the same time.

"Sara-Bella?"

"Sooty Sara?"

"Cinder-Bella?"

Immediately, Lady Mary clapped her hands twice and stared daggers at the ladies. "Leave us. All three of you. Not a word!"

At a concerned nod from his prince, Ajax left too. Once they had departed (Anne and Beth theatrically so), Lady Mary turned to the prince with a grave expression. "Your Highness, I place my family's good name at your feet by telling you this and can only trust to your discretion as a gentleman—even my daughters know nothing of this—but... how can I put this delicately? ... My late husband's daughter has no interest in males. Years ago I caught her doing unmentionable things with a childhood girlfriend in her chamber, and to this day all interest she professes to have in life lies in steam engines and the fairer sex. Why, I am actually forced to keep her locked up at night for her own sake, and that of her so-called *friends'* families' good names. If there was a way to disown her all the way to Australia I would in a heartbeat, but I cannot in good conscience rid myself of her by giving you her hand, what with your obligation to produce an heir."

Henrique looked appalled. "Do you have no love for your step-daughter at all, woman?"

She drew herself erect. "Love exists in many forms, sir. You will come to understand that when you become a parent, I dare say. Which brings us back to the business at hand: which of my daughters have you chosen for your bride? My eldest is the fairest, but my youngest has—"

"What are you prattling on about?" Henry said, irritated. "Your daughters are not interchangeable engine parts, you know!"

Lady Mary interlaced her fingers across her stomach. "The king your father has made his wishes widely known, sir—you are to be engaged before you return to the palace docks. And by coming here in your courting boat you have in turn made your intent to marry one of my daughters apparent to everyone in this entire fleet. Though you have spurned my daughters once, you will find either one fully ready to do her duty to King and Country."

"Duty." The prince turned to stare out the porthole. "Yes. Duty." He continued to stare. Peripherally aware that the woman was staring at him expectantly, he waved his hand in dismissal. Even though it was her ship, he was the prince. She withdrew.

"I brought you your shoe."

Sara-Bella's head whipped around to behold the prince in the hatchway to the engine room. She started to grasp at her skirt to curtsy, then, remembering she had doffed the detested dress for her trousers, gave up and sketched a bow. "Your Highness."

Taking in her appearance, sooty tear-tracks running down her face from the corners of her eyes, dress nowhere to be seen, Henrique made a guess: "You heard?"

"Anne and Beth eavesdropped, then they came down here to torture me with the news." She grimly tapped her left hand with the extra-long wrench in her right. "They won't be trying that again anytime soon."

"Ah." In an attempt to steer the conversation in a safer direction, Henrique held out her shoe and asked, "Why glass? Such a shoe is surprisingly impractical, for such a practical person as you seem to be."

"I'm conducting a stress test." She took it from his hand. "This is a stronger type of glass I was considering using in my next ship, and if it can stand up to me walking on it for a year, it's good enough for the ship."

"I see that you take design seriously." The prince took a seat on a closed coal bin. "Sara-Bella — if I may call you that — regardless of what your stepmother may have said, my offer still stands."

Her gaze dropped to the floor. "I thank the kind gentleman for being willing to honor his word, but for honor's sake in turn I must regretfully decline."

"Why?" Henrique asked.

It was harder, somehow, for Sara-Bella to reject a man she respected so, but in the end she stayed true to herself. "I choose to share my bed with no man. No heir would come of our union."

"Well, yes, what with my dynastic obligations, having no heir does pose a certain quandary. But that particular problem already existed before you came along. That's why father sent me out on this voyage around the kingdom — he thought if he dangled enough women in front of me, I would start to take a liking to them." Henrique peered at her in evident self-disbelief. "Oddly enough it sort of worked, though in my defense I thought you were a man when we first met. Now you have me all sorts of confused."

Sara-Bella's jaw had dropped. "Are you saying you..."

"Yes."

So that's why all the ladies call him Prince Charming. Wow. Sara-Bella cocked her head, set her wrench aside, and sat near him. "So, how would this work?"

"Freely. I see no reason for either of us to deny the other companion-ship of their choice when they find it, do you?"

Puzzled, Sara-Bella asked, "Why pursue this relationship, then? Other than appeasing your father, of what benefit to you is asking for a union with me, Your Highness?"

"Our union would not be all about me: from what I have observed you would lead a much happier life away from your stepfamily."

"That is true," she admitted. She did not mention the other option the Mer-matron had made available to her — the coat was behind the engine right now, where none of the other women on the ship would ever think to look for it.

"As to what benefit I would garner... Sara-Bella, talking with you last night was like talking to myself. Er, no, that came out wrong," he muttered. "What I meant was that it was almost like you were a part of me, not apart from me. We work well as a team — we're a natural fit — and I don't want to lose what we had last night over a question of who has what anatomical bits."

Sara-Bella placed a rough-skinned hand gently atop Henrique's. "Your Highness, please consider what you ask carefully. Would you truly be content in a loveless marriage?"

"Your stepmother was right about one thing, Sara-Bella: love comes in many forms. Just because we do not share one kind does not mean we cannot share another."

"Passionless, then. Would you be content in a passionless marriage?"

"We share a passion for steam engines, don't we? One might even say our relationship was steamy from the moment we met!" At her delighted laugh he took her soot-stained hand and lightly kissed the knuckles. "This isn't what either of us imagined for ourselves, I'm quite sure, but haven't some of the most amazing inventions of our time come about by accident?"

She considered his words, and decided. "Yes, Your Highness, they have. And, who knows? Maybe, some day, since you've already thought of me as a man, perhaps I can begin to think of you as a woman."

Henrique stood with a bemused expression for several seconds before admitting, "That concept is so convoluted I have no idea what to say."

Sara-Bella laughed. "Perhaps if we consider the creation of a child as an engineering project, your father might even get his wish for your heir!"

Laughing in turn, Henrique held up his hands. "Now, now, let's not get carried away. First things first." The prince got down on a knee. "Sara-Bella—"

"Cinderella."

"Cinderella, then: will you be my companion?"

Favoring her twisted ankle, Cinderella took a knee, too. "Sir, I will. Give me a moment to ready myself?"

"Certainly."

After Henrique had closed the door, Cinderella walked over to the porthole and, from behind the engine, pulled the selkie's coat. "Thank you, good mother, but I don't think I'll be needing this after all," she said softly as she draped the coat out the porthole.

Looking around the engine room, Cinderella walked over to the workbench, lugged the largest wrench over her shoulder, and opened the door. "Ready."

He blinked. "That's all? No hatboxes or such? Not even a valise?"

"Well, technically, this entire ship was supposed to be mine—Father and I built it together, after all—but my stepmother is in charge of the estate. Besides, if I took it with me right now, I'd have to take *them*, too."

"I can have Father insist that it be part of your dowry, if you'd like."

"A dowry." Cinderella shook her head, smiling. "Getting *married*. Never did I think to see the day."

"Nor I. But if it's any consolation, I think your stepmother is going to be more surprised."

She snorted. "Of that, sir, you may be certain."

"Married."

"Yes."

Lady Mary continued to look between Henrique and Sara-Bella as if waiting for one of them to tell her the joke was over, but neither did. Instead, she forced a smile onto her face and made the best of it. "Well, my sweet? When is the happy day?"

"One week after our return to home port," Cinderella said.

"One week?" Lady Mary said, shocked. "To plan a royal wedding? Why, the invitations alone will take a week to—"

"You needn't concern yourself with such details, madam," Cinderella interrupted her. "You will not be receiving an invitation."

The blood drained from Mary's face. "Not invite your own mother to your wedding? What would society think?"

"You've never taken that title upon yourself before today," Cinderella mused. "I do not find disinviting you to be so amiss."

"As to what society will think," Henrique added darkly, "it will think what we tell it to. You may even find that, someday soon, trousers will be considered the height of fashion for ladies. Come, my dear."

"You wouldn't just leave us like this!" Lady Mary said, clutching at Cinderella's arm.

"Like what?"

"Stranded!"

Cinderella rolled her eyes. "You're not stranded, you're in a perfectly seaworthy vessel. All you have to do is operate it."

Mary released her at once. "*Touch* that dirty, stinky engine? A woman of my stature? Never!"

"Then you're stranded by your own choice, not mine."

Lady Mary looked between her stepdaughter and her husband-to-be, and fell on her knees at his feet. "Mercy, Your Highness! I beg it, for me and my daughters."

"You're asking the wrong person," Henrique said stonily.

Mary swallowed, looked at the floor, and shifted her knees to the right. "Mercy, Your Highness," she said quietly.

The silence lasted for an uncomfortably long time. At last, Cinderella spoke.

"Ajax."

He stepped forward. "Yes, Your Highness?"

"Do we have any sailors or soldiers we can spare from our royal yacht?"

"A few, Your Highness."

"Then send them over to this ship to return these women to their home."

"Thank you, Your Hi—" Lady Mary began to say, but Cinderella was not finished.

"There they will remain under house arrest until after our honeymoon concludes, at which point they may be allowed to leave. But they are under no circumstances to be allowed near the palace grounds, nor anywhere we may be traveling."

"Yes, Your Highness," Ajax said.

Mary's voice was reduced to a whisper. "But society will ostracize us—not a man in the entire *kingdom* will call on your sisters! We will be ruined!"

Cinderella leaned closer to Lady Mary and spoke in a very distinct manner, as if quoting: "You've made it quite clear that you are not fit to be in society. It's as much for your own good as for everyone else's. Now stay out of sight until we're gone."

Henrique helped Cinderella disengage herself from the increasingly wan Lady Mary, and, hand-in-arm supporting her ankle, walked her up onto deck to the cheers and general acclamation of the surrounding ships' companies.

Under the cover of all the noise, Cinderella murmured to Henrique, "Do you *really* think trousers will become fashionable for ladies?"

Surprised, Henrique looked at her. "Why? Does it matter to you?"

She smiled. "You know what? I don't think it does."

The Clockwork Nightingale

based on The Nightingale

JEAN MARIE WARD

OF ALL THE SALOONS IN ALL THE BOOM TOWNS IN ALL THE NEW Dominion Territories, Shiro Shimotsuga walked into hers. Only Genny Teil didn't own Lodeville's Empire Saloon. She was just the canary on its gilded stage.

Her heart didn't care. The traitorous muscle leapt, the beat long enough to measure, then raced, drumming against the spelled diamond regulator implanted in her chest. The vibrations jarred flesh and bone, but after seven years, she'd learned to ignore the oddness and the ache, especially in the middle of a performance. Her yellow kid gloves with their fringe of yellow feathers never faltered as she conducted her audience through the refrain of "The Miner's Lament". The slight quaver in her voice as she launched into the final verse seemed nothing more than a fitting sorrow for the young miner who knew he must die.

She even managed to smile as she introduced the final number in her set—a galop to set their feet tapping and their mouths calling for another round. But Shiro was always in her field of view, weaving through the rambunctious crowd under the balcony, exchanging a word with the bartender at the saloon's imported mahogany bar, then heading for the room's only empty table, one row back from the stage.

She wasn't sure how her heart could be so certain it was him when so much about him had changed. Gone was the softness of the round-faced Shimotsuga boy who declared himself her personal *saburau* knight when they were six. You could carve stone with those sharp cheekbones, and cut your hand on his jaw. The brown eyes under his stovepipe hat, once so warm and merry, were as hard as the frozen mud of the streets outside.

Those eyes had wept the last time she saw him, standing beside her bed.

"I'll save you," he said.

"It's not a matter of saving. I'm broken, Shiro. My heart is broken."

"I'll mend it."

"You can't. Nobody around here can."

"When will you return?"

She didn't answer. She couldn't meet his eyes.

"I'll come for you. I'll bring you home."

But he hadn't. He'd come for Big Roy Lee. He tossed his hat on the table her boss reserved for his special guests, and dropped his fur-lined overcoat on a chair. So Genny did what she always did when her heart gave her pain. She poured it into her song. She wouldn't stop until her audience shouted and stomped their feet, and their applause rattled the bottles on the bar's long, mirror-backed shelves.

Was it her imagination that the cheers were louder tonight? Or was it what she wanted to hear as she took her bows? Her heart might owe its beat to a magic-powered metronome, but she still owned the sin of pride.

Like a goddess she descended from the stage to the main floor of the saloon, trading the smell of painted canvas and dusty curtains for the earthy funk of unwashed bodies and musky, sweat-stiff clothes. Her worshippers — gamblers, weathered prospectors, hard-faced miners from the Vale, men who would knife their brother for a poker stake — stepped aside to give her room. She favored them with smiles and nods, but neither stopped nor spoke until she reached the boss's table.

"Hello, Shiro."

He paused in the act of stripping the gloves from his long-fingered hands. For the briefest instant, shock knocked the frost off his manner, though she couldn't tell what startled him more, her voice or his name. His gaze flicked sideways, as if afraid of being discovered in one of their childhood scrapes. It was the first hint of her old friend in this well-dressed stranger.

And the last. The fine bow of his mouth thinned into something that wasn't quite a sneer. Not quite. But thanks to the upstanding matrons she encountered on her daily constitutionals, she knew the signs.

She lifted her chin higher. "It's me, Genny Teil. Though around here they call me Canary Diamond on account of my voice, and this."

She fanned her fingers next to the small, gold-framed socket holding the diamond in place. He could see where it cut into her breast, because the yellow taffeta of her sleeveless bodice barely crested the top of her corset.

Their audience murmured in agreement. She suspected that made it worse. His lashes flickered as he tried to look someplace less damning, and failed. Her feather-trimmed, canary-colored gown stopped well above her knees, exposing a greater span of silk-stockinged leg than decent girls showed on their wedding nights. Her powdered face, with its rouged lips, kohl-rimmed eyes and penciled brows, offered no respite. Her hair, which he would have remembered as a thick mane of golden brown tresses reaching to her hips, was dyed butter yellow and cropped like a feathered cap close to her scalp. There was barely enough left to secure the yellow fascinator angled over her forehead.

"I'll save you," he said.

Not that she ever expected he could. But his current contempt stung, made her cruel.

"Don't tell me you've forgotten," she drawled.

He snapped his gloves into his upturned hat like another man might crack a whip. If he thought that would stop her, he truly had forgotten.

She shrugged. "Sorry. I mistook you for..."

She never finished the thought. The door to the right of the stage banged against the hall behind it. Genny and Shiro flinched as one.

"Shimotsuga," Big Roy boomed, "welcome to the Empire!"

The crowd didn't so much part for Big Roy as get out of his way. Six and a half feet tall, he filled his claret-colored velvet coat near to bursting. It took a yard of heavy gold links to draw the steeple across his plaid silk vest. The jewel-studded gold watch tucked in his left pocket had been custom made as wide as a teacup so as not to get lost in his paw. The yellow diamond fob at the other end of the chain was as big as her thumb.

But the most desperate, most light-fingered among the Empire's patrons no more than licked their lips as he bulled past. Roy was rumored to have been a bare-knuckle champion in his youth. He was known to have a nasty way with a knife, and like most sporting men, he carried a pair of double-barreled Canova derringers in the pockets of his fawn trousers. But his true power lay in his wealth. The golden treasure splayed across his chest was no more than a symbol of the whole, a single chip standing in for a table stacked with golden crowns. He owned a part of everything worth owning in the silver-rich hills surrounding Lodeville—mines, railroads, water, judges, marshals, and all of the Empire Saloon.

He smiled the way he had the first time she saw him, standing beside her bed.

"How much will the operation cost?" she asked.

Her parents didn't answer. They couldn't meet her eyes.

"Three thousand gold crowns," the big man said. "A hundred pounds of gold. Metal on the barrelhead. They won't take notes or loans."

Her head rested on a bank of pillows, and still it reeled. Her life against her weight in gold. More gold than she'd ever heard of in a single place. More gold than her father's mercantile, the Shimotsuga forge, maybe their whole town saw in a year.

"No one has that kind of money."

"I do, and it's yours for a song, little lady. All you have to do is sing in my concert saloon."

"Exclusively. For twelve whole years."

"You have other plans?"

Seven years ago, she had. They hadn't included a man twice her age branding her shoulder with his hot, meaty hand.

She kept her expression bland, pretending her flesh was as hard as the rock for which Big Roy named her. Under the terms of her indenture, he couldn't force her to do anything but sing so long as she remained his headliner and continued to pay off her debt. But he could still make her life hell if she failed to maintain certain appearances.

Shiro remained seated while *she* spoke, but rose to take Big Roy's hand. The crowd bridled at the snub. Men who spent months living rough muttered about the stranger's manners. Their gallantry soothed her ruffled dignity, and for the moment, she felt a little less forlorn.

"I see you've already met the jewel of this establishment," Big Roy said.

He kept her pinned in place while he pumped Shiro's hand. She couldn't tell from his face whether he knew of their acquaintance or merely assumed her presence would make it easier to empty Shiro's pockets.

He didn't know the things Shiro kept in his pockets.

Used to keep in his pockets, she amended. Her memories didn't seem to apply to this tall, broad-shouldered swell dressed in black broadcloth and starched white linen better suited to a formal soiree than a frontier concert saloon. Frock coats didn't have any outside pockets. It would've ruined the line. But there was no telling what hid inside.

With a gracious gesture, Shiro invited Big Roy to sit at his own table. Amused, Genny turned to signal the bartender for her usual hot honey lemonade and found the Empire's prettiest bar girls already in motion, delivering champagne in a sweating silver bucket and a tray full of gold-rimmed crystal glasses. More intrigued than ever, Genny accepted a drink. She had another set to sing, but it was very good champagne.

Big Roy tossed back his champagne and held out his glass for another. "What's this marvel you couldn't wait 'til spring to show me?"

"Satchel," Shiro said, extending his hand to the black-cloaked figure at his shoulder.

Genny choked. Champagne bubbles burned up her nose. She'd been so focused on him, she never noticed his companion. Waving her would-be rescuers away, she studied the newcomer over the rim of her glass. The individual was so thoroughly swathed in fabric, she couldn't tell if it was a man or a woman, much less guess the reason behind his (her?) singular appearance.

Shiro drew a thick, clothbound ledger from the satchel. The label pasted on the cover read "Operating Instructions".

"It's hard to obtain first-rate entertainers for a concert saloon this close to the frontier." His smoke-seasoned baritone was so much richer than she recalled—husky and toe-curling like fine Logress whiskey, which irritated her no end.

"You trying to sell me a new act?" Big Roy interrupted, sounding like a jackdaw in comparison.

"Not an act, a solution to all the challenges you face on the concert side of your enterprise: singer of unparalleled range and musicality, whose every performance goes exactly according to plan. Nothing is left to chance. Every single show is as perfect as the last."

Was that supposed to be an insult?

Roy snorted. "So long as you wind it up every night. I swear, you magicanists are worse than snake-oil salesmen. You think nobody in the Territories ever saw a performing automaton before? Well, we have. Lots of times."

By now, most of the crowd had dispersed to the bar. Those who'd lingered to see what the champagne was about grumbled their agreement.

"Jes' an oversize music box," said one.

"Ya' think we spent our whole lives in a hole in the ground," said another.

"Three songs. I never heard one what had more."

"Give me a real canary any day," added Myrl, the staunchest of her devotees. The old prospector shot her an exaggerated wink from under eyebrows almost as bushy as his beard.

She flashed him her brightest smile. But instead of warming her, his praise raised goosebumps along her arms and lifted the fine hairs at the nape of her neck.

Every day brought some new magicanical marvel; she was living proof. It wouldn't be long before some bright spark found a way to preserve a live performance so it could be played like a music box. If you could have the best performance of the best singer forever at your command, why would you pay for anything else, especially when that anything else needed to be fed, housed, and clothed, and nurtured ambitions that didn't necessarily encompass the person who paid the bills?

When it came to gears, pistons, and selling the same, Shiro was as bright as polished brass. Whatever else had changed about him, she'd wager that remained true. He was too smart to waste an important man's time. Much too smart for unfounded confidence in a room full of less-than-friendly strangers. Yet there he sat, as cool and steady as the light from the mage-bulb chandeliers glowing overhead.

She stared at his cloaked companion. His attendant stood perfectly still, not even seeming to breathe. All logic to the contrary, her presentiment grew shivers. She set down her glass, because she was sloshing champagne over the rim.

"See what I mean?" Big Roy said. "Now you may have built the best automaton since the Painter of Cremeny, but it's still a one-trick pony tied to a box, and I'm not interested."

"I don't blame you. I wouldn't be interested, either. Boxes bore me," Shiro confided. Something sly glinted in his eyes. He commanded his companion, "Remove your cloak."

Miners, dealers, even Big Roy gasped. Genny was on her feet before the heavy black mantle hit the ground. An instant later she had to hop on her chair to avoid being crushed in the stampede to their table.

Shiro's companion was female, but no woman. She was a life-sized, fully articulated doll. Silky hair paler than Big Roy's champagne crowned a white china face. A heart-shaped patch of black enamel surrounded her right eye. Glossy red enamel painted her bee-stung lips, parted to show a hint of tiny, pearl-like teeth.

A smooth porcelain throat and the ball-like joints of the doll's shoulders rose over a skimpy, corset-like garment of white enameled panels embellished with black metal flowers and vines dotted with shiny jet studs. Black, fingerless mesh gloves hinted at the construction of her elbows while revealing the complex joints in her hands. An ostentatious black butterfly key too large for any gears the doll might contain crowned a bustle ruffled with thin, iridescent silk. The skirt itself was no more than a cage of vulcanized tubing. The knee-length costume—structure? assemblage?—bared the doll's white-stockinged legs from her black ankle boots to the briefest of black unmentionables.

The near nakedness of her artificial form should've been obscene. In one sense, perhaps it was. But in another, the brazen display was necessary. How else could Shiro demonstrate the perfection of his art? It was the magicanical equivalent of showing his cards, and what cards they were! People would travel for miles to see his creation, regardless of how she performed.

"Gentlemen…and ladies," he added belatedly to the dancing girls seeping from the door to the back, "behold the Clockwork Nightingale."

As soon as he said her name, the Nightingale's bottom lip and chin shifted downward. From her throat poured the note of A.

The tone struck Genny's senses like a hammer on glass. If it weren't for the men crowded around her, she would've fallen off the chair.

"See," Myrl said as propped her upright, "she only got one song, and it don't have words."

"No. You don't understand," she gasped, the note chiming inside her head like death's own bell. "It's perfect."

Miraculously perfect. Inhumanly perfect. Mechanically perfect. She bit her lip and tried to will the sound away, but the perfect pitch she was born with mocked her almost as much as the cocky lift of Shiro's mouth. She clutched her stomach and waited for the next disastrous knell.

Big Roy's chair creaked as he leaned back, eyes slightly narrowed. He had a fine ear and an even more finely developed sense of what people would pay to see. But a smart gambler always plays his cards close to his vest. He affected a lazy, stupid smile.

"Now I grant I never saw an automaton move on its own, much less one that did what you told it. But I agree with Myrl. One note ain't much of an act. How much more you got?"

"Three thousand more — three thousand songs, that is. The index lists them all."

Shiro spun the book around. It *shush*-ed across the table into Big Roy's hands. As if by magic, Genny thought a little hysterically.

She scrambled off her chair. She had to sit down. She had to put her head as far between her legs as her corset would allow. She was going to be ill, on two sips of champagne.

Three thousand songs… After years of study and coaching, her repertoire numbered in the hundreds, if you included operas. Her range, as much as the quality of her voice, had attracted scouts from some of the biggest theatrical companies in Logress and Yalevven.

But three thousand songs… It would take years to learn so many, and she'd never match the Clockwork Nightingale's perfect tone. She was obsolete at twenty-five. How would she redeem her bond? She had five years left on her indenture, and singing was her only skill, the only decent way she had of paying off her debt. What had she ever done to Shiro that he would do this to her?

"When will you return?"

Big Roy wanted the Nightingale. Where she shuddered at its potential, he smelled profit. She could tell from the way he stared at the air above Shiro's book, which he hadn't bothered to open. He was running the numbers in his head and plainly liked the sums.

She couldn't let Shiro's Nightingale supplant her on the Empire stage, not while Big Roy owned her service and her earnings. Not while, in the eyes of the Territorial Court, he owned her. The few safeguards in her contract existed to protect her ability to perform as a headliner. She couldn't afford to lose them to a machine.

Roy put on his haggling face and crossed his arms over his vest. "You're telling me that doll could sing a month of shows without repeating a single song? No offense, Shimotsuga, but that's a mighty big claim. You got some way of proving it?"

"You can prove it yourself. Pick as many songs as you like from the index, and I'll show you how to make her sing."

"Don't bother." Genny jumped to her feet. "Roy's already decided to buy her."

"Canary," Roy protested, "you know you shouldn't drink so soon after singing. That little bit of champagne went straight to your head."

"So what if it did? I'm only saying what everybody knows. You're crazy for machines. You go after every lightning-fired, coal-fueled, steam-powered, gear-driven dingus out there. It doesn't even have to work, so long as you think people will pay to see it."

His eyes narrowed. "Nothing wrong in wanting the latest and greatest."

"When it's my job on the line, I say there is."

"Aren't you the selfish one? We have a full house of people spoiling for a little kindness and entertainment. And what do you want to do? You want to deny them their chance to hear the latest marvel of the age."

"You got me all wrong, Roy. I want nothing of the sort. I want to give them the show of a lifetime. I want to give them both of us, woman against machine." She yanked off her right glove and flung it at the book. "I'm challenging that thing to a duel."

The new, impassive Shiro blinked. The house seemed to catch its breath in a single throat. Excited murmurs followed, like ripples from a stone skipping across a pond.

"Here, tonight, in front of all these fine people, you called me the Jewel of the Empire. A handful of minutes later, after hearing one note out of that thing's mouth, you started thinking you could replace me with a wind-up doll. Well, I won't let you, not without a fight. Three songs each. She—*it!*—sings one, and then I sing one. You pick *its* songs, I pick mine, and let the customers decide who they want to hear. They're the ones who pay for it, after all."

Roy's serpent smile eased into something that was almost genuine. He cocked his head at the doll. "You really think you can take her?"

"If I don't, how will I pay off my indenture?"

Another gasp circled the room. Everyone supposed her income matched her name. They assumed she dressed in the clothes Big Roy provided and roomed in his saloon because of some personal arrangement between them. Roy never bothered to enlighten them, and she'd been too embarrassed to admit she was little better than a servant. But now, with everything at stake, she wouldn't scruple at playing the sympathy card, not when so many of the Empire's customers owed bonds of their own.

Roy's lips skinned back from his teeth. "There's always upstairs work."

Upstairs work. Mattress work. Flat on her back with her legs spread. The kind of work that left healthy women damaged and diseased, if it didn't kill them outright.

"No, there isn't."

"You owe me, girl."

"Not that, I don't."

"Big words for such a little bird. You're forgetting who bought that diamond heart of yours."

"Pick your songs, Roy."

"Girl's got spunk," Myrl hooted. Other voices lifted in agreement.

"You think there's some other way of paying what you owe? Think again, little bird. As long as I hold your bond, you can't work anywhere else...unless you find a 'patron'"—his sneer turned the title into something vile—"with pockets deeper than mine."

Genny threw his sneer right back at him, goading him, willing him to say more. A hulking, red-faced bully threatening a woman less than half his size played *so well* in a room of homesick brothers and sons, she thought ironically. Miners and company agents grumbled at the edge of her hearing, for once in complete accord. Almost all of them were exiles from the Vale, and prone to be protective where women were concerned.

That didn't stop her legs from wanting to run. Roy couldn't abide any challenge to his authority. Shiro's succeeded because he was a magicanical genius, and everyone knew they were madder than rabid raccoons. She would pay for hers. Not today. Not in public. But as soon as Roy was sure he could get away with it, those heavy fists would batter everything that didn't show or sing.

She purged the thought from her mind. She couldn't afford the distraction. She had to win. She was staking her present, as well as her future. The stage was her sanctuary. He couldn't hurt her too badly without people knowing, and some would take it personally — especially those who made money wagering on this little singing match. From the gleeful exchange of sporting propositions, that number would include most of the people in the room.

"A duel," Shiro rolled the word around his mouth as if sampling the vintage. "This could be interesting. The Nightingale's songbook includes the most difficult arias in the operatic repertoire, including Nera's death scene from *Priestess of the Sun God*."

"The one with all the trills?" Roy asked.

"All twelve of them," Shiro replied. "There hasn't been a singer in fifty years who could manage the scales."

That wasn't exactly true. The scales might be tricky, but the real danger was boredom. Most productions of Priestess cut the run in half to prevent audience members from squirming in their seats or, worse, ducking out of the hall — which happened at the original command performance for the king of Logress. Her first vocal coach used the story to keep her students focused on the total effect of a performance, instead of their individual parts.

She'd told Shiro the tale. He said the same applied to the little tea-serving dolls that were his first automata. You needed to envision the whole or the parts would never fit.

She pulled her lower lip between her teeth, considering.

"And of course," Shiro continued, his face as unreadable as his creation's, "as the challenged party, you have first choice of material."

She'd already said as much, and received nothing but taunts in reply. But as soon as Shiro made the point, Roy flipped the cover of the book, knocking her glove aside.

"My first selection is Nera's aria."

"Mr. Lee." Eldon, the piano player, raised his beer glass to get the boss's attention. "I don't have the score for that. It's not on the rolls for the player piano, either."

"The Nightingale's voice needs no accompaniment," Shiro said.

"You hear that?" Big Roy asked. "Still think you can take her?"

"Does this mean you're thinking of replacing Eldon, too?" she countered. "What about the dancers? Why don't you have Shiro make you a few of those?"

"No! He wouldn't!" one of the newer dancers squeaked. "We sell too many drinks."

The room erupted in laughter. Lead dancer Lissa Katano shushed the girl and hustled her to the rear of the corps.

The twinkle in Big Roy's eyes was the glitter of mean. "Don't make this more than it is. You're as much a machine as she is. You wouldn't last a day without that regulator in your chest. It's what pumps your blood, not that stone you call a heart. That organ's as dead and hard as the diamond that supplanted it—the diamond I paid for—as every man here has reason to know."

She shook her head. "You paid me to sing in your concert saloon. Those are the terms of my bond. I'm just trying to satisfy them."

"Then, by all means, get on with it. Shimotsuga, you've got the stage."

"Follow me, Nightingale," Shiro instructed.

Genny tensed, but instead of another piercing A, she heard a barely audible click and a soft pneumatic hiss. The doll swerved as if her boots concealed ball bearings instead of feet. She skated up the steps to the stage, her movements smooth and economical. The crowd murmured their appreciation—and changed their bets again.

Not to be outdone, Genny sashayed up the stairs, all the while assessing her opponent. Thanks to Shiro, she'd learned a thing or two about automata over the years. Despite the name and the enormous key attached to her skirt, the Nightingale integrated too many functions in too small a space to run off a winding stem. Given the absence of visible vents and any trace of steam, the only thing small enough and strong enough to provide the necessary energy would be a series of spelled diamonds running in tandem, but the cost...

I'll mend it.

The low, smoke-tempered voice of the man replaced the boy in her head. She shivered anew. He swore he'd devise a regulator-sized battery that could be mass-produced like mage bulbs. Damn him for succeeding now. An internalized power supply made the doll all but impossible to disable.

Not that she'd dare. The folk who frequented the Empire might lack what society called propriety. But there was one class of person they would neither tolerate nor forgive: a cheat. Genny had to win fair or she wouldn't win at all. So what was the machine's weakness?

It wasn't presence. The contrast between Shiro's formal black suit and the Nightingale's skimpy costume called to mind a stage magician and his assistant. Genny didn't doubt the effect was deliberate. What was worse, their black and white outfits looked smart and fresh against the painted cage of brightly colored birds that formed the backdrop for her set.

In contrast, without her customary intermission repairs, her stage face had melted into dark smudges and shiny patches of skin. The bitten nails and ragged cuticles of her gloveless right hand were on full display. Her bustle dragged, and her mouth felt drier than if she'd been chewing sand. The Clockwork Nightingale was immune to all that, as indifferent to its condition as it was to its surroundings.

As it was to its audience. The doll's unblinking glass eyes stared at the people jostling for position in front of the stage. The automaton possessed the means of registering sound, or it couldn't respond to commands. But there was no flicker of reaction to the comments of the crowd, just as there had been no reaction to the dusky music of Shiro's voice. Genny would've gladly replayed his every word, even the insults, to preserve this bit of him she never thought to own.

The doll heard. The doll obeyed. It was a moving machine which could not be moved, not even by its maker. That was its flaw. That was the card to play.

"You might want to stand on the opposite side of the stage," Shiro suggested. "The Nightingale is programmed for a complete performance. Some of her movements can be quite dramatic."

Genny started. Her wayward legs had carried her close enough to smell the trace of cedar and smoke that managed to attach itself to even his newest clothes. Another time she might've laughed. For the moment, she couldn't let his instructions go unchallenged. That would make her no better than his toy.

"Why don't we divide the stage down the middle? You take stage left. I'll take the right. We can take our turns downstage depending on who's performing."

Shiro nodded. Whatever he thought of her as a person, it was the only sensible way to proceed.

Big Roy had other ideas. "You trying to fix this fight?"

The audience booed his insinuation. She opened her mouth to tell him she wanted to hear the Nightingale as much as anyone, but Shiro got there first.

"It wouldn't matter. The Nightingale's skin has been treated to shed water, resist soiling, and…"

A horn-handled folding knife appeared in his hand. He slashed the blade across the doll's throat. The edge squealed along the porcelain flesh like a butter knife on a dinner plate. The knife vanished quicker than the sound. *So the pockets hadn't changed.* An irrational thrill of joy accompanied the thought.

Shiro continued, "She's impervious to most forms of direct assault."

"Well, all right then," Roy crowed. "Let's get this show started."

Shiro tugged the snowy cuffs of his shirt. He pressed a pair of studs on the doll's back. Pistons sighed. The corset's side front panels lifted on short metal rods. Matching elbow joints folded the panels over the center of the corset. Hissing softly, the panels settled flush against the line of beads marking the corset's center front.

The operation exposed oblongs of stretched black mesh. Genny whistled softly. As if the Nightingale wasn't loud enough already, Shiro had incorporated covered horns, like the ones used in speaking tubes, to further amplify her voice. It wasn't the doll's movements Genny had to worry about; it was the volume.

She retreated upstage, trying to get behind the horns without spooking the crowd. For the first time in all her years at the Empire, she thanked the Saints for the perpetual glare of the Empire's mage-bulb chandeliers. The bright lights shining on the gaming tables meant there was no need for footlights. Stout metal casings shielded the mage-bulb spotlights suspended between the battens. Their glass wasn't as thick as the exposed bulbs of the chandeliers, but at that height, they should be safe.

"Please, turn to the song index at the back of the book, and read out the four-digit number next to 'Nera's Death Scene'," Shiro said.

After seeing what a pair of beads could do, it came as no surprise that the flowers on the Nightingale's corset served as dials. As Roy read each digit, Shiro twisted a different blossom on the back of the corset a corresponding number of petals to the right. Fascinated in spite of herself, Genny couldn't help but keep track: two, four, nine, one. Did each of the flowers, leaves, beads, and spangles govern a different function? No wonder the doll's instruction book was so thick.

Shiro called for silence. After a quick shuffle of feet and the scrape of a few chairs, the room quieted. Even the off-duty sheriff's deputy manning the gun check turned to the stage.

With a crisp flick of his arm, he presented his creation, exactly like the magician she'd compared him to. He pressed a white button between the automaton's shoulder blades and stepped back, somehow managing to draw level with Genny without glancing in her direction. She willed herself not to cover her ears.

"Woe!" the Clockwork Nightingale shrieked. In high C.

The crystal champagne glasses on Big Roy's table exploded in a hail of slivers. Sharp citrus fumes of champagne joined the odors of beer, sweat, and drying wool rising from the main floor. Roy started to swear, changed his mind and forced out a laugh as the bartender and waiter girls ducked under the bar. The mirrors shook in their frames, but withstood the blast as well as the thick, everyday barware. Not so the watch faces of the patrons near the stage.

A railroad engineer Genny knew by sight shouted at Big Roy: "That was my papa's watch, you son of a bitch!"

That's what she thought he said, at any rate. Thanks to the horns, the Nightingale's voice was big enough to fill the largest theater without sacrificing clarity, pitch, or the miraculous sweetness of its tone. Genny had never heard the aria sung so musically, as if some celestial instrument had been given human voice, or a siren had taken her melody to land. Eventually even the angry engineer succumbed. His eyes glazed with awe.

Only one aspect was lacking: the music had no context. Nera was being burnt at the stake. The infamous trills were her death throes, echoing the rising flames. Yet the Nightingale's voice registered neither the agonies of the fire nor the exultation of martyrdom. The stage directions called for Nera's chains to "miraculously" fall away in the middle of the aria, permitting her to clasp the flames in a final, symbolic embrace. But in the absence of emotion—or anything holding her down—the abrupt transition from singing stock to flailing arms looked more than a little ridiculous.

Meanwhile, the trills went on and on.

The reaction started with a quickly muffled snicker from somewhere near Roy's table. Soon there were more. Not many. The automaton's performance was a true marvel, worthy of the applause that greeted her final note. But it wasn't programmed for passion, and as for dying, it couldn't manage that at all.

At Shiro's command, the automaton retreated upstage. Genny minced forward, eyes as wide and girlish as her ruined make-up allowed.

"Oops," she squeaked in Soprano C, minus the Nightingale's glass-shattering force.

A few people tittered nervously. Big Roy snarled, "What the hell are you playing at?"

"I'm not playing." She pretended to pout. "That's the first note of my song."

With a snort of laughter Eldon slammed his shot glass on the bar. Over the course of the Nightingale's aria the pianist had lined up three empty shots in front of his beer. He turned unsteadily, propping his elbows on the bar for support.

"It's the opening to 'Sun Bird' from Brunello's *Princess Buttercup*. It's famous." '*Among real music lovers*' remained unspoken, but Eldon's tone got the point across. "You won't find it in the piano rolls. Player pianos can't handle the fingering. You need a real musician for that."

Scowling, Big Roy turned to the dancers in bright blue gowns roosting near the stage. The three Katano sisters had danced for the Western Logress Light Opera Company before heading to the Territories. Lissa, the oldest, boasted a knowledge of musical theater almost as wide as Genny's own.

"There's an aria that begins with 'Oops'?" Roy demanded.

Lissa nodded, setting her dark curls bobbing. She added diplomatically, "The tune's popular, but not the song. You only hear it in the operetta, and as far as I know, there hasn't been a new production of *Princess Buttercup* since before the Great Revolt."

It didn't help. A sizeable portion of the audience chuckled. Big Roy's nostrils flared. Genny was in for it now. She might've gotten away with dredging up an obscure hundred-year-old comic aria if Eldon hadn't turned it into an insult. Since he had, there was no way this could end well, even if she won.

Especially if she won. It was madness to pretend she was a person instead of a possession, bought and paid for the twelve-year term of her contract. Even the name he gave her was a thing: a rock as yellow as piss. Madness and pride. But damn them all, she was better than any battery-powered collection of metal and gears, no matter who put it together, no matter how perfect its voice.

She filled her lungs with the sharp ozone scent of the mage lights, the memory of bear grease and rice powder, and the dust clinging to the red velvet curtains on either side of the stage. Her chest expanded until her ribs ground against the metal bones of her corset.

"OoooooooOoooooOoooooOoooooOOOPS!"

On the tables nearest the stage, the remaining glasses cracked with a sound like buckshot. To cheers!

Her voice swooped and sailed through cadenzas as showy as anything *Priestess* had to offer, which wasn't surprising if you knew the score. The operetta was Brunello's comic take on the theatrical excesses of his day. People seldom performed it, because you needed to know the originals to get the jokes. But in this case, everyone had just heard the original. "Sun Bird" was Brunello's spoof of Nera's interminable dying breaths, only shorter, intentionally funnier, and a lot easier to sing.

By the time she got to the trills—and the commentary punctuating the vocal pyrotechnics—people were pounding the tables and howling. Her ovation didn't quite rattle the bar, but the shelves were still a little soggy from her opening note.

Big Roy was not amused. He wouldn't let himself be shorted twice. He'd avoid the cliché and stick with more modern material offering less scope for parody. Unfortunately for her, his taste in lieder was excellent. His next selection was "The Moon" from Vonallan's *Cycle of the Spheres*, a haunting, ethereal melody which derived its impact from pure technical brilliance.

Shiro ordered the Nightingale downstage, set the dials and started her song. Moistening her lips, Genny couldn't help but wonder what he'd thought of her performance. Had he smiled at the musical jokes they shared as children? Had he scowled at her impertinence like one of the ferocious *saburai* in the paintings his grandmother had carried with her from her distant home?

Why did she even care? He'd brought her to this pass.

I'll save you.

Destroy her, more like. The terms of her bond were tied to the terms of her contract—so many headline performances per year spread over a period of twelve years. She'd struggled with the circumstances of her employment. But the terms always seemed clear. She never imagined they'd become a trap. She never anticipated any long-term competition this far from polite society, much less from an overgrown toy which devalued her only skill.

He gave her Nera.

And destroyed her with "The Moon". She couldn't match the automaton's celestial perfection. When the Nightingale's song was done, she moved somberly, respectfully downstage and tipped her head in acknowledgment of a voice as peerless as the heavenly body it celebrated. Then she waited for the thunderous clapping to recede.

"That was amazing, wasn't it?" A fresh, dishearteningly enthusiastic round of applause greeted her question. She forced herself to smile. "It would be foolish and unmannerly to deny how beautifully my clockwork rival sang that song. I confess, I couldn't sing it so well. But there are many kinds of beauty. Sometimes you find it in the most terrible of places, like the Northern Wilds where my next song is set."

"The Elf King" was an old ballad set to a lush, romantic tone poem. It told the story of a man fleeing the lethal specters of the Elf King's Hunt. Riding in front of him on his lathered horse was his ailing child. The boy's strength ebbed with every verse, until at the last the Hunt claimed its prize: the child's spirit, ripped from his frail body, to ride with the Hunt for ever after.

The fraught emotion of the lyrics was the only possible counter to the Nightingale's sterile perfection. Still, it was a mistake. The song's themes of loss and desperate, hopeless flight mirrored her situation too closely. The loss of her health and the future she'd planned. The flight to the regional hospital. The mirage of medical hope that led to a different kind of loss. The loss of her freedom. The loss of her youth. The loss of her family for the term of her bond. Now she might lose them for good, racing to the doom she fought so long to escape.

And Shiro…Oh, Shiro…*He wouldn't meet her eyes.*

She couldn't say when she started weeping. Her cheeks were hot and damp by the middle of the second verse. Her nose held off running until the last. But the damage was done. Her voice failed on the final note in a strangled croak.

They were clapping. Why were they applauding? Didn't they hear her voice break? She'd lost, but nobody seemed to care. Her breath sawed in and out of her tear-roughened throat as miner and dancer, gambler and company agent, railroader, bartender and swell, stamped their feet and cried "Bravo!" to bring down the house.

No opening-night bouquet could compare to Myrl's tribute: a mug of honey lemonade just warm enough to drink. While she was still recovering from the surprise, he thrust a clean cotton handkerchief in her free hand. Where did somebody who slept with his mule find something like that?

Alone among the crowd, Big Roy scented blood. He waited his turn, sipping flat champagne from a beer glass. She fought not to shiver as he lifted his drink in an ironic salute. His eyes were opaque and unblinking, like a viper waiting to strike.

"For the Nightingale's final song, I choose a little number near and dear to the hearts of everyone here: 'The Miner's Lament'."

He thought he'd break her with that — her signature, the song her audience demanded night after night. If it weren't for Myrl, it might've worked. But when the time came, she'd have just enough voice for one final song. It wouldn't be concert quality. It didn't have to be.

There was one song dearer than "The Miner's Lament" to the men who toiled in the nearby hills. It was the one they never requested.

Calm flowed through her, warming her like the cup of kindness in her hands. A true predator, Roy sniffed out the change. He straightened in his chair, indifferent to the Nightingale's mechanical posturing as she belted out the chorus. Genny would've wagered no one in the crowd had ever heard the song sung with such exactitude — or felt it less. The Clockwork Nightingale would never mourn the miner who knew he must die.

The song ended in a spatter of applause. No cheers. No stamping. The only glasses that moved were the shot glasses of the gamblers who laid odds against her.

Genny stuffed Myrl's handkerchief into her corset and leveled her shoulders. "My final number will be 'The Vale'."

Big Roy's brows drew together over his nose. "Hillbourne's 'Veil'?"

"No. The other one."

All conversation ceased. The drinkers lowered their whiskey with exaggerated care. Eldon stepped away from the bar. Lissa braced her hands at the edge of the stage.

"Awake, Logressans bold?" Lissa asked, unconsciously slipping into the melody.

"Your time has come to fight," Genny sang in answer, "the tyrant's brutal hold..."

The song's original title was "War Song for the Army of the West". But everyone called it "The Vale" after the coal-rich valleys in northwest Logress where it was first sung.

The province was home to some of the most mule-headed, contrary-minded folk in a country famous for both. Fifteen years ago, the people of Vale supported Wynneth Pretender in the Great Revolt, and paid the price when he lost: their sons slaughtered, their daughters violated, their homes occupied by soldiers of the queen's army grown vengeful over the course of the campaign.

Those who could, fled. The wilderness of the overseas Territories was a good place for the refugees to lick their wounds and reinvent themselves. Miners by trade, many Vale natives gravitated to the rich ore deposits in the hills overlooking Lodeville, where few questions were asked of a man who knew his way around a blasting cap. Other "undesirables" were swept along with the tide: music teachers, piano players, even a dancer or three.

Genny wasn't one of them. She was born in the Territories to parents who'd immigrated for opportunity, not chased by war. She'd never walked Vale's flowered hills or seen the ocean lash its proud Iron Cliffs. But she knew what it was to lose, to bleed, to feel her heart failing in her chest, to yearn without hope, to hope without reason, and she poured it into her song.

"Link arms, citizens,
"Rise up battalions.
"March on, march on,
"Heroes resolved
"On victory or death!"

A hundred voices soared with hers. Two hundred! This was bigger than the Vale. Customers and saloon employees stood together, as tall as Nera on the pyre. Their stories might be different, but in pain, grief, and hope, they were all the same—people striving, failing, and trying all over again. The sound they made was too big for the room. It would've been too big for a cathedral. The notes lingered long after the song's final shout, becoming one with the ovation they gave themselves.

Dear as it was, she knew the victory would be short-lived. Next year or the year after, someone would capture a real singer's voice in crystal or teach a machine to feel. But for the moment she could stand like a hero with her legs wide and her hands fisted on her hips, drinking in the sight of Roy's curt, pucker-faced nod.

Myrl whooped and ordered a round for everyone. Eldon called out a toast to the Jewel of the Empire, which naturally led to more.

"Is this what you want?" Shiro's whisper lifted the feathery strands at the nape of her neck.

What she wanted was to pound his dense skull like pig iron on an anvil. Instead, she hissed, "I don't have a choice."

But the damned man wasn't paying attention. He bent over his infernal machine, fluffing her poufy behind like some dressmaker's assistant. Had she imagined the murmured question? He hadn't yet deigned to speak to her. Why start now?

The only thing that kept her from stomping off like a thwarted child was the jubilant crowd ranged around the stairs. She owed them. So she smiled and sparkled and thanked them all, letting herself be swept into their procession to the bar. The bartender had a fondness for horehound drops and a willingness to share. With enough water, honey, and throat lozenges, she just might be able to scrape through the night's second set. But she'd sip a proper drink or two, if only to raise her glass to the people saluting her.

Shiro strode toward the stairs, absently ordering the Nightingale to follow. He didn't sound angry or disappointed as much as abstracted, like one of his precious designs failed to perform as advertised, but he couldn't pinpoint the flaw. Disgusted, she wished him a headache for his pains — to say nothing of the pains he caused her.

"Leave her right there," Big Roy shouted. "I'm still of a mind to buy her."

Genny whirled. All thoughts of Shiro fled.

Myrl squalled, "Why you lying, underhanded son of a sidewinder! Canary won her duel fair and square. She's the one we want to hear, twice a night, same as always."

"You'll hear her. But she can't sing again tonight. Can you, Canary?" Big Roy asked, oozing false concern. "What with all that fancy vocalizing on top of your regular set, I suspect your throat is frightful sore. I'd hate for you to do yourself an injury. Why don't you take the rest of the night off? The customers won't mind. Not after your little show."

He smiled as he said it, anticipation flaring in his eyes. His thick wrist twisted, fingers curled as if around a knife, carving the air as if it were flesh, telling her exactly how the game would end.

Before tonight, she always believed her ultimate defense was the diamond in her chest. Roy might demean her, and try to whore what he couldn't buy. He might beat her black and blue, but he wouldn't risk losing his investment. She'd read him wrong. She'd pushed too far. He was going to make her an example. She'd heard tales of what he could do with a knife. Everyone at the Empire had. Now he would do it to her.

She jumped when someone touched her arm, half expecting to shatter. A gentleman gambler cocked his head toward the bottles remaining at the back of the bar. Gazing at him from under her lashes, she nodded. Let people think she needed a drink. It was safer than the truth.

She needed to think. She needed to plan. She had two half-crowns secreted in her boots — more than enough for a ticket to Buxton, the Territory capital, assuming she could make it onto the train. The few people she could trust to help her were either drunk or quickly getting there. The rest of the room lived in Roy's pocket or swam in his debt.

Big Roy waved Shiro to his table. "So how much is this little toy of yours going to set me back?"

"I don't see the point. Your customers prefer the current arrangement."

She needed warm clothes and a disguise, but she couldn't risk being trapped in her room. The Nightingale's cloak had to be around here somewhere. It wasn't as if the automaton could perish of cold.

Shiro reached for his hat. Roy snatched it from his fingers. "I didn't take you for a quitter, son. The Nightingale's something so new, folks don't know what to make of her. They'll come around."

"Not soon enough. I have a firm offer from the Grand Theatre in Buxton. I planned to close the deal over Winterfair, but Lord Hilltown insisted I talk to you first."

Buxton! Was he headed back to Buxton?

"And well he should. The governor knows I'm a forward thinker. I've got plans for Lodeville. Big plans. What would you say to a saloon where the entertainment ran non-stop, and it was all mechanical?"

Shiro snorted. "I'd say you're fishing for a discount."

"I knew you were smart the minute I saw you."

"No."

"What?"

"I'm getting out of the automaton business. A group of investors in Buxton have approached me about my work with compact power capsules and articulated mechanical limbs. The venture will occupy me full-time for the foreseeable future."

Buxton again. It had to be a sign. She could hide in Buxton. Wire her parents. Engage a lawyer. Shiro could get her there. He must have a wagon, something sturdy and defensible to transport his creations. He wouldn't have trusted something as valuable as the Nightingale to a train or the stage. She just had to convince him. *It might be easier convincing his doll.*

"In other words, the Nightingale's one of a kind, and likely to stay that way. That suits me down to the core. The law of supply and demand is a showman's friend, so long as he controls the supply. How much?" Roy repeated.

"Three thousand gold crowns," Shiro said. "A hundred pounds of gold or the specie equivalent. Metal on the barrelhead. I don't take notes or loans."

Sober as a widow's bonnet, and still she reeled. It couldn't be a coincidence—not those figures, not those words. *Her life against her weight in gold.*

The crowd muttered. That was more gold than they'd ever seen in a single place, more silver than all the miners of Lodeville together saw in a month, more money than any one of them would hold in a lifetime.

Roy laughed. He tossed Shiro's hat back onto the table, then poked his thumbs in the pockets of his vest, tapping the right one—the one that held his fob—three times with his fingers. The big yellow diamond wasn't just for show. It was spelled as a silent alarm, keyed to tokens all his bullies carried.

Rifle barrels poked through the gun slits secreted between the balconies' curtained boxes. The bouncers who'd emerged from the basement for her contest moved closer to the bar, the door to the street, and the door to the inside stairs, cutting off all visible exits. An off-duty sheriff's deputy mounted the stage and slipped into the wings. She bit her lip to keep from screaming. He was headed backstage. Backstage where there was a door to the alley. Backstage where she planned to make her escape.

"You almost had me there," Roy chuckled.

"Durn tootin'!" Myrl exclaimed, oblivious to the drop in conversation and the nervous, sidelong glances of the people around him. "A man'd have to be a fool to pay that kinda money for a jumped-up music box, when we got ourselves a real, live Canary."

Shiro shrugged. "It's my price. If you won't pay it, others will." He retrieved his gloves.

"Not so fast," Roy growled. "We don't take kindly to cheats in Lodeville."

Genny wasn't the only one who gasped. Shiro's forehead creased in confusion, the well-remembered expression sitting oddly on his grown-up face. Her corset seemed to tighten all by itself.

"I assure you, the offer from the Grand is legitimate. If you don't believe me, wire the manager. Wire the governor, while you're at it. He's the one who thought you'd do better."

"That's not what I mean, and you know it," Roy snarled. "You think I missed the way Canary stared at you, or the way she cozied up to you on stage? She's never done that before, not even with those she owes. Then there's you, mooning after her when you think no one can see."

He did? She snorted at her own stupidity. Roy would say anything to get the crowd on his side.

"Now you want three thousand gold crowns for a jumped-up music box, which just so happens to be the exact price of the operation and the spelled diamond that keeps my little songbird singing."

A flash of understanding lit Shiro's eyes. Then his features settled into the bland, impervious mask of the stranger he'd become. He wouldn't be so composed if there was anything to Roy's charges. He was the worst poker player in town. *As a child.*

"Can't blame a man for having a soft spot for an old friend. Since when is that a crime?"

At least he had the decency to call her a friend and not something worse.

"It's a crime when you come into my establishment under false pretenses."

"I did no such thing. I came here to offer you the ultimate entertainer, a one-of-a-kind mobile musical automaton which performs exactly as advertised. The going price for stationary automata is a crown a song. The Nightingale has a three thousand song repertoire. She's mobile and responds to voice commands, which makes her worth even more."

"Liar!" Roy's face bulged like a thundercloud, veins shooting across his forehead and down the side of his neck. "You came here to steal my Canary Diamond. Don't try to deny it."

The edge of the bar bit into her stays as she instinctively backed away. Shiro went deadly still, an answering threat in every line of his form. "You wrong me."

Roy surged to his feet, nostrils flaring. His thick fingers clenched and his arm eased back, but something in the shorter man's face stopped him from taking the punch, even as the corners of his mouth went white.

"I came here to *buy*" — Shiro's smoke-stained voice deepened into a growl — "the remainder of Miss Diamond's contract."

The raw, animal sound shook her insides. Then her mind caught up with the words.

I'll come for you... I'll save you. For the second time that night, Shiro knocked the world out from under her. She clutched the bar for support. *No, no, no! The blazing idiot! How could he do anything so stupid? Roy would kill them both.*

"And just how do you propose to do that?" Roy sneered.

"With the proceeds of the sale of an automaton worth the full amount of her spelled diamond and the operation that put it there. There's nothing dishonest about that."

"If everything is so honest and above board, why'd you pretend not to know her? Answer me that!"

"This is ridiculous. I don't have to justify…" Shiro clamped his mouth shut. He took a slow breath. "The governor and Lennessee Falchion both told me you'd drive a hard bargain. I wanted an edge."

If the situation hadn't been so dire, Roy's sour face would've made her laugh. The head of Falchion Apprehension Services wasn't a man to be crossed, even at one remove. Roy settled back on his heels, baring his teeth in something that tried for a smile and failed. The chuckle that accompanied it was worse.

"Well, you should've said so. The Canary's contract isn't for three thousand crowns. That was just the cost of her operation. A debt like that comes with interest: twelve percent compounded annually for the twelve years of her contract. The total comes to just under twelve thousand crowns, one thousand crowns for every year she sings at the Empire."

Shiro's heavy-lidded eyes rounded. "That's obscene."

"The Territorial court didn't think so. There's a copy of the contract in the court records, signed, sealed, recorded, and archived for anyone to see. So unless you're hiding something like this in your pocket" — Roy drew his fob from its resting place and swung the cone-shaped yellow diamond in a languid arc — "you can't afford her."

A grumble shuddered through the crowd like the grinding of rocks before an avalanche. The girls and boys upstairs sold their bodies for a handful of coppers a night — a week's wages for a miner, dancer, or clerk. The fancy ladies in the private boxes commanded all of a testoon, and the lot of them owed Roy three-quarters of their takings. The refugees of Vale had mortgaged seven years of their life for the fifty silver pieces it cost for passage overseas. Gamblers all, they knew their sums. Fifty silver testoons equaled two gold crowns. Equaled less than a day of her debt.

Equaled less than a spark from the diamond on Big Roy's chain. Their gazes tracked the sullen slash of yellow through the air, considering things (if only briefly) that could get a person killed.

"Now I'm a fair man," Roy continued. It was such a bald-faced lie, none of the staff even blinked. "I can see now how you misunderstood the situation with Canary and me, and I wouldn't want anyone to think you came all this way for nothing. So I'm willing to make a counter offer. Let's draw for it: your Nightingale against the remainder of Canary's contract, double or nothing."

Shiro shook his head. "Five years is too much to wager on a single card."

Retrieving his hat, he finally caught sight of the bouncers massed at the front door. He scanned the room for another exit, registering the proliferation of armed toughs and the blue steel barrels protruding between the gilded pilasters of the private boxes.

Roy smirked at Shiro's expression. "Maybe so, but you opened this hand, and you're not leaving 'til you play it through."

"The pot's too big for one card."

"Fine. We'll make it five. Five-card draw—one card for every year left on the Canary's contract. I'll even let you cut the cards."

This time, he didn't wait for Shiro to agree. He staggered Shiro with a bruising slap on the back, and sent downstairs for his favorite dealer.

Now was the time for Shiro to play the magician for real, and pull a rabbit out of his hat. Or his pockets. Or something! Instead, after a soul-breaking night of pretending she was a bug to be crushed under his heel, he shot her a wry, half-smile that lit his face like sun on gold.

Something pulsed inside her. It could've been something feminine and foolish. But it felt more like anger winding itself around a knot of fear, turn by turn by turn.

Did the fool man think Roy would let him win? The Empire had a reputation for honest play, and mostly it was true. To a point. To the point of exactly one thousand gold crowns. Once upon a time, the story went, the roulette wheel paid out the equivalent of two, supposedly to cancel a debt. But the debtor was shot on his way out of town, and all the money vanished.

That wouldn't happen to Shiro, not with friends like Lennessee Falchion to guard his back. The dealer smoothing the felt across the cleared table was the best of the professionals working the high stakes tables downstairs. Like the house, he had a reputation for honesty. They said he didn't even cheat at faro, where cheating was practically part of the game. The truth was he wore spring-loaded dealing boxes underneath both shirtsleeves and had twenty years' experience palming the cards.

Shiro wouldn't die. He'd simply lose. That was how saloons worked. It didn't matter if it wasn't fair, as long as he could walk away.

Her chances didn't look half so good. Gnawing the cuticle of her thumb, she searched for a way out. A fight would work, one big enough to draw the bouncers off the door to the back and give her a chance of escape. But nobody was fighting. Nobody was placing side bets, either—a situation entirely unique in her experience. By the numbers, this poker challenge had a bigger pot than any in the Empire's history. There should've been wagering galore, with paper money waving and bags of dust bouncing in twitchy hands. There should've been a run on the bar's remaining liquor as folks toasted their wagers with a drink. No one so much as lifted a glass. The only sound was the occasional scuff of boots against the hardwood floor.

She stripped off her remaining glove and rubbed her goosebump-covered arms. In the normal course of things, the steam piped beneath the Empire's floors and the press of people in the room meant neither she nor the dancers ever got cold. But tonight was the opposite of normal, and she was as cold as if she was standing naked at midnight in the bitter winter wind.

The dealer shuffled and offered Shiro the cut.

Shiro's hand paused an inch above the deck. "Just so I understand: I'm staking my Nightingale against Miss Diamond's contract, winner take all."

"That's not what I said," Roy drawled. "The remainder of Canary's contract is worth two of your toy. You win; it's yours. You lose; she works off the remainder of her debt. Either way, the Nightingale stays."

"How do you figure that?" Shiro demanded as protests sputtered across the saloon.

Roy grinned, thumbs in his vest pockets, patting his gut. "Cover charge. You came into my establishment, drank my liquor, enjoyed my entertainment, and tried to lure away my principal attraction under false colors. Now that may not be illegal, but it comes at a price. Tonight that price happens to be one singing automaton, and if you've got any complaints, you can wire your good friend the governor and see what he says about it."

Shiro stared. He couldn't have been more surprised if his own hand slapped him across the mouth. By the Saints, there were *rules* in his world—the safe, comfortable world she'd left behind. Honesty and fair dealing, promises made to be kept. Tonight proved he still held those rules as immutable as the energy exchanges that powered his machines. The terror and rage in her gut twisted tighter.

"There's one at every table," Roy confided to the crowd. "Quit your stalling, boy. Didn't your mama tell you? The house always wins."

I'll come for you.

I'll save you.

The house always wins.

She knew the instant it hit him. She felt the blow as if his emotions were bound to hers by strands of telegraph wires. The fix was in. The cut didn't matter, neither did his hand. He was going to lose. He was going to be made an example. *See what happens when you get between Big Roy Lee and what he wants.* If he was lucky. She wouldn't think about the alternative. She couldn't go on if she thought about that.

Shiro didn't storm or go red in the face. He accepted his cards like the young miner in the song accepted his death. She pushed the image away, but the dread remained, the coil ratcheted tighter by each precise mechanical beat of her heart, until she thought the pressure would snap her in two.

As if the imaginary wires between them ran both ways, he glanced up from his cards. Their eyes met, locked, crashed head-on like two trains on a trestle bridge. Everything she thought she knew about necessity and survival came uncoupled. Burning metal cried, tumbled, plummeted into the waters of a fathomless ravine. He fell with her, his hard mask shattered with the rest. His gaze held no judgment, only trust. The tight coil inside her exploded like a broken spring. The eagle screech of ruptured steel rang inside her skull.

This wasn't some mournful ballad. Shiro wasn't some half-dead stranger already growing cold. He was the friend who came for her. He was the man who made a miracle to save her.

The house always wins? *Not tonight.*

Genny eased away from the bar. Eldon tried to hold her back, but the gentleman gambler caught his arm. One of Roy's bully boys moved to intercept her. Lissa Katano pressed a flirtatious hand against his chest and whispered in his ear. Her sisters positioned themselves next to the stage. The other dancers flitted into the space between them and the stairs, their *special friends* close at their heels.

From the vantage of the stage, the air was thick with tobacco smoke and simmering discontent. Some of Roy's men looked as unhappy as the customers. After all, they were gamblers, too.

The three men at Roy's table paid the room's atmosphere no mind. Fresh from the hermetic confines of the basement game room, the dealer knew nothing about what happened before, only that his boss had to win. Shiro focused on his hand; Roy, on the least suspicious draw.

I'll save you.

Nobody was looking at the stage or Shiro's Clockwork Nightingale. Genny almost smiled.

Her nails were bitten to the quick. Her inflamed fingers bled as she worked the dials, weeping red on the white.

Two.

"How many cards?" the dealer asked.

Four.

Shiro shook his head. It wouldn't have mattered if he held a royal flush.

Nine.

The dealer turned to Roy. "Sir?"

"One," he said.

Genny pressed the button on the Nightingale's back and stepped aside.

The Nightingale bellowed, "Woe!" in glass-shattering Soprano C.

The unsuspecting dealer jumped. Cards exploded from his sleeve, spraying the crowd with aces. The answering roar of outrage shook the front windows in their frames. A whole shelf of bottles dived to the floor, crashing in counterpoint to the bartender's leap over the bar.

The *thunk* of steel in wood was almost swallowed by the din. Not so the dealer's shriek. The people clustered around him drew back, finally giving her a clear view of the table. Roy was on his feet, struggling in the grip of a half-dozen spitting, swearing customers. The dealer was pinned to the table by the horn-handled knife protruding from his right sleeve. There wasn't any blood that she could see, but Shiro's blade had caught a fold next to the thick, starched fabric of the cuff, and no amount of desperate tugging and jerking would tear it free.

Shiro produced a pair of shears from another interior pocket. Knocking the dealer's left hand aside, he slashed his pinned sleeve to the elbow, exposing the spring-loaded container strapped to the dealer's wrist. The last remaining card was the ace of spades. The dealer's cry and the apex of the Nightingale's trill struck the same piercing note.

Shiro thundered, "Is this how the house always wins?"

Two hundred voices answered, "No!"

The Nightingale launched into another trill. Roy wrenched free and lunged at Shiro. Three men tackled him before he connected. The customers at the windows cut the silk cords from the curtains, and flipped them around the necks of anybody who looked like a dealer. People pulled billy clubs, knives, and brass knuckles from their pockets—though mercifully, so far, no guns.

Genny retreated toward the Nightingale. Lissa rushed past her. The lead dancer heaved the backdrop further upstage, creating an escape route off stage right. Steadying the canvas with one hand, she waved Genny and the corps backstage.

The deputy assigned to guard the alley barreled through the opening from the other direction. He took one look at the melee and retreated into the gloom. Genny felt more than heard the thud of the backstage door against the inside wall. A lash of frigid air struck her exposed skin.

The Empire dancers charged into the cold. Genny turned to follow. A fleeing patron knocked her aside. She got her feet back under her, and found herself facing a stampede. There were too many people, too close together, for her to cut in.

Heart pounding fit to knock the regulator from her chest, she wheeled downstage. The room had a hazy cast as if all the patrons' cigarettes had been left to smolder. The salty taste of smoke clung to the back of her throat, making her breathe faster. She told herself it was fear. She couldn't see any flames amid the welter of people pounding each other with fists and furniture. But it was a certainty not everyone put out their smokes before joining the fray. She prayed they'd been ground underfoot and not found their way to a forgotten card or scrap of felt— or worse, a trailing curtain.

Stray bellows punched their way through the Nightingale's song. "Cheat!" "Thief!" "…'longed to my wife!" "Lost my house!" "Crooked scum!"

She couldn't find Shiro. There were too many dark coats. Wait. There in front, forcing a path to the stage. Once he got to her, they'd need a way out. The door to the landing was almost clear. From there they could get to the employee entrance or one of the first-floor windows. All she had to do was get to the front of the stage and jump.

Part of a table went flying across the room. Roy used the wreckage to clamber onto the bar, kicking and stomping Myrl and anybody else who tried to grab his legs.

"This is your fault, bitch!" he howled, reaching for his guns.

Genny didn't wait for the rest. She dove behind the Nightingale.

His first bullet caught the automaton in the chest. The impact rocked her upper body backward over the joints of her hips. Nera's aria ended in a lop-sided clang. Gears whined.

Genny clawed at the backdrop rail, trying to lift it. She'd be safe if she could get behind the canvas. Roy couldn't shoot what he couldn't see.

Something heavy landed downstage. She glanced over her shoulder. Shiro hurtled toward her. He flattened her against the boards, shielding her with his body as Roy's second bullet tore through the canvas close to his head.

She didn't hear the third bullet. She felt Shiro spasm against her back. He collapsed on top of her. He was so heavy she couldn't breathe. For an interminable, heart-stopping moment she thought he was dead. Then he grunted, and some of the weight shifted off her back. He was alive. She could've wept with relief.

Roy's last shot went high, tearing into the canvas near the top of the painted cage. She and Shiro were safe, for now.

"Let me up," she said. "I know you were hit. I can help."

Nothing moved except for his chest, which heaved against her back like a bellows. His breath puffed hot over her shoulder.

"It's all right," she insisted. "Roy's only got four shots."

Shiro still didn't respond. You'd think he hadn't heard, though she'd spoken plainly enough. A few strands of damp hair slicked across her neck. He must've turned his head. Why didn't he say something?

Finally he rolled off her. He settled on his left hip. The movement left him perspiring, his teeth bared in a grimace.

Ignoring the burn of her skinned knees, she crouched beside him. She caught a strong whiff of meat and metal. She couldn't see any blood on his coat, not that she would, necessarily. Black wool could be tricky that way.

He hiked up the hem of his right trouser leg, wincing as the fabric tore clots off a finger-length gouge in the muscle of his calf. The wound bled freely. Dark, tacky blood stained his calf from the cut to the top of his sock. But the wound wasn't gushing. It was a graze. Just a nasty graze. The breath rushed out of her lungs so fast it left her light-headed.

"Handkerchief." She held out her hand. She couldn't use Myrl's to stop the bleeding. It was caked with make-up and drenched in sweat— and to be mortifyingly honest, she was afraid of leaving her diamond unprotected so long as the Nightingale was set to Nera.

Shiro blinked. He angled his head and smacked it with the heel of his hand like he was trying to shake something loose. Whatever he intended, his widened eyes said it wasn't working. Then his gaze lifted higher, to the Nightingale, who remained bent back from her hips, her arms spread wide.

"Forget the doll," she told him.

Or tried to. Her lips moved. Her throat vibrated. But she couldn't hear any words. She'd thought the wailing in her head was panic compounded by a roaring pulse. But it was the Nightingale. Her aria had devolved into a single impossible note: Eighth Octave C, two octaves higher than High C, the highest note on the piano, a note never meant for human throats. But this wasn't the weak cheep of a hammer striking a single short wire. It was an endless, overpowering shrill that, once acknowledged, sliced through her brain like glass knives. She clapped her hands over her ears. It did no good at all.

Shiro forced himself to his knees. He grabbed the Nightingale's skirt and scooted closer. Hands spanning either side of her waist, he pressed his thumbs against a pair of buttons partially obscured by the key. Genny guessed it was the kill switch. Nothing happened. Gritting his teeth, he pressed harder. Still nothing.

Releasing the brakes on the back of her boots, he swiveled the doll to the right. Genny would've sworn the din couldn't get any worse. But sound is directional. Turning the doll to face them exposed them to the full force of her voice.

Shiro jackknifed over his legs, arms wrapped around his head. Genny spun away from the blare, swearing things she couldn't even hear in her head.

Stupid Roy's stupid bullet had punched a fist-sized dent in the front plates of the Nightingale's corset. A person would've simply died. But the stupid automaton was built to last. Caving in its stupid chest turned it into a sonic weapon, which stupider Shiro tried to fix, because that's what the stupid idiot did. He mended things. He saved things, instead of running when he had the chance, and now...and now he was going to get himself killed.

Panting from pain and fear, she grabbed the Nightingale's waist. She wrenched it around until it faced stage left, and pushed. The doll outweighed her by almost as much as Big Roy, but damned if she was going to let that stop her. She shoved the Nightingale into the thick folds of the house curtain and dropped its brakes.

The pressure of the sound eased. She still couldn't hear anything over the Eighth C echoes banging around her head. But the hammering at her temples receded. She'd be fine, she told herself as she grabbed the nearest lift line and hauled herself to her feet.

Deaf to his approach, she started at the warmth of Shiro's hands on her shoulders. He turned her to face the house.

The crowd retreated from a wall of blue, alcohol-fueled flames blazing the length of the bar. Behind a burning barricade, Big Roy stuffed a bar rag into a bottle from the rail, and hurled it through the blaze. The rag ignited as it sailed through the fire. It streaked toward a miner still struggling to stand.

Genny screamed a warning. He didn't hear. Nobody heard. The Nightingale's infernal note had silenced her as completely as a knife across her throat.

The bottle crashed on the miner's shoulder, igniting a line of fire from his hat down his sleeve. His beard lit, carrying the flames down his flannel shirt and wrapping his head in fire. His face split in a terrible, soundless shriek. He snatched off his smoldering hat and pounded his face with it. Someone threw a coat over him. Together they dropped into a roll.

More burning bottles crashed into the floor around the bar, pushing Roy's attackers back. It was a dangerous play, unless the rumored secret passage under the bar was real. Even then it was risky. The bottles that struck bare floor flared and guttered, checked by the mud and melt carried on the customers' boots. But you couldn't have a fight without debris—splintered chairs, torn clothes, dropped hats, and trash of all description. Where the blazing alcohol struck those, the fire caught. Smoke cried from a dozen hungry orange mouths.

The wiser patrons broke and ran for the front doors. The majority stayed. Singly and in groups, they tested the limits of Roy's throwing arm. Smothering the fires took second place to searching for an opening in Roy's defenses, even as he fed more spirits to the flames on the bar.

They'd all run mad. Lodeville was nailed together with wood and hope. One bad fire could gobble it up in a single night. Add the gusts of late-winter wind blowing through Sawtooth Ridge, and the conflagration could jump to the mines. Then they'd be doomed. There were fires set in the coal mines of Logress during the Pretender's Revolt that would burn until the hills themselves collapsed.

She couldn't let that happen. She couldn't let Roy destroy the lives of a whole town. She rapped Shiro's hand and aimed him at the sandbags used as counterweights to the drapes and soft scenery run from stage left. Bless him, he understood immediately. He limped to the rigging and pulled out another large knife. His shears were too small for the job.

The sand-filled fire bucket was too heavy for her to lift. The strain would've torn the regulator housing from her flesh. But putting her back to it, just like she had with the automaton, she shoved the bucket to the edge of the stage.

She pelted the nearest men with handfuls of sand. One clump struck the freshly barbered back of a wind-burned neck. Its owner whirled. Violence blazed in his glare until his gaze landed on the big red "FIRE" painted on the face of the bucket. He punched one of his colleagues in the shoulder and pointed. Together they hefted the bucket off the stage. As the rest of the group gathered around, the first guy gestured toward Shiro and the sandbags suspended in the wings.

Panting, sweating, muscles burning, scrapes stinging, she raced to the other side of the stage. The bucket there was only three quarters full, but it felt heavier. Thankfully, she only had to push it as far as the drape. Myrl had taken shelter behind the player piano next to the stairs. Ignoring the chaos around him, he calmly and methodically wiggled the teeth on the side where Roy had kicked him.

A weight she didn't know she was carrying lifted from her chest. She snapped his suspenders to get his attention. He jumped, twisting in mid-air like a startled squirrel. Indicating the bucket, she mimed throwing sand on a fire. Then she pointed at the men working to release the sandbags on the other side of the stage.

Myrl's face lit. Scanning the crowd, he pointed in turn to a handful of fellow old-timers at the fringes of the fight. She nodded and gave his shoulder an encouraging pat.

The first sandbag hit the boards with a teeth-rattling thump. Freed from its counterweight, the curtain jetted to the middle of the stage in a sluice of red velvet and dust. The Nightingale's voice swelled anew, hammering Genny's skull inside and out.

Behind his wall of fire, Roy's head jerked up. His burning hatred was a fist. She stumbled as if hit, pawing the curtain for support. He hurled the next bottle at her head.

She flew across the stage, losing her silly hat as she thrashed and fell. A knight armored in wool and linen caught her in his arms. His features drawn in pain, Shiro swayed but didn't fall, even as tempered steel might bend and still return to true.

Behind her, fire raced the folds of the stage-right drape. The heat flashed against her skin, building as the fire grew, fueled by the fabric and more of Roy's damned bottles.

Nothing could stop the fire now. The flames had reached the proscenium. A mist of molten gold drizzled over the stage. It charred a line across the boards and smoldered in the fringe of the surviving drape. The smoke spread faster than the fire. The stench burned her eyes as well as her nose.

They had to get out. Now. Backstage was a powder keg of paint, scrap lumber, grease for the stage machinery, canvas, and papier-mâché props. The rigging for the curtains and fly lines would act as a giant fuse. The ropes spanned more than half the building and reached all the way to the third-floor joists.

They couldn't exit through the wings. One was barred with fire, the other with frantic men. There was only one way to go: through the painted canvas backdrop three ropes away from the burning curtain. The first rope caught as she turned.

Flop sweat broke from every pore. It cemented her stockings to her shoes. They kept trying to trip her as she ran upstage. Her damp hand slid over the little knife holstered in her garter. She nicked herself on the draw, but she didn't feel it until she stabbed the blade into the bullet hole at the top of the cage and tried to pull.

Shiro thrust his bone-handled knife into the hole next to hers. Their blades sheared the canvas in a single mighty stroke. Cold from the open stage door blasted into the fissure. They plunged through the tear, and half-pushed, half-dragged each other to the door. Against the fire's glare, the alley seemed doubly dark. Without pause, they hurtled toward the end of the block, instinct guiding them until they could use their eyes.

They coughed out the smoke as they ran, barely smelling the odors of garbage and waste riding the stinging air.

Undulating waves of moon-silvered rats lapped against their boots. Erupting from between the buildings, the torrent fanned into a delta of lesser currents, each stream taking a different course. Some scuttled toward the shadows of the alley across the way. Others raced for the frost-blasted kitchen gardens further up the hill.

The miners who'd been working the rigging caught up with them on the street. The group's momentum carried them down the hillside faster than they could've run on their own. Genny's ears popped. She began to hear snatches of wind, stray shouts from the street fronting the saloon, and Shiro muttering, "Just a little further…"

Half the town had gathered along Placer Street despite the lateness of the hour. A dozen pairs of arms reached out to them, catching them before they crashed into the porch of the hardware store catty-corner from the saloon. Blanket-draped dancers and upstairs girls surrounded Genny and Shiro. Their breath steamed as they pelted her with questions she almost heard. Empire regulars and townsfolk she only knew by sight crowded behind them, blocking the cold she hadn't had a chance to feel.

Shiro folded the front panels of his coat around her like a pair of giant wings. The gesture warmed her as much as the cloth. Mindful of his injured leg, she nestled against him, pacing her respiration to his, aware of his body – the taut muscles of his arms, the contours of his chest, the pressure of his hips against her bedraggled bustle – in ways she scarcely understood seven years ago. She cherished scant expectation of satisfying the low ache his nearness inspired, but for the moment it didn't matter. They were together. Alive.

Heat radiating from the Empire kissed her upturned face. As yet, the building's three-storied, stone-and-brick façade remained untouched by the fire. But the two rows of seven tall windows marking the upper stories blazed as bright as opening night. All the scene needed was a troupe of actors – or fancy ladies – parading their talents along the projecting balcony that shaded the width of the main floor. Instead the upstairs girls gathered around them raised a chorus of racking sobs.

A gush of stragglers spurted through the posts supporting the balcony. The light from the windows and the entertainment district's only street-corner light pole illuminated singed hats and reddened hands waving the smoke away from their clothes. Beyond them, a score of men and women wearing coats over their bedclothes formed a basket relay to convey the belongings of the tobacconist next door across the street to safety.

A distant-seeming tintinnabulation pricked her ears. People turned toward the steeple at the end of Placer Street. The House of the Saints was always lit, so it was easy to see the bell swinging in the spire, warning the town of fire. A minute later, the street echoed with the ululating wail of the fire department's hand-cranked siren.

A solitary figure tumbled down the cross street into the light. Genny joined the cheer as the old prospector lurched to his feet. Aside from a fresh shiner, Myrl's weathered face didn't look much worse for wear. In fact, his gap-toothed grin outshone the moon, the corner mage light, and the fire behind him.

He waved an arm over his head, whipping a thick gold chain through the light. At one end flashed a bedizened gold watch; at the other, a piss-yellow rock as long as a woman's thumb.

The crowd responded with a roar that blasted the last vestige of the Nightingale's song from her ears. The night was suddenly alive with yelling, whistling, clapping, stamping feet, excited questions, and yelps of surprise.

Shimmering in the heat of its own making, the Empire's flat-topped façade almost seemed to glower. A tremendous boom echoed from the heart of the building. The lower story windows shattered, spewing smoke and glass into the middle of the street. The glass bulbs of the saloon mage lights exploded. The resulting flare of white clawed the eyes the same way the Nightingale's song had gouged their ears. The release of the bulbs' magic, charmed against fire, momentarily sucked the force from the conflagration.

Its effect had dissipated by the time Genny blinked the spots from her eyes. But by then, the larger of the fire department's two horse-drawn engines had arrived at the neighborhood water tower. The crew connected the hoses. A moment later the engine's eight clacking pistons started pumping water into the Empire's shattered windows, pushing the fire back. Further up the hill, the crew of the smaller engine doused the rear. Volunteer firefighters armed with vulcanized water bladders swarmed the roof of the tobacconist, soaking it and as much of the saloon roof as they could reach. On the street, bucket brigades and sandbag haulers joined the people emptying the store. Others readied hooks and dynamite for a fire break.

To Genny's left, Lissa hugged her dancers as if she needed their support to stand. The fire hadn't broken them as it had those who lived at the Empire. But she and her sisters would have to start over—again— in a town that no longer had a venue for their only skill, their only decent way to make a living. Their misery and loss were reflected in the faces of all the Empire employees Genny could see.

Even the customers mourned. Whatever they'd brought to the tables or sought to wring from Roy's exposure was gone as surely as if it had disappeared in Roy's special vault in the Lodeville Bank.

She'd done that. She'd taken something needful from people who'd already lost so much. She hadn't meant to. She was only trying to survive and protect what she held dear. The world was supposed to be a better place when wickedness received its comeuppance. People weren't supposed to lose their possessions, their homes, and their livelihoods. Guilt clogged her throat. Her fingers clenched over Shiro's lapels, spotting the fabric with fresh blood.

His arms tightened around her. Her senses drowned in cedar and smoke, sweat-damp wool, and the steady throb of his pulse against her forehead where it pressed against his throat. It felt so right. But with everything that had happened, she couldn't help questioning whether this, too, was wrong.

He jogged her elbow under his coat, a little shake to draw her from her reverie, test her temper, ask a question and offer comfort all at once.

"I was thinking about the people in there tonight," she said. Carefully, so as not to bang his jaw, she cocked her head toward the gutted saloon. "I hope they all escaped."

"Even Roy?"

"Even him."

Shiro had come for her. He'd certainly mended things, if not in the way he planned. Without the Empire—so long as hers wasn't the hand that physically destroyed it—her contract would be void. She had no doubt a good lawyer and a word from one of Shiro's influential Buxton friends would make it so.

But Roy had saved her. Once. And thought he owned her ever after.

She shivered at the precedent. Never again, she promised herself. Never again would she surrender her liberty to another, no matter how worthy. No matter how dear.

Shiro tensed, drawing himself as straight as a western blade. "Are you all right?"

"I will be as soon as we get a doctor to patch you up," she asserted with a cheer she was far from feeling.

A soft laugh huffed through his chest and teased her tousled hair. He eyed the former customers who'd set up triage stations on the street. "There seem to be enough of them milling around. But would you trust your leg to a doctor who couldn't diagnose a crooked saloon?"

She couldn't help but smile. That was so much the Shiro she remembered. Maybe some things never changed. She sighed, unwilling to let the illusion fade.

After a minute he asked, "And then?"

He sounded more than hoarse. She slanted him a concerned look. Was it the smoke or something more? He'd lost as much tonight as anyone in Lodeville. No machine crafted by mortal hands could survive the destructive forces at play in the burning saloon. And the Clockwork Nightingale wasn't just a machine; she was a masterpiece. From the very first, Shiro poured himself into his creations. They were children of his mind and heart, and almost as dear as a pet. Losing the Nightingale like this must have cut deep.

But the strain on his face didn't look like pain or grief. It in no way resembled the bleak expressions of her colleagues. In fact, it was somewhat comical. The big, grown-up, master magicanist, the man who could make metal walk and stared down Big Roy Lee in his own saloon, worried his bottom lip like a school boy. You'd think his whole future rode on the answer to one impossibly vague question.

"Other than finding a warm roost for the night, I hadn't given it much thought. I'd like to do something to aid folks dispossessed by the fire. Maybe a benefit concert…if they'll let me."

"I have friends who can help with that. But afterward, would you…" He faltered, then fortifying himself with a deep breath, took another chance. "Would you like me to take you home?"

"Did you just ask my permission?"

"Well, yeah."

Deep within the Empire rose a groan like the hinges of a rusted door. Deep within Genny, a wounded dream, imprisoned and discarded, lifted its wings and soared.

They made their home in Buxton. Shiro founded a company to manufacture articulated prosthetics and other life-saving devices.

People called him a wizard for the wonders his engines performed, though he didn't own a whit of magic, except for his craft.

They called her Genny Lark. They said her voice could heal the ailing heart better than a Shimotsuga Regulator and a team of doctors combined.

Genny wouldn't go so far as that, but she knew the comfort music could provide. So between touring the Territories and overseas, she gave concerts in the park outside the city's new Magicanist Hospital.

One warm spring day many years later, as she glanced over her audience on the hospital lawn, her gaze lit upon a familiar face among the row of wheelchairs lining the open air stage. Big Roy Lee was much changed. His shoulders hunched over his sunken chest. His blue-veined hands fretted the padded leather armrests of his custom-built, steam-powered chair. From his color and the particular attentions of his nurse, she guessed he'd come for an operation much like hers. Thanks to Shiro's mass-produced steel regulators, the operation now cost little more than the surgeon's salary and hospital fees—though judging from the private nurse, the costly chair, and the cashmere blankets bundled around him, Roy could still afford far more.

All at once, her past rose before her, roaring like the Great Empire Fire. Compassion warred with anger which—despite all that she'd been given, all she'd achieved, all she'd won—burned like coal dust underground to that day.

So she did what she always did when her heart gave her trouble. She took the heart she gave Shiro, and the heart he gave her, and put it into her song.

The Walking House

based on Baba Yaga

JEFF YOUNG

"UNCLE, TELL US WHY THERE IS AN OAK TREE IN THE YARD."

Piter looked down at Alexei and his little sister Tatiana. Her fingers gripped Piter's pant leg and she pulled insistently. He put a hand on the young boy's head, ruffling his dark hair. Then he led them over beneath the shade of the tree. "You know these don't grow this far north and certainly not like this one. So why don't you sit down, and I'll tell you the whole story the way your father told it to me." Piter pulled out his ever-present journal and paged through it until he found the story. Then he began, "A long time ago, your father lived in Moscow and one day he went on a journey with two friends..."

"Nikolai, wipe the borscht from your beard. You look like a Cossack." Svetlana handed him his napkin from the table. Then she turned away, her cheeks reddening as she hurried to the doorway.

"She is too forward with you, Nikolai," Ivan said, pointing with his knife.

"No, she is right. You do look a bloody mess." Piter laughed and sipped his tea before turning to the other guest, "Be kinder, Ivan, you don't want her mother against you. After all she merely tolerates Nikolai and he pays her to keep the house. Although that is not a bad thing now that his parents are gone, else he would be like a house spirit with no tenants. A little *domovoi* on his lonesome."

Nikolai sighed and daubed at his beard. Svetlana was right. More often than not she was right.

Ivan rapped his knuckles on the table and the others turned to him. "Congratulations, dear Nikolai, on your new assignment. It is always good to be noticed and very good to be noticed by the Tsar."

"Even if you are being sent out into the woods to chase a ghost." Piter's cup occluded his cockeyed grin.

"That may be my fault," admitted Nikolai running his spoon around the bottom of the bowl. He looked to the mantelpiece at the photograph of his parents in front of their balloon. Perhaps it was his turn to explore and hopefully his luck would be better. "When I spoke of the drawings I found by Sasha Gubernetsky I had little idea things would turn out so."

"Why do we need a machine that walks anyway? Didn't we free the serfs to raise an army? You tell him, Piter; you know I am right."

"No, Ivan. The Tsar freed the serfs because it was the right thing to do and the right time to do it. What is this walking machine anyway, Nikolai?"

"Gubernetsky's machine was two-legged and had a gyroscope inside to keep it balanced. It was big enough that it could step over most obstacles. Imagine how you can march men over areas you could never drive a wagon through; that's what Gubernetsky envisioned. Unfortunately, all I have is a picture and some vague sketches that were given to the Tsar by a mysterious source.

"Since I met Gubernetsky a while ago, I am considered familiar with him and his work. The military is always looking for ways to keep the borders more secure, such as those with the Ottoman Empire, and stop unrest in places like Poland."

"You sound like you should be recruiting for the army, Nikolai," Ivan said with a laugh.

"No," Nikolai replied, "I've just heard it too many times. One of the generals is taken with the idea of a walking machine and pushed the plan up to Alexander II. So I am commissioned to find Gubernetsky and retrieve him."

Piter leaned forward. "But that still doesn't tell us why Svetlana is going along with you, much less why you are taking the balloon."

Nikolai found he couldn't meet the other's eyes for a moment even though the reason was perfectly honest. "She is from the Ural Mountains north of Perm where Gubernetsky was last seen. So she will serve as a guide. As for the balloon, there is an immense amount of land to cover in our search and we will do it more quickly from the air. The plan is to stop at villages here and there and ask after Gubernetsky until we find him."

"You make it all sound so simple, Nikolai. But when you come right down to it, it is you and a young lady in a balloon in the wilderness. I know Mistress Kasinov well enough that she would not allow that for her daughter. So is this where you come in, Piter?"

With a glance at the doorway, to ensure he was not being watched, Piter replied, "Yes, I am the chaperone, but only because my uncle married Mistress Kasinov long ago. Even though she is sharp of tongue, Svetlana is family and I shall look after her. I am to keep our young man here a dreaming inventor and not a wild beast that the young lady should fear. Also I am a writer. The opportunity to chronicle this adventure is too great to pass by."

"And Mistress Kasinov trusts you to not spend your days head down over your notebook?" Ivan laughed, shaking his head. "I don't know who is the greater fool here, you or Nikolai for chasing a ghost in the wilderness."

When his guests left, Nikolai climbed the staircase to his room. As he packed his clothes, a light evening rain dimmed the lights of Moscow. In a day or two they would be far enough away that he would no longer see those lights. A day or two more and they would be farther away than any *dacha* he had ever visited. In a week, farther than he had ever traveled. He reached out to put his sable hat into the trunk and stopped when he heard a board creak. Looking up he caught Svetlana glancing at him from the doorway. She pointed to the hat and then shook her head. It was so quiet that the long black hair spilling from her headscarf rustled against her back. Then he smiled and set the hat aside. She was right; something so fine would make him stand out as from the cities. As always her advice was sound. At least some things would not change.

The seats of the train encouraged one to sit upright. Nikolai groaned at his resulting stiff neck. The Gubernetsky drawings were spread over his lap again. But they never made any more sense despite how many times he went over them. There was a drawing of Gubernetsky on a smaller piece of paper as well for when they started asking after him. Nikolai stared at the images as he had done day after day until it became a ritual. He'd also gone back to check on the balloon in the rail car after every stop, but eventually gave up after the fifth time.

At that point Piter had said, "Weapons, tools, money, or food might go missing, but what fool would steal a balloon?"

"Perhaps they'll try to live in that small little house," was Svetlana's reply.

"Gondola," Nikolai corrected, "small or not, that will be our home while we search."

"Why it's barely bigger than the bath house from where I grew up."

"Then let's hope we only have to share it with Piter and not a *bannik*."

The train hit a rough join, causing the carriage to buck, which drew Nikolai's thoughts back to the present. He carefully gathered up the drawings and put them away. So far the Tsar's orders bought them passage without a problem. But the farther they went the more likely they would need to start paying their way in rubles. What had Piter said? "A ruble is a ruble everywhere and no one turns it from the door." Much to his amazement he'd caught Svetlana grinning at the comment.

Now when he looked over, Piter was asleep with his head thrown back and Svetlana was leaning against the window, wrapped in a blanket, the waning light of the day scattered across her features. For a moment it looked like she had a mask of gold. In a blink the image was gone. Reality was aptly represented by the old man across the aisle, who cracked open hazelnuts, casting the shells into his left shoe. Nikolai rubbed his neck and leaned back wishing he could sleep as easily as Piter. *Only a few more days,* he consoled himself with the thought. When he woke he was surprised to find that Svetlana had tucked her blanket around him.

"Uncle, why do you use so many big words? What's a gyroscope? Was the train like the one you carved me only bigger?"

"Alexei, don't you want to hear the rest of the story? Save your questions like your little sister."

"You only say that, Uncle, because she doesn't talk yet."

"Yes, I can hardly wait for the day when you both chatter like pigeons. Enough. Let me finish the tale."

While the train ride was quiet, the day they launched the balloon was not. After a ride in several wagons to a field away from the factories of Perm and the banks of the Kama River, Nikolai found his little expedition had gathered a crowd. It had been some time since he'd taken his balloon, *The Swan*, up. Feeling for once in his element, Nikolai guided Piter and Svetlana as they tied ropes, drove in stakes, and unfolded the gasbags. The bystanders gawked, elbowed each other, and occasionally got in the way. Svetlana bustled about checking knots and shooing away small children who clambered over the gondola. Once it was set up, Nikolai admitted to himself he was rather proud of the way *The Swan* turned out. The little building was round like a cake whose center was cut out. In the opening was a stove whose chimney led to the bottom of not one but three gas bags that formed the lifting part of the balloon. The inside of the gondola was broken into three rooms, from the walls of which tables, beds, and chairs folded out. Practical Svetlana noticed immediately there was no kitchen space.

"Don't worry," Nikolai said, "We'll be landing often. Besides there are places on the stove to cook. The weather won't always be kind, and we'll want to stay those nights on the ground as often as possible."

Piter tapped against the side of the round tube that ran about the perimeter of the gondola, "So, is your little house wolf-proof?"

"I'm afraid that's up to us. But the part you're tapping is where those barrels go." Nikolai pointed over his shoulder at a wagon pulling up to the gondola. "We'll have water for when we need it and ballast too. Sveta, move the others back; I've got the fire lit so the gasbags will start to fill soon." Nikolai engaged a few of the men standing about to help ensure the netting about the gas bags would not tangle. Just before noon, Nikolai was satisfied with the state of things and, to a chorus of cheers, the balloon lifted from the ground.

Piter tossed kopecks from the gondola to the children below who scrabbled like hens in the tall grass. "So why do I suspect that was the easiest part of this journey?" he asked Nikolai who was putting logs into the maw of the stove.

Nikolai laughed. "This is the part I have been waiting for. Up here there is not a care in the world."

"Don't forget why we are here," reminded Svetlana, who was already peeling potatoes and tossing the skins over the side. "We need to go north."

Nikolai nodded, and after pulling a series of levers, a pair of propellers unfolded below the gondola. He checked the gauge measuring the steam built up by the boiler under the stove and then fired up the props. Slowly *The Swan* turned under his hand and started toward the river Kama. Below the boats looked like twigs afloat in the current.

"Uncle, it's just not right."

"What do you mean, Alexei?"

"There should be three brothers or three sisters in a good fairytale."

"It isn't enough that there are three of us in the story? And who said this was a fairytale?"

"But there are no horses of power, no talking fish, no — "

"You mean that Tsar Alexander II sending us off on a long journey in a balloon isn't enough?"

"Please, Uncle, I've grown up enough to know that never happened."

"Really now. You'll tell me what is true and what is not? Well then, here is the rest of your story. Our three heroes went into the woods. They fought off the wolves. They traveled for many days. They found the walking house built by Gubernetsky. They completed three tasks given by the owner of the house. They lived happily ever after. Wonderful. Hope you enjoyed it. Now I'm going to stay under this tree and you can go fetch me some tea." Tatiana tugging on his boot tops, brought Piter's tirade to a halt.

"Uncle, you can't finish your story like that. Look at her. Tatiana can't tell you so, but she was listening. Please, we promise to let you finish." Alexei looked down at his feet, *"Even if you do want to tell it the way you were."*

Piter leaned his head back against the twisted trunk of the oak and sighed. *"Very well, I will continue. But I suspect I will need some tea when this is through, for there is much more to tell."*

"So now we know wolves can't get in the gondola."

"There's no need to be so sharp, Piter."

"Sorry, Svetlana," Piter replied, pouring her some tea from the *samovar* and then filling a cup of his own. "They can, however, howl at us for the better part of the night."

"Look, a village."

"Well, Nikolai, I suppose that's what passes for a village around here." Then Piter sighed and added, "Sorry again, Svetlana," when he heard her sharp intake of breath.

Leaning on the levers that controlled the propellers, Nikolai turned *The Swan* toward the group of huts and fields of barley below. It would be good to talk to some other people again. The little gondola became quite close after a time and every opportunity to be free of it was one to be treasured. Nikolai did have to admit he was enjoying the adventure. He was no longer so sure of how the other two felt. They'd stopped in five towns and villages so far and no one had seen or heard of Gubernetsky. But there were a number of instances where people would not meet his eyes when he questioned them and were occasionally nervous. It just made sense to Nikolai that an inventor like Gubernetsky would use the factories of Perm to build his masterpiece before escaping into the wilds.

However, the evidence was lacking. Perhaps things would be different in this village. If nothing else, it wouldn't take long to question the inhabitants since there couldn't be many. Nikolai brought *The Swan* down near the small stream that ran by the village.

Svetlana and Piter quickly disembarked. When Nikolai stepped down he noticed that Svetlana carried an armload of clothes. "Washing?" he asked, "I thought —"

"No, Nikolai, you didn't. If you did you would have realized I am off to talk to the women. You and Piter find the tavern and ask your questions. I will see if I can find out the truth for you."

Her tone started off sharp, but it did not stay that way for the whole of her statement. Nikolai found himself watching her move through the grass, the stalks swaying much the same way her hips did as she went. Svetlana's jet-black hair was a stark contrast against the fields of barley. It took him a moment to realize that Piter was talking to him. "The mind of a woman is like the wind in summer." Then the other man turned away and walked toward the huts of the village whistling tunelessly as he went.

The men in the tavern talked about the weather, the number of eggs their hens hatched, when the barley would be ready, the last time they'd hunted, the strange number of trees that had fallen over recently, and anything else at all...except inventors who visited their village. A few hours later, sitting on the woodpile outside of the tavern, Nikolai was a good deal less happy. "We are getting nowhere."

"No," replied Piter, who'd been enjoying just about anything to drink that was put in front of him. "We are well and truly far from Moscow. We've done that very well."

Nikolai looked down at the cup of kvass that he was making last. The moon shown on the surface of the drink and for a moment in the reflection Nikolai spied a strange shadow at his back. Piter's hand fell on his shoulder roughly and when Nikolai turned he found Piter staring intently at the woodpile looming behind them.

"What?"

"Give me your cup and be quiet."

Nikolai handed over the *kvass* and watched as his friend picked up a dried up leaf from the ground. Since the edges were curled up, it acted as a makeshift glass when Piter poured some of the *kvass* into its center. Then he very carefully set the leaf down at the edge of the woodpile and stumbled backward to fall down next to Nikolai. Rescuing his cup,

Nikolai started to ask what Piter was about when he noticed a long skinny arm reach out from the woodpile. The limb was covered in matted gray hair. The rest of the creature came slowly into sight as it settled itself on its haunches in front of the leaf. For a brief moment, its head spun round as if it were an owl and two large yellow eyes which were mostly pupil stared at him from amongst the hair that covered the little fellow's body. Then it picked up the leaf and proceeded to sip delicately at the *kvass*.

"Picture," Piter hissed, his hand outstretched.

"What?"

"Don't be stupid. Give me Gubernetsky's picture."

Nikolai was stunned enough that he did not argue. He pulled out the drawing and unfolded it. He watched as Piter struggled to lean forward and place it on the ground without sliding off the woodpile and onto his face. The little mannikin put down the leaf for a moment, picked up the paper, turned it all about and stared at it from all angles. Then, dipping a finger into the *kvass*, it huddled over the uneven wood floor and started to draw in the dried mud that was on the planks. First it drew a circle, then a dot within the circle and finally lines radiating out from the center.

Both men sat there staring at the image, recognition not settling in until Piter muttered, "Wagon wheel?" Then he jerked himself up to his feet and pulled Nikolai along. Piter leaned down and scooped up Gubernetsky's picture, which the mannikin had dropped in favor of its *kvass*. He shoved the paper into Nikolai's hands and snatched away the glass of *kvass*. Turning back, he placed the cup in front of the creature. Bowing, Piter said, "Thank you, old father. Enjoy your cup. May your house always be safe and warm." Then Piter was spinning about again to grasp Nikolai's arm and pull him away.

"Where are we going?" asked Nikolai.

"To find the man with the wagon because he's the one who knows where Gubernetsky is. If you think about it, it makes sense. If your inventor made it this far then somebody carted about all of his wares."

"What was that?"

Piter came to a halt turning to Nikolai. "Were you raised in a hole? That was the house's *domovoi*."

Nikolai crossed his arms, staring hard at Piter.

"No, before a word passes your lips about how much I have drunk, that has nothing to do with this. That was the guardian of the house.

Surely you've heard of such things before." Piter shook his head as if in disbelief.

"Heard of and discounted, shared my *kvass* with, no."

"Nikolai, we are very far from the safe little place that you grew up in. The world works differently out here and just because your science doesn't explain something, it can still help or hurt you. So open your mind, your eyes, and be a little cautious. After all the gray father you don't want to believe in just gave up our first clue to finding Gubernetsky."

Sighing, Nikolai shook his head, "When I see proof—"

"What more proof do you need than the *domovoi* you just saw? You've heard the wolves at night. Do you need to have one bite your hand off to believe in them? Come, let's find Svetlana and see if the women know where the man with the wagon is now."

Nikolai allowed himself to be led off as Piter continued. "That was just perfect. I need to sit down and write this all out before I forget it. Absolutely amazing."

"It's just all one big adventure to you, isn't it?" Nikolai huffed, looking away across the barley fields as the late day sun cast shadows from *The Swan*.

"If it wasn't, it wasn't worth the trip and I certainly wouldn't be writing about it." Piter came around the balloon and nearly ran head long into Svetlana, who was draping their laundry over the rails of the gondola. "We need to find the man—" he started.

"Who is the wagon owner, right?" She finished for him, while tossing a pair of his trousers over the iron railing.

Piter drew back briefly, his mouth hanging open.

"Yes," said Nikolai, "so we've heard."

"Good. Here, put these few things over the rail there."

Nikolai found himself draping his shirts over the rail and then fumbling as he tried to do the same with one of Svetlana's underskirts. "Shouldn't we—" he began.

"Be talking to him?" Svetlana concluded his thought and, tossing the last pair of pants over the rail, turned to point at a wagon approaching the village. "Yes, the women told me as we washed. It's nearly sun down. He's coming home."

So they strode out to meet the man as he drove his wagon up to the village. At first his sun-beaten face was all smiles as he pushed his long mustaches into some semblance of order. Then when Nikolai showed him the picture and asked of Gubernetsky, his countenance drew up tight. He shook his head, abruptly turning away his face.

Piter, however, was not deterred. "Little father in the tavern house is the one who told us to look for you. If you want to settle down day after day for a drink after your work undisturbed, you'd best help us."

Now the wagon owner's shoulders slumped, and he shook his head. "You cannot know who I have promised. No, I will not say."

Svetlana stepped forward and gestured for the man to lean down. She whispered in his ear for several moments. As she did so the man's eyes grew wider and wider and when she stepped back, he jumped down from the wagon and bowed low to her. Then in a rush of words he told them how he had been hired to gather wagons from the surrounding villages several years ago and drive down to the river Kama. There they had picked up a cargo and the very man that Nikolai's picture described. This little village was where the man came to, bought all of the wagons and then drove off down the road that led further into the woods. The wagon driver was indebted to the stranger because he now had this nice new wagon bought with his payment for service. Taking off his hat, he bowed to all of them again and then climbed up to his seat to drive off.

Watching the wagon roll away, Piter turned back to Svetlana. "But his promise to Gubernetsky isn't what kept him silent, is it?"

She regarded him darkly for a moment and then turned away to shake some of the wrinkles from the drying clothes.

"What was that about?" asked Nikolai.

"Something I am certain we should let be for the moment," Piter answered. "Come, it's getting dark. Let's stoke the fire in the stove. Tomorrow is a better day for answers. The morning is wiser than the evening, and I must write in my journal while it is still fresh in my mind."

"You are making this up. How could he not believe in a domovoi?"

"Alexei, just because you have always known the little father of the house does not mean that others grew up so. Look at where we are, far from the cities and the fools that live there. We know about the vodyanoi, dvorovoi, and domovoi because they are with us every day and here they do not have to hide." Piter slapped the cover of the book in his hand. "As for making it up, this story is Nikolai's words written down by me. But you are right, I am a teller of tales, so I do make things up. Go ask Nikolai and see what he says. But for now shall I keep reading?"

"*Of course, Uncle. I don't mean to be rude. People who don't believe in domovoi...what will you tell me next?*"

"*Why, little man, how about the walking house, for we are nearly there. Just listen.*"

On the second day of flight, after their stop in the village, Nikolai changed directions. Piter noticed it and looked up from his book. Svetlana thrust her needle through her sewing and came to stand by his side.

Clearing his throat and raising an eyebrow, Piter made to get to his feet. Nikolai waved him away. "I think I've seen something I've been looking for. Bear with me, I only wish to be sure," Nikolai said. Svetlana leaned against the railing near him and for a time Nikolai simply enjoyed her presence. He took a moment to show her the dials on the control box, the compass, and the steering levers. Then he let her fly *The Swan* for some time, calling out right and left as necessary to keep her on track. Sveta quickly noticed what had caught his eye and was soon following the trail below. Finally, Piter could stand it no more and lurched to his feet, stretching like a cat that had lain in the sun.

When he looked over the side, Nikolai shared a grin with Svetlana over Piter's shoulders. "I don't see why we left the road," complained Piter.

"Keep looking," encouraged Nikolai. "Do you see this line of lighter leaves?"

"Well, yes," admitted Piter, leaning out farther over the railing.

"You have to stop thinking that what we are looking for is like anything else. A walking machine like a man would have a stride and leave a series of foot prints."

Piter's sudden intake of breath made Nikolai chuckle.

"So it's real."

"Funny, isn't it, that I'm willing to believe in a walking machine in the wilderness but not a *domovoi*?" Nikolai laughed, clapping his friend on the shoulder.

They followed the footsteps of the walking machine for another day until Nikolai saw the river. The more he looked at the course of the water below the less sense it made. So he pulled the cords and dropped ballast allowing *The Swan* to ascend. The higher the balloon rose, the stranger the landscape below became. The river was bent about nearly in a great circle and its course in the arc of the perimeter was fretted with loop upon loop. The whole of the land encompassed by the river was more than four miles across. There were clumps of woods and rich, green meadows all fenced in by the water. The footsteps of the walking machine ran all about, crossing the enclosed area. It was Piter that saw the roof. Nikolai worked the controls diligently, venting the hot air to allow *The Swan* to descend. When they were a few feet from the ground, Nikolai's heart hitched briefly for the little house below was akin to the gondola of *The Swan*. There was no sign of the walking machine.

As they drew closer, Nikolai could see two chimneys that rose from the back of the house. Both were plumed with heavy gray smoke. The house itself sat upon a small, circular hummock. It was late morning when Nikolai glided *The Swan* to a rest a respectable distance away and the balloon's passengers prepared to greet the inhabitants. Nikolai put on the best clothes he'd brought along and Svetlana drew a brush through his errant hair. He couldn't help but notice the way that the house repeatedly drew her gaze or the intensity of her consideration. Piter picked up his notebook, dusted off the cover, and then dusted off the top of his boots as well. Then they stepped down from *The Swan* to walk up to the house.

The closer they got, the stranger the structure appeared. There was a fence about the perimeter of the house that every so often was topped with a white round knob. Nikolai noted that there was a gap between the fence and the grass in front of it. There was no path or road leading to the house, which was also strange. It was about that point he noticed the white knobs on the fence were actually skulls lit from within by some eldritch light. Then the chimneys belched forth pure black smoke. A low rumbling broke the silence and the entire hummock and house lifted up into the air on a giant pair of iron legs. The whole great machine began to turn about in a circle, the legs moving purposefully looking for all the world like those of a giant chicken despite their gears and pistons. The ground shook with each iron footfall.

Nikolai couldn't help himself. He fell backward in the grass and lay there, his mouth opening and shutting like a fish pulled from the river. The air filled with the sharp odor of burning wood. Piter's journal hung limply from his fingers. Only Svetlana was unaffected. She strode forward nearly to the walking machine's shadow and cried out, "Izbushka! Izbushka! Turn your back to the wood and your front to me!"

Piter was mumbling to himself, backing away as Nikolai found his feet. Walking as calmly as he could, Nikolai went to stand next to Svetlana. She looked at him briefly, a smile on her face, before crying out again, "Come out, come out, Baba Yaga. Your child's child calls to you."

The circling hut came to an abrupt halt, legs folding as great jets of steam shot out from the undercarriage. Nikolai desperately wanted to get a better look at the mechanism of the walking machine's legs but he remained at Svetlana's side.

Piter's mumbling grew more audible. "You called her by name. You called the witch with the iron teeth. The witch that eats up bad little girls. You called that nightmare your kin!"

Svetlana turned and, reaching out, struck Piter a slap across the cheek. "Yes, I did, and when I was a young girl and uncontrollable, my mother sent me to spend summers with Baba Yaga. She used to look at me and say 'long of hair, short of wit.' I will tell you that time with my grandmother took the wildness from me and instilled discipline like nothing else could."

The front door of the house opened wide and out strode one of the thinnest women Nikolai had ever seen. She wore a long gown with a red collar and her nose jutted before her like the prow of a boat. Voluminous gray and white hair billowed about Baba Yaga like a cape. She carried the long handle of a pestle in one hand. When she passed Piter, who quivered like a hare before a serpent, she struck out with the pestle at his knee and toppled him to the ground. The muscles of her arm were like knobbed wood. Then she walked the last few steps to stand before Svetlana and Nikolai.

Her dark black eyes raked Nikolai from head to toe and when she swung her pestle at him, he was fortunate to maintain enough wits to sidestep its blow. Her head cocked to one side like a crow and she grinned abruptly, gray iron teeth glistening wetly in the sunlight. Her other hand shot out and grasped his shoulder, digging painfully into the muscle there. Nikolai did his best to look her directly in the eye and breathe evenly as she appraised him. Baba Yaga made a deep coughing sound, "Huh," and then turned to Svetlana. The two of them stood there for a time staring at each other. In that moment, Nikolai could see the similarity of features. Then Svetlana tipped her brow down and bowed to her grandmother.

"Good," rasped Baba Yaga, "Too much longer and I might have felt the need to bend that stiff neck of yours." Turning back to Nikolai, she asked, "What would you have from me, you who smells of far-off Moscow?"

Nikolai forced himself to speak, "I would learn all I can about the walking house and speak to Sasha Gubernetsky."

Something changed in Baba Yaga's expression and some of the furrowed wrinkles on her forehead smoothed briefly. Then she turned and pointed at a small stone lying in the grass close to the wall of the house. "Talk to Sasha all you want, but you're too late for conversation.

He fills up the ground there. But he did build me something like no other in exchange for a peaceful place away from men who only wanted to use the walking machine for war. Sasha gave me a home that matched the foolish legends made by half drunken farmers.

"If you want to learn about the walking house, that is another matter. You do three tasks for me, and I will let you learn its secrets." Her smile was once more a crescent of shining iron.

Again her gaze met Svetlana's. "I know what you want, daughter's daughter. If he succeeds you shall both receive what you wish. But I warn you, you may help and counsel, but you must not do. That is his alone."

Finally, she turned to Piter who still lay sprawled on the ground and would not meet her gaze. "What would you have?"

"Only peace with you, grandmother, and nothing else."

"So your head is not as empty as your courage. Well enough. There is an axe around the back of the house. You chop wood."

Piter scrambled up and bowed deeply. Then he scurried away around the side of the house. Nikolai couldn't help but notice the notebook open in Piter's hand and the pencil running across its pages as he stumbled along. If Piter was lucky Baba Yaga might not notice.

"First task," said Baba Yaga, facing Nikolai again. "You must start fire with water. Find me when your fire is burning and tell me how you have done it." With that she turned and reentered the house, the front door slamming closed behind her.

For a few moments, Nikolai simply stood there trying to take it all in. It did make a sort of sense. He'd heard stories about the walking house of Baba Yaga. Sasha had come here to the wilderness. But those were the easy parts to accept. He looked at Svetlana, "Your grandmother is the stuff of children's nightmares and fairytales. Piter cannot even look her in the eye."

"She had to be someone's grandmother," was Svetlana's short reply. "Do you know the answer to her riddle?"

"I have an idea. But before I begin, we will need wood to keep the fire going once it starts." Nikolai pointed to a nearby grove of trees. Together they started out through the rough grass. It came upon him slowly, but Nikolai realized how much he was enjoying picking up the small twigs and tufts of dried grass. Perhaps it was the mere fact that he was closer to the goal now or maybe even just that he was accomplishing something. A thought crossed his mind and he admitted that maybe it was simply because he was spending time with Svetlana. Then he turned back to the task at hand. When they gathered enough tinder, they returned to the walking house.

At the base of the fence, Nikolai and Svetlana scraped clear a small circle and placed the tinder within. They built up a tiered mound with the small twists of dried grass at the center. Leaving Svetlana with the wood, Nikolai walked to the river that flowed behind the walking house. He gathered up a handful of water and slowly walked back. Once there he asked Svetlana to hold out her hands and poured the remaining water into her cupped palms. Selecting a long piece of grass, Nikolai dipped its tip into the water until a single droplet clung to its end. Then ever so carefully he made his way to the little pile of wood. There, after a brief glance at the position of the sun in the sky, Nikolai used the water droplet like a lens to focus the sunlight on the curls of dried grass.

"Clever," said Sveta with a smile.

"Perhaps," Nikolai replied, "but do not lose all the water. I am fairly certain it will take more than one drop to start this fire."

In fact it took three tries, but eventually a thin wisp of smoke rose from the center woodpile. Nikolai saw something move out of the side of his vision. When he spun around one of the curtains of the walking house's windows slid back. Aware he still had just the beginnings of a fire, Nikolai leaned in close to the wood and blew gently. Flames curled about the fuel and the fire strengthened. For the next few moments Nikolai was thoroughly involved in keeping the little blaze alight. When he dared lean back, he found Svetlana close by his shoulder. She smiled at him. "Well done," she said.

"Indeed," Baba Yaga interjected, causing them both to jerk away and turn about. The old witch crouched just behind them. "That was well done, boy. Your next task will not be easier and the final one — well as they say, the final one pays for all. Now I want you to fold air not once, not twice, but thrice." With that, she stood up, smiling as she loomed over them. Then, as before, Baba Yaga returned to the walking house.

Nikolai's brow drew up in thought as he pushed the branches together, causing the fire to smother. He carefully tamped down the small pile of ashes with his boot after Svetlana poured the remaining water over them. "Folding air, that I have no idea."

Sighing, Svetlana rose from her crouch. "I do not either, but I suspect that much as starting fire with water seemed impossible, there is a way."

They stood there in the field for a time and then Svetlana suggested that they go back to *The Swan* for a cup of water or tea. An hour or two later when they were having something to eat Piter returned to the balloon. He had shed his shirt and already his shoulders gleamed red from the sun. Sweat streamed from his brow. He looked at the two of them and shook his head but did not turn down the offer of water. Finding some shade, Piter leaned against the side of *The Swan* and listened to their story.

"Well, it is just as well she asked you something you knew how to do first. I've certainly done better to be chopping wood. I do find it interesting that you weren't shown the pointed end of the stick during the brokering of the deal."

"What do you mean, Piter?" asked Nikolai.

"I keep forgetting what an innocent you are in these things, Nikolai. Baba Yaga is every child's worst nightmare. Behave yourself or bony shanks old mother will come along and gobble you up blood, skin, and marrow with her sharp iron teeth. In every story with Baba Yaga making a deal, the participants are offered enticement or dismemberment. I find it odd that you are only denied what you desire, Nikolai. It seems uncharacteristic, doesn't it Svetlana?"

When she answered, Svetlana met Piter's stare, "Perhaps she knows that Nikolai will be most hurt by such a denial rather than childish fears? After all, he is a thinker, which is why he was able to overcome the first task and how he will conquer the others."

"I salute your faith, Svetlana, for I would like to see Nikolai succeed as well. But for now, I see no way to fold air even once so I will take a brief rest before I return to chopping wood. I have been working like I have my tongue over my shoulder. Don't worry, I have enough fear of Baba Yaga for both of us, Nikolai, if it comes to that." Then Piter tipped his head back and closed his eyes.

They sat down in the shade beside Piter for the moment and relaxed. The gasbags of *The Swan* rippled overhead in the breeze. Sveta stared at them for a moment, her gaze gone distant. A slow smile crept across her lips and then she rose to her feet, drawing Nikolai with her. She clasped his hand, pulling it up to touch the fabric of the balloon. Realization came over him and using his captured hand, Nikolai pulled Svetlana into a brief embrace. Her black hair rustled all about him before she drew away. Nikolai couldn't help but notice Piter's eye closing when he looked at the other man, but Piter gave every impression of remaining asleep.

Stepping around his friend, Nikolai led Svetlana into the gondola. He pulled out various boxes and pouches until he discovered the patching material for the gasbags. Together they spread out the cloth on the grass and cut it into a long rectangular shape. Svetlana showed Nikolai the best stitch to use and he set about sewing. After the two long sides were done and the bottom sewn as well, Nikolai ran with their creation held over his head until it filled with air. After sealing the top with more stitches, they brought their balloon to the walking house.

There Nikolai laid flat the rectangle folding inward a quarter of its size. He then folded over the quarter so the balloon was half its former length. Finally, he folded over the remaining piece. He'd successfully folded the air inside the flat balloon thrice. When Nikolai looked up, he saw the pestle of Baba Yaga plunging down. The grinding implement plunged through the balloon so swiftly that it burst.

"Well done again, young man, but there is one final test." The grin she wore frightened Nikolai. He backed away from Baba Yaga as she reached into her gown to pull forth a pouch that hung on a cord about her neck. She drew open the top and reached within. When she drew forth her hand, in the center of her shriveled palm lay a single acorn. "If you are so clever, then tie a knot with this." She dropped it without waiting for him to put out his hand.

Nikolai dug about in the grass until he found the nut and clasped his fingers about its smooth shell. This time when he met Svetlana's gaze her confidence had vanished. Streaming peals of wicked laughter, Baba Yaga left them sitting in the field before her house. "Take as long as you like," were her parting words.

All the rest of the day, Nikolai and Svetlana said little to each other as both lingered deep in thought. When Piter came back they told him of the final test. He could only shake his head. Even after dinner little was said. Long after Piter fell into an exhausted sleep and Svetlana crept away to her bed, Nikolai sat in front of the stove turning the acorn over and over in his fingers. When the wolves howled in the distance, he did not even twitch.

Morning found him with his fingers tight about the nut still seated in front of the now-cold stove. Nikolai decided that a walk would wake his stiff muscles and perhaps his mind. He moved away from *The Swan* until he came to the bank of the river. The water's oxbow loops were so tight it was only a short distance from one to the next. The banks were deep cut and Nikolai sat on one, his legs dangling down. The sun reflecting off of the water made him drowsy and his head began to drop forward. That was when he noticed the two pinpoints of red that lay under the surface of the water. In fact the lights almost looked like eyes. When the round, bloated face came forward, breaking the surface, its green hair and mustaches plastered back against black scales, Nikolai pulled back, the all-important acorn spilling from his fingers into the dark water below.

The *vodyanoi* caught the nut in one of its webbed hands and held it up before its red gaze. When that look was turned on Nikolai, he felt the spirit of the river's calculating glare. "Where did this come from, I wonder?" it croaked. "Surely only the witch travels far enough to find something as strange as this."

"Yes, it belongs to Baba Yaga," Nikolai said hoping that might encourage the creature to return the acorn to him.

"Then what are you doing with it?"

"I've been given a task to accomplish with that acorn. I suspect she will be very cross if I do not complete it." Nikolai could feel a bead of sweat slide down between his shoulder blades.

The *vodyanoi* looked at the acorn once more and then returned to staring at Nikolai. "What if you were to tell me the truth?" it asked.

Feeling as if he had no choice, Nikolai told the spirit of the river how he was to tie a knot using the acorn. It looked at Nikolai a while longer saying nothing, simply staring with its unearthly eyes. Then it tossed the acorn back to him.

"I can tell you how to complete your task."

"How?"

"You can do as the witch asks if you will do something for me."

"What do you wish?" asked Nikolai, relieved that the answer to his problem was within reach.

"I will ask that of you later. Your task will take time and you will only get one chance so you must be patient. When the witch tells you that you've succeeded you must come to me. Swear this on the blood of your sons and daughters."

"But I—"

"Swear it on the blood of your children to be then."

After Nikolai swore to the *vodyanoi*, he ran back to *The Swan*. When he saw Sveta stepping down the small steps, Nikolai thought that she was the most beautiful thing he'd ever seen. He swept her up in his arms and kissed her hard. She didn't struggle and sank into his embrace, her lips meeting his joyfully.

Together they found a level place near the stand of small trees and scraping away the grass planted the acorn. They carried water from the river to the patch of earth and doused it good. It did not surprise Nikolai that Sveta's hand found his as they walked back to *The Swan*. Piter was there already writing in his note book and a knowing grin chased itself ever so briefly across his lips. He ducked his head and went back to work once more. Later he gave them time alone by returning to chop wood for Baba Yaga. That evening they found a basket of food on the steps of *The Swan*.

So their days fell into a cycle. Three times a day Nikolai and Sveta walked to the river and brought back water. Then Nikolai would chop wood for Baba Yaga and study the nearby walking house from the outside. Sveta would go inside and work the witch's loom until they broke their fast at midday. They spent their afternoons in the woods and each other's arms while Piter chopped wood and wrote. In the evening they lay out under the stars and told each other the stories of their lives.

The oak shoot grew a foot tall and Nikolai took a cord and tied its top to the ground near the trunk bending it over in a loop. Gradually, day-by-day he was able to bring the trunk about into a complete loop. When the oak was two foot tall, the loop was complete and Nikolai set about training the top of the little tree to come around behind the loop. When the oak was three foot tall its trunk completed the knot. The next morning when he and Sveta arrived with their pail of water they found the witch standing over the little oak tree. She said nothing but took the water from them and poured it carefully about the roots of the oak. When she turned to leave they followed. Baba Yaga took them up to the door of the walking house. She threw open the door and waved them inside.

Nikolai was amazed at the interior. Great gears, shafts, and pistons rose from the floor and the walls. Yet there was still plenty of room to live within. On a nearby wall were framed the very plans that he carried except they were complete and covered in notes. Then Baba Yaga reached out and grasped both of their hands. She brought them together and clasped their joined hands within her own. For a mere whisper of a second Nikolai thought he saw the glimmer of a tear in her raptor-sharp eye, then she turned away, leaving them alone.

Nikolai wished he was Piter then. The man always had something to say. "So was this your desire then?" he asked, looking at their joined hands.

"For such a brilliant man, it took you quite some time to figure that out." Sveta's smile was as bright as the shining tears that stood in her eyes. Then she stepped forward to fill his arms, her kiss a sweet, unexpected miracle. He had all the time in the world now to learn the wonders of the walking house and somehow he had gained something even more important.

"There you have it," Piter said, slamming the pages of his journal closed. He stretched his arms over his head and yawned. "It is most certainly time for tea and after such a fine tale as that you must certainly get it for me from your mother."

"Because you know there is a much better chance of tea if I ask, right, Uncle?"

"Most certainly. You are as smart as your father, Alexei."

"I am smart enough to know that you did not finish the story."

"What?" Piter cried as if aggrieved.

"Listen, can't you hear Tatiana say that the story is not done?"

Piter bent his head to the little raven-haired girl who promptly blew spittle bubbles in his ear. "Ahhh, she's said no such thing."

"But I am right, Uncle," Alexei prodded.

"You children will be the death of me as I perish from thirst. Yes, your father went back to the vodyanoi and kept his promise. The spirit of the river made him agree to build his home and raise his children here so that Baba Yaga would spend her time with them instead of meddling with the river, making it go where she willed. In fact, when you go fishing next, have a good look and you will see that the river has already begun to straighten out its course once again."

"Why do you stay here, Uncle?"

"That is a silly question. Here is where the stories are. I tell them to you and I write them down. In Moscow or one of the cities, everyone is always convinced they know all the answers and how things must be. Out here on the edges, things can be as they are and the unbelievable does not hide away. Maybe one day I will go back to the city and tell my stories, or perhaps one day instead of having her for dinner your great grandmother will find a young maiden for Piter. But until then, it will be time for tea. So off with you, fetch my tea. Tatiana, you go with him and be certain he doesn't fail." With that Piter laid his head back against the great knot in the trunk of the oak tree that shaded Nikolai and Svetlana's home. He kept his eyes closed until the children left. Then, as always, his hands, almost of their own accord, grasped his notebook and pencil once more.

The Patented Troll

based on The Three Billy Goats Gruff

GAIL Z. AND LARRY N. MARTIN

NCE UPON A TIME, IN A WORLD OF GEARS AND STEAM, THERE LIVED an inventor. Now this was no ordinary dreamer. This was an inventor of clockwork creatures so amazing that they could learn tasks and follow orders. He developed all kinds of mechanical wonders, each more ambitious than the last, all beyond the limits of what others had considered possible.

The brilliant inventor's fame grew, and people came from all around the world to see his amazing creations. Some of his clockwork creatures had the shape of men, but they could work for days at a time and never required sleep or food. Others resembled dogs, but the steel and steam dogs could hunt for a week and never lose the scent of their quarry. His iron horses were a wonder to behold, powerful and regal, stallions that could run as fast as a train. Audiences swooned at the beauty of his mechanical falcons and aluminum eagles, with cameras for eyes that beheld the world beneath them.

But all too soon, the inventor came to the attention of those who could not appreciate his clockwork creatures for their elegant beauty, and saw in them only a means to create profit and inflict pain.

"Sell us your fantastic creatures," the men from the army said to the inventor. "We will make you a hero! Your steel dogs will run enemy soldiers to ground and your iron horses will trample the enemy under their hooves."

"Sell us your amazing inventions," the men who ran the factories said to the inventor. "We will make you rich! Armies of your mechanical men will run our factories, men that require no pay and no sleep, who never feel pain and cannot die, and we will work them until they fall apart."

"Sell us your clockwork monsters," the criminals said. "You will be powerful! With control of such creatures, we can best our rivals and eliminate anyone who stands in our way. We will rule the world!"

Now the inventor had never imagined such horrors when he created his mechanical wonders. He had a brilliant mind, but he was childlike when it came to the darkness of the human heart. When he saw what others wanted to do with his creations, he refused their offers in horror.

"I will never sell my fabulous animals and mechanical men to help you kill and enslave and destroy!" the inventor said. "They were created to improve the world, not to make it a place of bloodshed."

But powerful and greedy men do not listen to the likes of a poor inventor. And so they broke into his laboratory and stole his wonderful creatures and his clockwork men and they beat the inventor senseless and left him for dead. "If you will not accept money, fame, or power, then you are a fool," the men said. "We are going to change the world."

And change the world they did. The inventor did not die, though he was badly injured. Some days, he wished he had perished, because it broke his heart to see what the men who stole his mechanical creatures made of them. Governments waged war without end, pitting clockwork soldiers on iron horses against each other in battles that never ended, fighting men that could not bleed. Steel dogs killed without remorse, wiping out villages and farms in their path. Criminals used mechanical monsters to terrorize cities and hunt down anyone who opposed them, until no one was safe.

Factories filled with metal men worked around the clock, belching smoke and sending flames into the night sky. Outside their gates, the human workers and their families starved, their labor no longer needed.

The inventor saw all of this, and wept. "I have brought this on the world. I have failed my precious creatures, and let them be enslaved. If anyone discovers that I am still alive, the powerful and greedy men will take me prisoner and make me invent more horrors for them. I cannot let that happen."

So the inventor went away, to a secret place only he knew existed. On an island in the middle of the deep woods far away from cities or towns, he had built himself a cabin and a workshop. Not all of his beautiful steam creatures had been lost to the profiteers, because he had already begun to move them, slowly and secretly, to his sanctuary in the forest. He had planted a garden to grow his food and he had outfitted his laboratory with all the tools and materials he might need, intending to spend his old age tinkering. He planned his escape, and slipped away one night, making certain to take with him or destroy any of his notes that might be used to exploit his inventions. But in his hurry, he forgot one of his notebooks.

And so it was that when the cities fell and the skies burned, the inventor was far away, living with his beloved clockwork creatures. Smoke carried on the wind from the conflagrations, and the night trembled with thunder from the explosions that lit the horizon with false sunsets. The inventor sobbed for his part in the destruction, and none of his fabulous animals could console him.

"I must never let anyone misuse my creatures again," the inventor said. His island had a single, wooden bridge that connected it to the mainland, since its shores were steep and rocky and unfit for a boat to land. To protect himself, the inventor built a large, powerful mechanical man with a broad chest and thick arms and legs.

"I will call you 'Troll'," the inventor told his creation. "You will stand guard over this bridge and keep away any intruders."

Troll did as he was told. Like all of the inventor's creatures, Troll was able to learn tasks and follow orders. He watched the animals in the forest, and they watched him. When he made no move to hunt or hurt them, the birds and rabbits, foxes and bear cubs dared to come closer. Troll watched them jump and play, and saw them tend their young. It occupied his circuits while he waited.

Sometimes, the inventor would come across the bridge with one of his mechanical dogs to visit Troll and check on his gears and wiring. The inventor was scarred from the attack that nearly killed him, and he walked with a cane. When the inventor visited, he would talk to Troll of this and that. Troll learned the words, and when he was alone, he would speak to the animals, and they would bark and howl in return.

Years went by. Troll saw the animals in the forest find mates, give birth, grow old, and die. Troll never changed. The mechanical dogs that came with the inventor never changed, either, but the inventor grayed with every turn of the seasons. His visits, once frequent, came less and less often. After a while, the inventor did not come at all.

Twenty years went by. Troll counted the winters and summers to pass the time, though he did not change. He looked across the bridge for signs of the inventor or his dogs, but nothing stirred. Troll did not have instructions to go back across the bridge, so he stayed where he was. Generations of birds and animals took him for part of the forest. They ran across his broad shoulders and perched on his head. Troll learned to make their songs and noises, and they considered him one of their own. But always, Troll waited for his inventor to return.

Far away, in the ruins of what was once a vast city, a young man named Tad spent his time tinkering with bits of metal. He scavenged the pieces he found in old buildings and garbage dumps, and took what he needed from the rusted hulks of long-silenced factories and huge, broken machines.

"I have no money and no prospects, and barely enough food to eat," Tad said to himself. "But with a few tools and some old junk, I can amuse myself and pass the time."

Tad had no family and few friends. He spent his time searching for food and materials, exploring the wreckage of the buildings destroyed in the long-ago war. Sometimes he found books, and Tad taught himself many things. He liked numbers the most, because some of the books showed him how numbers could help him build wonderful things.

One day, Tad found a room in an old, deserted building that was full of strange equipment, disassembled and badly damaged. He moved his few belongings into the room so he could examine the odd tools that had been left behind and read the books that were filled with drawings and numbers.

At first, Tad tinkered with making small clocks and little machines. He built a mechanical mouse, and then a clockwork cat to go with it. As he learned more, he built a steel dog he called Gear and a donkey he named Trouble. Now he was not alone.

Though the war had long been over, the city and its streets were still not safe. Wild animals walked the ruined boulevards, and gangs of desperate men were a law unto themselves. Tad ventured out from his hiding place only when he needed food, or water, or equipment. He dreamed of going somewhere with all of his mechanical animals where he could build new wonders and not be afraid.

One day, Tad found a notebook that had fallen behind a bookshelf. No one else had found it in all the long years, and its hiding place had protected it from the elements. The pages were yellowed and the ink was faded, but Tad discovered the most wondrous drawings he had ever seen.

"I must find the person who wrote these notes," Tad said to Gear, who wagged his steel tail. "But where could he have gone?"

Then Tad found a piece of a map stuffed into the back of the notebook. He knew where there was a building full of a lot of old books,

and he took the fragment with him, daring to go searching for a clue to where the inventor might have gone. Many of the old books had burned in the great fire, and others had been damaged by time and water, but Tad finally found a map that matched the fragment in the notebook.

"This is where we're going to go," he told Gear. "This is where we'll find the inventor."

Then Tad realized how far away the place on the map was, and he grew sad. "The road is long and dangerous. I'll need a way to protect us on the journey."

So Tad build a large metal man. The metal man moved with springs and gears like his other inventions, and he could see and hear and speak. Tad called him 'Billy'. Billy had room to carry Tad inside his big, broad chest. Tad could also see through Billy's eyes and speak through Billy's mouth.

"Cat can scratch and Gear can bite. Mouse can run and Trouble can kick. Now Billy can protect us, too," Tad told his creations. "We're ready for our adventure."

So Tad packed up his few possessions and took his mechanical creatures and struck out to seek his fortune. He carried Mouse in his pocket as he rode within the mechanical man and Cat and Gear walked alongside Trouble and Billy. Soon, they left the city behind. Tad had a compass and a supply of candles, and he had learned how to trap rats and rabbits for food. He had a knife to protect himself and to cut wood for a fire, and he had enough bits of metal and tools to fix anything that might go wrong with his clockwork companions.

Tad and his mechanical menagerie walked for many, many days. By now, the ruins of the big cities were far away. They passed abandoned homes and farms fallen into disrepair. All of the people were gone. The weather grew colder as they went north, and by the end of the summer, they had found the forest on Tad's map. On they walked, deeper and deeper into the woods.

Tad had never seen a forest, except in books. He marveled at the smells and sounds, and feared the noises he heard in the night. Animals were all around them, watching from a distance. By now, Tad had learned which plants and berries and nuts were good for eating, so he did not have to harm any of the forest creatures. They followed Tad and his companions at a distance, as if they were curious to see where they were going.

"There it is!" Tad stopped Billy on a rise overlooking a large lake. In the distance, he could see a few buildings on an island, and a long wooden bridge. "That must be where the inventor lives!"

So Tad and the others headed for the bridge. Cat and Mouse played chase with each other. Gear wagged his tail and pranced. Trouble picked up his plodding pace. But when they reached the bridge, Troll was waiting.

"You cannot pass." Troll's voice was metallic and scratchy.

"We've come to see the inventor," Tad said, still riding inside Billy's big chest.

"No one can cross," Troll warned.

Just then, Mouse scampered around Troll's feet. Troll reached down and picked up the mechanical rodent, holding Mouse in his big metal palm. "Nice," Troll said. He let Mouse down, and immediately Mouse ran toward the bridge with Cat right behind him.

"You cannot pass!" Troll warned, but it was too late. Cat and Mouse were already halfway across the bridge.

"Don't worry about them," Tad said through Billy's mouth. "They won't cause any harm. The inventor has clockwork animals of his own, doesn't he? Maybe they would like company."

Troll had not seen the inventor or his mechanical dogs for a long time. The clockwork dog with this newcomer looked like one of the inventor's favorites.

"That's my dog, Gear," Tad said. "He's very friendly."

Troll threw a stick like the inventor had taught him. Gear brought it back and wagged his steel tail. Again and again, Troll threw and Gear fetched. While Troll and Gear played, Trouble edged closer to the bridge. Before Troll could stop him, Trouble ran across the bridge after Cat and Mouse.

"You cannot pass!" Troll called after him, but it was too late. Cat and Mouse were on the island, and Trouble was most of the way across the bridge.

"Gear can get them to come back," Tad said. "I'll send him after them." Gear followed Cat and Mouse and Trouble across the old wooden bridge.

Troll stood between Tad and the bridge. "You cannot pass!"

Tad was still inside Billy. Billy and Troll were nearly the same size. But while Billy was shiny and new, Troll was weathered and stained. His metal was dented in places, and Tad saw a few spots of rust. He looked at the weathered old bridge and at Troll and knew that the inventor must be dead.

"You've been guarding this bridge a long time," Tad said.

"A very long time."

"Have you seen beyond the hillside?" Tad asked. "The forest is very big and filled with beautiful things. There are waterfalls and ponds and flowers and animals."

As they stood there, the forest creatures came closer. A bird landed on Troll's shoulder, and a squirrel skittered across his big metal feet. "Your friends could show you where they live," Tad said. "It isn't far. I will guard the bridge for you."

"You cannot cross!"

"I'll stay right here until you get back," Tad promised. "And when you return, I'll keep you company, and so will Cat and Mouse and Gear and Trouble."

"Stay?" It had been a long, long time since Troll had company.

"Yes. I'll stay and guard the bridge. Go and see the animals. I'll be here when you come back."

The rabbits and squirrels seemed to understand, because they headed up the ridge, and stopped to see if Troll would follow. Troll took one step and then another, and looked back uncertainly. Billy waved, still standing at the end of the bridge. No one would pass. And so Troll followed his animal companions, up the rise and over the ridge.

When Troll was out of sight, Tad climbed out of Billy and closed the metal body back up again. "Stay here, and keep Troll company," he told Billy.

"Stay?" Billy asked. Tad had taught him to follow instructions and do many tasks during their long journey, but Billy had never been away from Tad before.

"Yes. Here with Troll. Help him guard the bridge." Then Tad hurried across the bridge, leaving Billy on the other side, to keep watch.

Cat, Mouse, Gear, and Trouble were waiting for Tad. Together, they explored the island. There was an overgrown plot for growing vegetables and plenty of fresh water. A barn held more crates of parts and tools than Tad had ever seen. Tad found several mechanical dogs that had wound down, and when he turned their keys, the dogs and Gear played a game of chase.

The cabin was tidy and comfortable, with a fireplace and a stove and a table with chairs. Shelves of books lined the walls, and there were lanterns to read by and a bed to sleep in, along with a trunk full of clothing that was close to Tad's size.

On the floor, Tad found the inventor's body, shriveled to mere bones. It made him very sad that he could not talk to the man whose notes had inspired him. But as he looked around the cabin, he realized that the walls were filled with new drawings and numbers, plans for all kinds of wondrous creatures the inventor had not lived to create.

"I will pick up where you left off," Tad promised. "I will build your dreams and take care of your inventions." He looked at his companions.

"We're home now."

After a while, when Troll had followed his animal companions to see the forest, he headed back to his bridge. There stood Billy, just as promised. And for the first time in many years, smoke rose from the chimney of the inventor's cabin. Mechanical dogs chased and barked on the far shore.

The inventor waved to him from the window of the cottage. Troll settled into his place at the end of the bridge, next to Billy. All was as it should be.

A Cat Among the Gears

based on Puss 'n Boots

Elaine Corvidae

"You put my brain into a cat."

"Exactly!" Master said, gleeful as a kid with a new toy.

I stared down in horror at the silver-furred forelegs stretched out in front of me instead of arms. At least I could still stand on two feet. "You. Put my brain. Into a cat."

"Yes, yes." Master's enthusiasm dimmed slightly, as he peered down at me. "You seem to be having trouble comprehending simple language, though. Perhaps this is a side-effect of the feline biochemistry?"

I tried to slap my palm over my face in exasperation, but instead bopped myself on my little pink nose with a paw. And those claws were sharp. Maybe I ought to use them on him. "Why in the nine hells did you put my brain in a cat?"

"I needed to test my size-adjustment ray."

"We already tested it on that annoying minstrel last week, remember?" Master had shrunk the poor lad so small I suspected one of us had accidentally inhaled him.

Master leaned against the device in question, a rather large and bulky contraption of brass, gears, and lenses. I didn't have a clue how the thing worked; I was just the gal who handed him the right wrenches, fetched the occasional corpse, and swapped out the punch cards in the automatons.

Except now I was apparently the *cat* who did that.

"We'd done a whole-body test, yes," Master agreed, "but it occurred to me to try it on body parts instead," he said.

"And you couldn't have waited for the next castle-to-castle salesman?"

He almost looked guilty. "Well, I happened to have some of my sleep syrup in my pocket, and your wine was right there…"

In this business, that almost qualified as an excuse. I came from a long line of minions, and trust me, the mad-genius types seldom have good impulse control. Mostly they just do whatever damn fool thing comes into their heads. With a nutter like my current master, well, you learned to watch your drink, count your limbs, and hope to come out the other side with a nice pension. Or at least a sack of gold you managed to loot after the local do-gooder reduced the castle to a smoking ruin.

But really, I had to draw the line somewhere. "So you took out my brain and shrank it."

"Exactly! It was so cute and tiny, it seemed a shame to waste it. So I asked myself: 'What else is cute and tiny? Kitties!' The solution was obvious."

Great. "So where is my old body? And how soon until I get it back?" I might be able to handle being a cat for a little while, but the novelty was bound to wear off.

The abashed look on his face didn't bode well. "There was an accident..."

I extended my claws and lashed my tail, and if you don't think that felt damn weird, you've never had your brain stuck in a cat's body. "What. Happened. To my. Body?"

"I used the size-adjusting ray to make one of the automatons larger—just to see what would happen, of course—and well, the 'ton stepped on you. Um, what used to be you."

That was it. I drew myself up, as best as I was able with only two-and-a-half feet of height to work with, and stalked to the door. Pausing at the entrance, I turned and pointed a paw dramatically at him. I intended to make some dramatic statement which would strike fear into his heart, but he'd already lost interest and had his head stuck underneath the ray gun, tinkering away.

Muttering under my breath, I dropped onto all fours and left with whatever dignity I still possessed.

I spent weeks plotting. And getting used to being a cat, since it looked like I was stuck this way. Do me a favor and don't even ask about my first tongue bath. My cat body was good for being cute and getting free handouts from sappy villagers, but not so good for wreaking vengeance. For that, I was going to need help.

My ex-master's tower was on the edge of a prosperous kingdom, just far enough from any villages to be a real bother. I'd heard rumors the king wasn't the shiniest 'ton in the workshop, if you know what I mean, and his daughter the princess was the real power behind the throne. There had to be a way to get them on my side.

They say providence smiles on little children and discarded experiments. Certainly it smiled on me the day I chanced by the cemetery in a small town not too far from the palace. Three men, who I assumed were brothers, all stood at the side of a freshly-filled grave. The oldest and the middle one weren't much to look at, but the youngest was hotter than a boiler explosion.

"I can't believe all Dad left me is this stupid broken 'ton!" the oldest said, gesturing to a small auto-tailor, which let out irregular gasps of steam.

"I can fix it!" said the youngest eagerly. Ooh, handsome *and* smart. I liked him more all the time.

"Nah, just scrap the stupid thing," the middle son said. "Besides, what are you complaining about? All I have is blueprints for a pie-making machine that doesn't work."

"I can make it work," offered the youngest.

"Forget it, Peter," the oldest sneered. "Dad didn't leave you anything. Go back to your workshop."

Shoulders slumped, Peter left the cemetery and went to a tiny cottage on the outskirts of the village. I followed him, of course, and jumped up on the windowsill to look inside. I was pleased to see the entire house had been converted to a workshop, filled with brass tubes, wrenches, welding equipment, and the like. Peter had already sat down at the worktable and wore a pair of goggles outfitted with at least a dozen different lenses.

When he saw me at the window, however, he smiled. "Oh! Hello, puss! Are you looking for some cream? I might have some here…"

Cream? Oh, yeah, he was a keeper. "Thanks," I said.

He stopped rummaging for the cream and blinked at me through his goggles. "You-you talk?"

"Of course." I jumped down from my sill and stood on my hind paws, executing a credible bow. "Didn't you know? I'm your inheritance," I added, in case the idea of a random talking cat was too much for him.

He looked puzzled. "Dad had a cat? Huh. I didn't know that." He looked around the workshop. "I'm sorry, kitty, but you might be better off finding a different master. I'm just a poor tinker."

Tinker? This guy was seriously underselling his talent. Probably thanks to his two idiot brothers. "Don't worry," I said, "I'm here to help you. We're going to turn your fortunes around." And get my revenge while we were at it, though I kept that bit to myself.

Peter crouched down to be on my level, and I gave him marks for politeness. This guy had major potential, all right. It was just up to me to tap it.

"How?" he asked guilelessly.

I smiled as best I was able with a cat mouth. "Settle in, and I'll tell you over cream."

My plan included a lot of travel, so the first thing I had Peter do was make me a pair of boots. Not just any old boots, though: these babies would let me run seven leagues faster than a horse. Plus the shiny brass gears and brown leather looked great against my silver fur and dark stripes.

Hey, if I was going to be stuck as a cat, I might as well be stylish about it.

While he was working on the boots, I did some reconnaissance, going to the palace and pretending to be an ordinary cat. The clockwork guards didn't even look at me twice, and I strolled right into the throne room, the king's bedroom, the larder...pretty much anywhere I wanted to go. I wasn't thrilled about being a cat, but at least my ex-master hadn't stuck my brain in a cow. That would have been awkward.

Once I'd figured a few things out about the king, I told Peter to whip up a few gadgets. As soon as he was done, I popped the first one in a bag and headed off to the palace, decked out in my nice shiny boots.

This time, the clockwork guards paid attention, since I was clearly not an ordinary cat. "State your business," one of them clanged.

"I am here to see the king, on behalf of my master, Lord Gearsly," I declared.

The guards ground loudly for a moment, as I'd expected, since they would have no Lord "Gearsly" stored in their memories. Lights began to flash, and a few minutes later, a human guard appeared.

This was what I'd hoped for. 'Tons were easy to fool, but never so easy as a person. "I have a present for the king!" I declared imperiously. "Take me to him at once!"

I'd learned through my surveillance that the king loved presents. The guard knew as well, and it would be on his head if the king found out he'd turned away a really good one. If I'd looked like a beggar or a madman, he might have taken the chance, but it takes real gumption to say no to a talking cat. "This way," he said grudgingly.

The king received me quite kindly. I strode up to his throne and offered my most extravagant bow—I'd been practicing since I met Peter. "Your Highness, thank you for granting me this audience," I said.

"You're a kitty!" he exclaimed, clapping his hands in delight. I did mention he was a bit simple, didn't I?

Not only was he simple, but he loved gadgets, the more useless the better. Reaching into my bag, I pulled out a mechanical partridge. Like a real partridge, it didn't do much more than scratch on the ground and peck, but it looked wonderfully complicated while it did, what with all its gears and gyros and such.

"A present for Your Highness, from my Lord Gearsly," I said. Then I took my leave quickly, before the king could notice, because nothing sharpens interest like unanswered questions.

I repeated this act for the next two weeks, taking first an automatic shoe-tying machine, then a small 'ton which recited poetry at random intervals. Both of them delighted the king, but I made sure to slip away before he — or any of his sharper ministers — could inquire any further as to my master.

As for Peter, he was as confused as the king. "I'm sorry, Miss Purr," he said, which was what he'd settled on calling me. I must admit I rather liked it. "I don't see how giving the king presents in a fake name will make my fortune."

"Don't worry, my boy," I said, patting his knee. "You'll make your own fortune tomorrow by the river."

"How?"

"By getting robbed."

"Help!" I cried, bursting from the underbrush just as the royal carriage rolled by, "Lord Gearsly has been set upon by bandits! Oh, help, please!"

The carriage came to a stop, and the king flung open the door. The princess peered out around him. I had to suppress the urge to purr, because her presence meant my plan couldn't fail.

"Oh!" said the king. "It's the kitty! You say the man who made all those delightful inventions has been attacked?"

"Alas, Your Highness," I gasped, clutching my chest as if in terrible distress. "He went to bathe in the river, and robbers stole all of his clothing and coin! Please, help him!"

The princess leaned further out of the carriage. "I have heard of your master," she said, skeptically. "Let us see him, if he has been truly set on."

It was what I'd counted on from the beginning. I went back to the riverside and coaxed poor Peter out from the weeds where he hid. According to our story, he'd been robbed blind, and thus had on not a single stitch of clothing. I'd told him it was necessary, since we didn't have any coin to buy the fancy clothes expected of a lord. But, let's just say I had an ulterior motive as well.

As he came reluctantly out, his face burning with shame, the princess shoved past her father for a better look. Although Peter tried to conceal his private bits…well, let us say his hand wasn't entirely up to the task. Being a woman of taste, her scowl was immediately replaced by a smile. "Oh, you poor thing!" she exclaimed, catching hold of his naked arm. "You must come into the carriage with us!"

"Guard, give him your clothes!" the king ordered, to the princess's obvious disappointment. Fortunately, the guard was smaller than Peter, so the shirt strained across his broad shoulders, and the trousers clung to his rear. The princess was too refined to actually drool, but I'm pretty sure she purred.

"So, Lord Gearsly," she said, putting a hand a bit higher up than his knee, "tell me about yourself."

We'd rehearsed this bit multiple times, and fortunately Peter stopped making doe eyes at the princess — who was a looker herself — long enough to remember his lines. The tale he spun about his extensive holdings in an obscure corner of the kingdom was a fine one — as it should have been, since I'd come up with it.

"Really?" the princess asked, with a skeptical arch of her brow. "I'll send for a contingent of soldiers, and we'll see these lands of yours."

Like I said before, not much was getting past the princess. Which was just as I'd hoped.

The carriage started off, and so did I. In all the commotion, no one had noticed I'd remained outside. Now I put my seven-league boots to good use, easily outstripping the horses and reaching the lands I'd told Peter to claim as his own. If you've been paying any attention at all, you won't be shocked to hear these lands actually belonged to my former master.

'Tons worked the fields to either side of the road, mechanically harvesting wheat, turnips, and a dozen other crops. Having spent several years maintaining them, it was a simple matter to pull their punch cards, do a bit of reprogramming, and slip away.

I hid in a hay bale and watched as the carriage drew up to the first group of 'tons. As it came to a stop, the princess leaned out of the window and called, "Hail, you workers! Who is your master?"

"Lord Gearsly," they replied in their monotone voices.

A smile of surprised pleasure crossed the princess's face before she disappeared back inside.

Satisfied things were going according to plan, I put my boots into high gear and got to work.

I won't say the castle had fallen into disrepair without me, but the outer defenses would never have gotten so rusty or slipshod if I'd been there. It didn't take much for me to get inside and locate my ex-master in his workshop.

"Master!" I exclaimed, as I rushed inside.

He blinked owlishly at me. "There you are! Where have you been? I ought to dock your pay!"

I'll be honest: I'd hoped to make a resounding speech about how I'd seen the error of my ways and come back to him. The fact he'd barely noticed I was gone took some of the wind out of my sails.

"I'm sorry, Master," I said. "I got word your enemies were conspiring against you. Don't you remember?"

Rule one in the minion handbook for dealing with mad scientists: they'll never admit they don't know something. "Of course I do," he grunted. "But you took a wretched long time!"

"Forgive me," I said, bowing low. "But, Master, you are in danger! The king is on the way, leading an army to kill you!"

"What?" he ran to his far-seeing device, which actually worked for once. After a few minutes of adjustment, he spied the king's carriage and leapt back with a cry. "Dear heavens, you're right! The king is on his way! With soldiers coming behind him! It's an attack!"

I wrung my paws in a show of distress. "Quick, Master! Use your size-adjusting ray to make yourself a giant, so you can stomp them all flat!"

"Excellent idea, minion!" he said, and rushed to the device. Within the space of five minutes, he had swelled to gargantuan size. His head brushed the rafters, and the floor groaned beneath his weight.

"Yes!" I said. Then I glanced between him and the door. "But—oh no! You're too big."

"I'll just shrink back down and move the ray apparatus into the courtyard," he said. Of course, once he was normal size again, he saw the problem. The size-adjusting device was far too large to move.

"The castle will surely fall," I wailed. "We're doomed. Doomed!"

"Perhaps the 'tons will hold them off."

"There's no time for that, master. You must flee to save yourself, and have your revenge another day. I know — shrink yourself to the size of a mouse! That way you can sneak past them without being seen."

"Yes, yes!" He hurriedly poked at the ray, and a few moments later, he was the size of a mouse.

"Now, minion, I shall escape!" he squeaked.

"I don't think so," I replied, just before I ate him.

We all lived happily ever after. The king and princess arrived, looked over "Lord Gearsly's" castle and lands, and were satisfied he really was a noble. Peter's looks had done most of the work, but this sealed the deal, and the princess married him a month later. Peter was smart enough to keep his mouth shut, pretend he'd always been a lord, and continue inventing distracting gadgets for the king. Eight months after the wedding, the king was thrilled to have a grandchild.

As for me, I'm Lady Purr now, thank you very much. I live with Peter and his family, and yeah, I'm stuck as a cat. But I have all the cream and fish I could want, and there is a handsome tom in the castle next door.

Plus, these boots do look amazing on me. What more could a cat ask for?

The Steam-Powered Dragon

based on The Dragon and His Grandmother

DAVID LEE SUMMERS

ARLOW AND DANIELS WERE STROLLING THROUGH THE MARKET OF Peshawar Town, admiring the work of local weavers, when Carlyle ran up to them, out of breath. "The Russians jus' crossed the Oxus River. They're fightin' the Afghans at Panjdeh."

"Good for them," declared Daniels with a laugh. "Keeps the bloody Afghans off our backs for a while."

Marlow scowled. "That's not going to sit well with Parliament. The whole reason we get to enjoy this mild climate is to keep the Russians intimidated. They push in on us, we'll have to push back."

Carlyle nodded. "Bad enough fightin' Afghan tribesmen. Them Russians is trained soldiers, they is. The last thing I want to do is face them — and that's bloody desert over there by Panjdeh."

"All I ever wanted was to be an artist." Daniels looked off toward the tall peaks to the north. "We could always go into Kafiristan and set ourselves up as kings. We'd be wealthy and do what we wanted."

Marlow folded his arms. "That's just dreaming. You know the tribesmen up there would tear us apart as soon as look at us."

Carlyle followed Daniels's gaze. "He does have a point, though. If we was up in the mountains when the army moved out, we wouldn't have t' march across the Afghan desert."

Marlow snorted. "They'd still shoot us as deserters if they caught us."

"And who'd catch us?" Daniels asked. "If we run off, they'd assume we went down the road to Lahore."

"Best if we're not deserters." Carlyle tapped his pith helmet's brim. "We could suggest a scouting tour in the mountains — requisition some guns and disappear for a few days. By the time we get back, the army's sure to have moved on to meet the Russians. We'll be able t' stay here in relative comfort with the garrison what's left behind."

Marlow considered the proposition, then nodded. "Now that's an idea I could get behind."

Daniels sighed. His gray eyes lingered on the mountains, whether studying them or dreaming of distant kingdoms the others didn't know. "All right then, I'm in."

With that, the three men returned to the garrison headquarters and reported to their commander. Once in his office, they snapped crisp salutes. Carlyle stepped forward. "Sir, we's heard that the Russians have invaded Panjdeh. We respectfully request that we lead a scoutin' party into the mountains to make sure there's no Russians spyin' on us."

The lieutenant returned their salute and placed his hands behind his back. "And why do you think the Russians would be spying on us?"

Daniels stepped forward. "Surely they'll overwhelm the Afghans. If that's the case, isn't it likely we'll be sent to fight them?"

Marlow nodded and joined Carlyle and Daniels. "Surely the Russians will want to know what they're facing. Spies with telescopes could be lurking up there right now and we'd never know it...unless we go look."

The lieutenant pursed his lips and sat behind the desk. "Very well. I need to check with the colonel, but if he approves, you can go. At least I'd get some useful work out of you three. Make a list of the supplies you need and see me in an hour's time."

The three saluted again, turned on their heels and left the office.

The lieutenant granted the three soldiers permission to conduct their scouting expedition. "Take only a week's worth of supplies," said the officer. "The colonel agrees the Russians might be snooping about, but we could be marching out soon. I want you back here when we do."

The three soldiers snapped salutes and left for the mountains as soon as they could.

Their foray into the mountains was a quiet one. They encountered no Russian spies and stayed clear of the villages. Nevertheless, Marlow couldn't shake a feeling they were being watched. Six days later, they hiked out of the mountains into the foothills above Peshawar.

Daniels retrieved a spyglass from his belt and examined the city. "They haven't been ordered west yet," he growled.

Carlyle took the spyglass and confirmed Daniels's observations. "I say we's stay put fer a few days an' see if they depart."

Marlow shook his head. "You heard the lieutenant. He wanted us back in a week."

Carlyle shrugged. "So we go back in th' hills, fire off some rounds, eat s'more of our rations and say the tribesmen gave us trouble. No one'll

be any the wiser." With that, the three men were agreed and they went up into the hills for three more days.

When they returned to the foothills, they saw that the garrison had still not been ordered west to Panjdeh.

"What do we do now?" Marlow's shoulders drooped. "We're nearly out of supplies. If we stay in the mountains we'll starve. If we return to the garrison, we'll have to face the Russians. If we sneak east to Lahore, we'll be shot as traitors to the Crown likely as not."

"I vote we stay in the mountains and make friends with one of the tribes," said Daniels.

Carlyle shook his head. "I say we's takes our chances on Lahore."

"I think it's best if we accept our fate and return to the army," said Marlow.

Just then, a great wind swept up clouds of dust. A loud, screeching roar like a broken-down freight train pulling into a station sounded. A burst of flame ignited a nearby bush. A moment later, a great, copper-colored dragon appeared in the sky above and descended to the rocky ground, scattering dirt and pebbles. As it landed, they heard tickings, whirrings, and clackings from within the beast. Steam issued forth from between its joints. The dragon was not alive at all, but rather a great automaton. Nevertheless, it looked them over with green, emerald-like eyes and let out a hearty mechanical laugh. "You men seem to find yourself in a predicament. I think I can help."

Daniels rubbed his goatee. "And just what do you think you can do for us, eh?"

"If you promise to give me service," said the steam-powered dragon, "I will carry you across India to the coal fields of Raniganj. There you will buy a coal mine and work it for seven years. Once you have done that, I will come for the coal and give you a choice."

Marlow held up his hand. "Now wait a minute there, Mr. Dragon. In principle, this all sounds very good, but we're hardly rich men who can go about buying coal mines."

"That is easily solved," said the dragon. He opened a leather pouch that he wore around his neck and pulled forth a small machine, which he placed on the ground. Then, he opened a door in his belly and retrieved a chunk of coal. He placed the coal inside the machine, then turned a crank on its side. Steam issued from the machine and it glowed red. Before it was cool enough for human hands to touch the exterior, the dragon reached in and plucked forth a diamond with his claws. "I think this would serve as a down payment for a coal mine. I'll leave you with the diamond engine in case you have…other expenses."

Carlyle stepped forward. "You said we'd have a choice at the end of the seven years. Wha' choice would that be?"

"Ah." The dragon's metallic lips creaked upward in a toothy smile. "I will give you three puzzles — one for each of you — and if you solve them, you shall have your freedom. If you don't solve them, you shall continue to serve me for the rest of your days."

Marlow and Carlyle looked at each other and nodded. Daniels narrowed his sharp gaze. "What if we're not there? What if we just make some diamonds and skip out on you?"

"A clever man. I like that." The dragon tapped his forehead with his metallic claw, then his devilish smile turned into a fearsome scowl. "If you try to cheat me, I will hunt you down. Human flesh won't burn as efficiently in my belly as coal, but it will do for a while." The dragon let the implications of the threat sink in.

"I see no choice then but to accept your terms," said Daniels.

Without another word, the dragon scooped the soldiers up in his claws and carried them through the air and across the entire subcontinent until they reached Raniganj near the Damodar River. He set them down. "Enjoy your time in Raniganj. When I return in seven years, I expect to have coal enough to power my burners for many decades to come."

They watched open-mouthed as the dragon lifted himself high into the sky and disappeared from sight. Marlow held up the diamond the dragon had given them and nodded slowly. "I suppose we better get busy and buy a coal mine."

Good as their word, the three soldiers soon acquired a mine. They took the occasional hunk of coal and placed it in the alchemical diamond engine. Not lacking for wealth, they soon acquired waistcoats, cravats, and tailcoats. They burned their uniforms and put the military life behind them.

The men threw parties and became well known to the railway owners and steamship operators. Soon they had good wives and luxurious mansions with numerous servants. Remembering their harsh days in the military and the poverty they encountered throughout India, they treated their servants well. In fact, their wealth overflowed so much that they gave it away to the poor of Raniganj.

The time flew and soon the three friends realized only a month remained before the seven years would draw to an end. They met at the mining company offices. Marlow wrung his hands and Daniels paced the floor. Carlyle entered the room, opened a wooden box, and grabbed a cigar. "Brothers, I 'ave a plan to keep us from th' dragon's service."

"You can't hope to trick that Satanic monstrosity," said Daniels. "We'll have to rely on our wits and hope he plays fair with whatever puzzle he gives us."

Carlyle clipped the end from the cigar, thrust it in his mouth, and lit it. A moment later, he exhaled smoke, looking something like a steam-powered machine himself. "Let's beat 'im at 'is own game. We can take the train to Peshawar Town an' hike into the mountains. That dragon is too big an' loud to hide. Surely someone else has encountered 'im and can give us insights into the way he thinks. We'll solve the puzzles before 'e even asks."

"And what if we fail?" Marlow steepled his fingers, appraising Carlyle over the apex.

"What if we do?" Carlyle took another puff of the cigar. "We'll 'ave 'ad a good vacation in the mountains, which'll clear our heads. I see no way it can do us 'arm."

Daniels leaned in close. "What about the army stationed at Peshawar? What if someone recognizes us?"

Carlyle shook his head, but frowned. "After all this time, I doubt anyone is goin' t' recognize us. You worry too much!"

A week later, the three friends stepped off the train at the end of the line in Peshawar. They collected their belongings from the baggage car and cast about for someplace to eat.

"Well if it isn't Thomas Daniels, Peachy Carlyle, and Rudyard Marlow," called a man from up the street.

The three friends turned and saw a man in red uniform coat with a bandolier and a pith helmet. It was the lieutenant from their army days, only now he wore the insignia of a major. "When you disappeared in the mountains, I thought the dragon got you chaps."

"Dragon?" Carlyle's eyebrows came together. "Wha' d'you know about the dragon?"

"Why he's been harassing the railroad for years. Comes down out of the mountains and steals coal. We've tried to stop him, but the bullets bounce off that cursed metal hide of his. Best we can figure, he lives on Mount Ilam."

"As a matter of fact, we're looking for the dragon. Hunting him, you might say," said Daniels. "He carried us away years ago. Kept us from returning to the unit." All three looked downcast, as though terribly sorry they had not returned before now.

"Well, by the looks of you, it didn't do any harm," said the major. "If I were you, I'd stay away from that dragon."

"We would if'n we could." Carlyle opened his bag and handed the major a diamond. "Can you tell us th' way t' the dragon's lair?"

The major sighed. "March up through the Swat Valley. As you skirt Mount Ilam, you'll see a stream that has cut a deep culvert. Follow that until you come to a rock fall. They say the dragon makes his home there."

"If you know how to find the dragon, why haven't you gone after him?" Marlow asked.

The major shook his head. "That's rough terrain. Can't get in with more firepower than men can carry. It would be tough going even on horseback. Going there, you're just asking for that dragon to tear you to shreds."

Marlow and Daniels looked at each other and swallowed. Carlyle smiled and tipped his top hat. "Thanks fer all your help." Once the major was out of earshot, Carlyle clapped his hands together. "Wha' a piece o' luck! We know exactly where t' find th' dragon."

Daniels shook his head. "You heard what the major said. It's dangerous to go up there."

Marlow nodded. "The more I think about this, the more I think we should find a nice hotel room and leave on tomorrow's train."

Carlyle shook his head. "You two 'ave gotten soft. I'm going up t' Mount Ilam whether you two come wit' me or not."

The three men did secure a hotel room. Marlow and Daniels decided to spend the night, but Carlyle changed into hiking gear and set out at once. He hiked through the Swat Valley and stopped at an inn, paying for a night's lodgings with a diamond. The innkeeper's wife confirmed he was on the right path for the dragon's lair, but cautioned Carlyle to turn back. "You have done a good turn, giving us a diamond," said the innkeeper's wife, "so I will return the favor. That is not only lair to the dragon. That is lair to the dragon's grandmother."

"Grandmother!" Carlyle's eyes widened. "How can a steam-powered, mechanical dragon 'ave a grandmother?"

"She's a witch at any rate," said the old woman. "She practices the ancient art of *rasayana*—Hindu alchemy—and they say her blacksmith son forged the mechanical dragon. Beware her as much as you beware her pet."

Soon afterward, Carlyle went to bed, where he spent an uneasy night tossing and turning. The next day, he arose just as the sun peeked over the horizon, packed his gear and set out on the trail for the rock pile where the dragon made his home.

He found the rock pile around lunchtime. Inside, he saw a tidy home, and a hunchbacked woman swept the floor. Aside from being a home built inside a rock fall, nothing suggested danger. What he saw looked much like the humble inn where he stayed in the valley. He took a chance and knocked on the door.

It creaked open and a woman with skin like wrinkled shoe leather peered out. "Who are you and what do you want?"

Carlyle grinned and tipped his hiking cap. "My companions and I 'ave entered into a bargain wit' your...grandson."

She smiled openly at that. "Yes, the dragon is like a grandson. My son forged his body and sculpted him. I devised the clockwork mechanisms that give him life...wrote the chemical equations that give him consciousness." She invited the former soldier inside. "The dragon is a good boy and he protects me from those who would accuse me of witchcraft and do me harm, but he is strong-willed and mischievous."

She indicated a chair at a rough-hewn wooden table. Carlyle sat while the old woman shoveled coal into a stove and set a kettle on. While she worked, the soldier explained the bargain he and his friends had made. "We 'ave families and careers we like. I think we've done more good than 'arm. We'd like t'stay where we are."

The grandmother poured two cups of tea and passed one to Carlyle. She sipped as she considered his words. "I think I can help you," she said at last. She stood and hobbled over to the far wall, then rolled away a stone. "Hide in here. You can hear everything spoken in the house. Sit still and don't move a muscle. When the dragon comes, I'll ask him about the puzzles. He'll tell me everything and then you will know the answer."

At twelve o'clock that night, the dragon landed on the rocks outside the house with a loud clang. He squeezed through the door and sat on his haunches at the table like an obedient dog. The old grandmother took a hot mitt from a hook and opened the boiler in the dragon's belly. She shoveled in several scoops of coal. "How was your day, my love? Did you capture anyone?"

"No, Grandma," said the dragon with a wheezing sigh of steam. "I had bad luck today, but, I have three soldiers set aside nice and safe."

She took an oilcan from the shelf and placed two drops in his elbow joint. "Are these the soldiers you gave the diamond engine to?"

"Aye, they're the ones." The dragon's jaw squeaked as he spoke and she oiled the hinge. "I hoped they would make mischief with the diamonds they created—people are always so grateful when I dispatch those types—but they've done nothing but good." The dragon snorted black smoke. "I'll find a way to make them mine yet."

She nodded, then attached a set of magnifying lenses to her glasses and inspected a rusty spot on the dragon's tail. "I don't understand why you hate the English so. It seems like you're always harassing them."

The dragon frowned. "You once lived in a palace and had many servants. The English killed my father and sent you into exile. I shall have my revenge."

"But soldiers?" The grandmother clucked her tongue. "They're just as much victims of the British Crown as we are. Most of those soldiers are working men who get duped into the army up in London and dragged here."

"It doesn't matter," said the dragon. "They are all part of the problem." He folded his great metal arms across his chest.

Satisfied with her inspection, the grandmother sat down at the table and lifted the magnifying lens with a sigh. "If that's how it will be, I know you will succeed. Your clockwork logic is sure to come up with puzzles that mere humans cannot solve." She put her elbows on the table. "What did you come up with this time?"

"My puzzles are inspired by our home in these mountains. Men cannot come up to this mountain in motorized vehicles. They must come by foot or horseback. There are no linens or silks here, only coarse wool. The only goblets you can find are rough wooden ones, nothing splendid or nice. Only one who knows these things can solve the puzzles. The English are so self-absorbed, they have no hope."

After gloating, the dragon yawned, then clanked over to a cozy corner formed where two rocks met. He shut his great emerald eyes and a faint rumbling issued forth that sounded a little like a snore. The old grandmother moved the stone and let Carlyle out. "Have you paid attention to everything?"

"Yes," he said. "I know enough to 'elp myself."

He went through the window to avoid being seen and, with all haste, made his way back to his companions in Peshawar. He told them how the old grandmother had outsmarted the dragon and what he had overheard. They were so joyous with the good news that they fed a lump of coal to the diamond engine and once it had cooled enough to remove, ordered a sumptuous feast.

A few days later, the train carrying the three friends arrived in Raniganj. It also happened to be the seventh anniversary of the day the dragon had rescued the soldiers from their fate. They found him waiting at the train station with great metallic arms folded across his copper-plated chest. "I see you've been on a trip, but the time has come to travel with me to my mountain home. Don't look so downcast, I've brought fine German motor carriages for you to ride in." With that, he stepped aside revealing three magnificent vehicles with fresh, black paint and gold trim.

Marlow snorted. "Motor carriages cannot drive up a craggy mountain such as the one you live on. You're a dragon with a forge. I suspect those are nothing but empty shells." He stepped over and threw open the engine compartment revealing an empty box. "Were you planning to carry us back to Peshawar in our 'fine carriages'?"

That devil of a dragon was vexed and his clockworks spun with a sound like "Hm! Hm! Hm!" After a moment, he pointed to Daniels, "I see you like to wear fine clothes." The dragon produced a bolt of cloth from his satchel. "There is no finer silk than that from Mount Ilam."

Daniels rubbed his goatee and considered. "We used to live in Peshawar. The mountains are too cold for silk worms and the valleys below too dry to grow cotton. At best you'll have goats and coarse wool." Indeed, when the men examined the dragon's bundle, it became clear he held wool and not fine silk or linen.

Steam issued forth from the dragon's ears and again the "Hm! Hm! Hm!" sound came from his inner clockworks. He turned to Carlyle. "The cloth may be coarse, but there is fine wine to drink from golden goblets." The dragon withdrew a beautiful goblet from his satchel.

Carlyle stepped forward and took the goblet from the dragon. He scraped gold paint from the wooden cup with his thumbnail. "As I suspected, this ain't nothin' but wood, an' poor quality at that." He tossed the goblet aside. "Dragon, why d'you try to trick us with your foolish puzzles? We serve you well righ' where we are. We're rich men, content to pull coal outta the earth."

"I am a creature of clockworks. Once I make a promise to return, it cannot be broken...unless the clockworks run down."

Daniels folded his arms and narrowed his gaze. "But there's something more, isn't there?"

"It's my grandmother. I do not fear for her life because her alchemy will keep her alive, but I fear for her health. She used to live in a palace with servants to see to her needs. You English took that all away. You killed her only son."

"Ah." Marlow shoved his hands in his pockets and looked to the ground. "I don't doubt English soldiers had a hand in your father's death, but rest assured it wasn't us that killed him. It may be small comfort, but I think a woman with your grandmother's abilities would be most welcome in our operation." He looked up at Carlyle. "What do you think?"

"Absolutely. We could set 'er up in a house righ' here in Raniganj with a nice garden and a well paid staff to see to 'er every need."

Daniels stepped forward and put his hand on the dragon's metallic forelimb. "And you can visit any time you'd like. We'll make sure to feed you plenty of coal—as long as you promise to stay out of mischief!"

The dragon's lip creaked upward into a snarl. "I do not like the foreign invasion of our land." The dragon's expression softened. "Nevertheless, I believe your sorrow for my father is genuine and you have proven yourselves by helping the poor." His head drooped forward and the steam issuing from the dragon's nostrils faded to gossamer tendrils, as though the hatred had finally burned itself out.

Marlow and Daniels called to the train's fireman, asking him to bring a shovelful of coal. They opened the hatch in the dragon's belly and dumped it in the firebox. Refreshed, the dragon roared "I'll be back," then unfurled his metal wings and flew away, leaving the alchemical diamond engine behind. The three men kept it and made as many diamonds as they wanted for themselves and others and lived joyously until the end of their days.

All for Beauty and Youth

based on Hansel and Gretel

KELLY A. HARMON

OME ON, GRET, RUN FASTER!" HANSEL SAID. HE GRABBED HER HAND
and pulled her down the cobblestone street toward the rail
station. She'd long ago lost her hair clips, and her long, blonde
curls tumbled down her back, tangling in the wind.

"You go," she said, trying to shake off his hand. "I'm only slowing
you down. You can catch the train without me." Her voice was ragged as
her lungs sought air. Large clouds of breath swept past her as she ran,
visible in the damp winter evening. Her carpetbag beat heavily against
her thigh at every step. "Send for me when you get established."

She heard the shrill whistle of the train two blocks away, and even
from this distance, the sound of exploding steam as the conductor freed
the brakes. *They wouldn't make it.*

"I can't leave without you," Hansel said. "There's no telling what
she'll do."

"I can't run any farther," Gretel said. Fog twisted the shadows into
monstrous spectors, frightening her. For just a moment, she squeezed her
eyes shut. She stumbled.

Hansel tightened his grip and pulled her to her feet, almost losing his
grip on his own small suitcase. "We're almost there, Gretel. You can do
it. Come on." He tugged her a bit faster down the foggy side street. *She
had to hurry,* he thought. *Everything depended on their making it onto this
train.*

They turned the corner and the Bahnhof Hamburg came into view.
Gas lamps enveloped the platform in an orange glow where Vapourer
moths and mosquitoes danced in the wan light. Only a few remaining
passengers boarded, lifting their valises and carpet bags to porters, then
mounting the steps to the car.

The teens arrived in a flurry, scaring off a dozen clockwork birds
pecking at metal shards cast from the train wheels.

Hansel reached for the gleaming brass handlebar of the last car coupled to the train just as the conductor blew the shrill whistle once more. He abandoned the effort when a figure stepped out of the shadow of the train station, the point of her black-frilled parasol brushing against the leather toe of her lace-up ankle boots.

"Going somewhere?" She grabbed Gretel's free arm and pulled her away from the steps.

"Stepmother," breathed Gretel, under her breath. Her carpetbag fell limply out of her hand onto the platform.

Their father stepped out of the shadows behind her, the brass buttons on his Hussars' uniform gleaming in the orange glow of the gas lights. He twisted his hat in his hands.

"Yes, *Franziska*," Hansel said. "Since you ever complain of having to feed and clothe us on a military man's salary, we thought we would make our way back to relatives in the Old Country."

Shunk. A blast of steam powered the escapement and forced the train wheels a quarter turn forward.

"*Step-mama*," Franziska corrected through gritted teeth, her smile turning to a grimace. "But you're children," she said, lightening her tone. "You can't be allowed to travel so far alone."

Shunk. Another blast of steam, another quarter turn of the wheels.

The crowd, having seen their relatives off, began to stand around them, interested in the family squabble.

"Come home with us," she said. "Now. We have a carriage waiting."

Hansel gripped Gretel's hand more tightly and looked to his sire. "Father?" he said. "We—"

"Do as your step-mama says, Hansel. She knows best."

"But—"

"Not another word," their stepmother hissed from behind clenched teeth. She bent forward, reaching for Gretel, then grasped her fragile wrist in leather-gloved hands and gave it a quick twist.

"Ow!"

Still in a low voice, their stepmother said, "Come with me this instant without causing a scene or there will be worse for you when we reach home."

Gretel nodded and picked up her bag.

Shunk-shunk. Shunk-shunk. The steam came faster, building up momentum, and the train slowly pulled out of the station, its steel wheels screaming atop the rails that would have carried them to their freedom.

Hansel knew he could still make it aboard, but he watched it slowly depart from view before following his family. He couldn't leave Gretel alone with that witch.

"Stepmother is in one of her famous moods," Gretel said to Hansel as he entered the kitchen.

"She's always in a foul mood," Hansel said, sitting down heavily on a wooden stool. His hands, red from the work of binding brooms his father sold for a bit of extra money, shook from exertion. Gretel handed him the scrap of sheep's fleece she kept in her apron pocket. When he couldn't smooth it over his own trembling hands, she took it back and wiped it across his palms and between his fingers, soothing the redness with a bit of natural lanolin in the wool.

"It's near used up," he said. "Keep it for yourself. You'll need it for your ankle."

Gretel looked down at the shackles chaining her to the heavy wooden table. The chain reached to the stove so she could cook the family's meals and out to the small herb garden behind the brownstone, but not far enough for her to reach the W.C. She had a bucket in the corner for her private use. But that did not bear thinking about.

"I don't mind sharing."

"You should have pots of creams like *Step-Mama*," Hansel said, emphasizing with a sneer the endearment their stepmother preferred. "You should have her new, *and very expensive, Youth and Beauty Elixir*."

"The lanolin is better than her pots of creams," Gretel said. "There's simply never enough."

"There's never enough of anything, thanks to that old harpy," he said, fingering the threadbare cuff on Gretel's sleeve. "Father should never have married her after mother died. I don't know what he was thinking."

"He was thinking that we needed a mother," said Gretel. "I can't fault him for that. I just wish he'd chosen better. She doesn't want us. Why can't she just let us go?"

"She's willing to let us go. She just wants to make certain she gets something out of the deal. We've got to get out of here," Hansel said.

"Go, while you have the chance," Gretel said. "You're not chained. You could leave now while she's out. You'd get away free and clear."

"I can't." He pulled his goggles from around his neck and untied the heavy canvas apron that protected him while he worked. One scratched eye from the clipped binding wire was all it took to convince him to wear them. "She'd find some way to take it out on you. She knows I won't leave you because of that. I ensure your protection."

"I can handle whatever she might do," Gretel said. "I've gotten stronger over the months."

"I know," said Hansel, "but so does she. That's why she keeps you chained. I can't leave you."

"Then you're bound just as tightly as I," she said softly.

Franziska flounced into the room, in a new lavender dress, her titian hair swept up and away from her face, held back with a diamond clasp. Her three terriers barked and nipped at her heels, dancing around in circles on their hind legs once they realized they were in the kitchen.

"I've finally decided on your punishment," she said, smiling and reaching for the cookie jar. She opened the lid and took out three bone-shaped cookies, one for each dog. She bent for kisses from each one, then handed over the treats. "Run along," she said, and shooed them out of the kitchen.

"Being bound like a slave isn't punishment enough?" asked Hansel.

"It's what gave me the idea," Franziska said, laughing. The warmth drained from her face, leaving nothing but her cold, unapproachable beauty. "And quite a delicious one it is, too. It's the best of all possible worlds."

"I can't imagine anything worse than being chained to a table in the kitchen," Gretel said.

"Then you're in for a learning experience." Franziska pulled a packet of papers out of her apron pocket and spread them on the table.

"I've contracted you both into indentured servitude," Franziska said. "Effective tomorrow."

"Father would never agree to that!" Gretel said. "*He* loves us."

"But of course he does!" She laughed again, and turned to the third section of the documents where all the signatures lined up on the page. "It took some convincing to prove to him that a loving father could both punish his children for disobedience and at the same time provide them with skills they could use to support themselves when their indenture is over."

"I don't believe you," Hansel said, red-faced. "Father wouldn't sell us into bondage."

"Here it is." Franziska pointed to the last signature on the page. "Your father's name."

"But indentured servitude is no better than slavery!" Gretel said. "It's a measure to force criminals to pay off their debt."

"Not so," said Franziska, turning back to the first page. "At the end of your contract you'll have a nice little nest egg to show for your trouble — that's better than being apprenticed." She tapped a lacquered nail on one paragraph of the document. "Better still, *thanks to me*, the contracts stipulate payment up front. Your father and I will invest the money for you while you're away. Imagine the sum which will be waiting for you when you return home."

"I don't imagine we'll live long enough to see it," Gretel said.

"Gretel!"

"It's true, Madame, and you know it. Less than half of indentured servants survive the duration of their contract."

"Have no worries," Franziska said. "You'll be close enough that your father and I can keep an eye on you."

Hansel froze. "There are few families in this neighborhood well-off enough to afford one indentured servant, let alone, two. Who did you make this contract with?"

"Frau Kleinschmidt."

"The witch!"

"The *apothecary*." Franziska smiled a cheshire grin. "She told me herself she had lots of use for the two of you in her laboratory."

Frau Kleinschmidt stood behind the glass counter of the storefront, a pristine white apron covering her fashionable gown. She lectured Hansel and Gretel, even while she refilled a candy jar, then straightened the post cards on the shiny surface.

"Hansel, you will lift boxes, stock the shelves, and carry large packages out for the customers. Also, see that the store is kept clean, the windows polished, and the sidewalk outside swept clean."

"Yes, ma'am."

She lifted a hand to tuck a stray hair behind her ear, drawing attention to her delicate beauty, then looked at Gretel with an appraising eye. She stepped around the counter and moved closer.

"You're a handsome enough child. How old are you?"

"Thirteen, ma'am." Gretel curtsied, as she'd been taught by her mother. Frau Kleinschmidt grabbed Gretel's chin in her fine, delicate hand, and pulled her face into the light of an open window. "We'll tell the customers you're older," she said, "twenty, at least, and that you use *Frau Kleinschmidt's Youth and Beauty Elixir*." She nodded once. "I'll want you working the front counter during my absence, although I have another job for you as well."

"But Hansel is older than I!"

"Not anymore."

"But—"

"Another word and I'll sell one of your indentures to America." She pierced the two of them with a look from her steely black eyes. "I'll have no backtalk from either of you, and require complete obedience. Do I make myself clear?"

Gretel felt the tears sting behind her eyes. Working here was going to be just as unpleasant as living with her stepmother, perhaps worse.

She nodded, as did Hansel.

"Very good. Then follow me."

Frau Kleinschmidt opened a door behind the counter in the back of the store and led them down a set of steep, narrow stairs.

She turned left off the shallow landing at the bottom and said, "Welcome to my laboratory, children."

At the foot of the stairs, a copper, clockwork man unloaded a box of glass vials from a wooden shipping crate, stacking them onto a shelf. Beside him, atop a rosewood cabinet, a row of clocks ticked away, all the times set to a different hour. He seemed to work to the rhythm of the ticking, his round head, with the flat, painted face, nodding in time. He was barely as tall as Hansel, but built solidly, and looked strong enough to lift great weights. He ignored them as they walked into the laboratory.

The long, narrow room ran the length of the brownstone basement. Books lined the staircase wall on shelves from ceiling to floor. One section held hundreds of scrolls housed in a honeycomb shelf.

The opposite wall held scientific equipment: beakers and bowls, coiled lengths of rubber tubing, and glass pipettes all hanging on or balanced upon or thrust onto a thousand wooden pegs.

A black marble counter ran the length of the room. On its surface sat the apothecary's various projects. Inside a large glass cabinet, thick smoke whorled and eddied, making it impossible to see what might be sitting on the small black platform inside. Next to it, a mortar and pestle rested, along with a balance-scale and several sets of weights. Carved out of the end of the counter was a deep, narrow sink with a tall, hooked spigot. A drying rack beside it held copper pots, iron tongs, and test tubes and flasks, each with graduated markings painted on the outside.

"Here is where all the magic takes place," she said, walking to the far side of the room, adjusting this or that on the counter.

"There's no such thing as magic," Gretel said.

"There's no reason we can't pretend!" She smiled at the children, her thin lips parting wide to reveal a tiny gap between her two front teeth. But it was her expression that made Hansel leery. True, the apothecary could rival any of the local beauties, but she seemed to have the wisdom of someone much, much older. She'd been in this neighborhood as long as they had, and hadn't seemed to age a day. *Was* there magic in this place?

"What's more magical than being sick and drinking one of my elixirs to make you well?"

"It's science," said Hansel.

"To be sure, to be sure," said Frau Kleinschmidt, "but it's not exact." She picked up a small bottle on a shelf near the stairs. "Perhaps this one works for you, but not for your neighbor. There's a guessing game to it all. If it works...*magic!*"

"Where's your cauldron?" Gretel asked.

Hansel's eyes opened wide. He yanked on her elbow. "Are you trying to get us killed?" he mouthed.

"No cauldrons here, *liebling*," said Frau Kleinschmidt, once more offering the thin-lipped smile to Gretel. "There's no witchcraft here—as your own brother points out, merely science. This is my latest experiment."

She pointed to a round-bottomed flask sitting on a wire shelf above a burner. Glass tubing sprouted out of the corked top and circled down like a spring into another stoppered flask on the counter-top.

Next to the burner and flask, a machine about the size of a hatbox wheezed and pumped. A small bellows expanded and collapsed from the rear of the machine, driven by a steam-powered wheel-and-pulley system just visible through several air slits in the machine's outer metal casing. Red rubber tubing connected one end of the machine to an intake valve on the heated flask. A second rubber tube, attached to the opposite side of the machine, snaked across the counter and sat idle. Poppet valves between the machine and this tube controlled both intake and exhaust, to and from the device.

As the bellows opened and closed, a globe-shaped spinner on the top of the machine turned clockwise and then counter-clockwise, lighting an amber bulb each time the bellows contracted, spinning the globe clockwise. A green bulb remained dormant next to the amber one.

A small dial on the front of the machine had four settings: *Normal, Vacuum, Reverse,* and *Propel.* The dial pointed to *Normal.*

Frau Kleinschmidt turned up the flame on the burner and motioned Gretel over. "Come closer, *liebling.* I want you to do something for me."

Gretel hesitated.

"It's all part of the indenture," she said. "If you don't do my bidding I can have you whipped. Or transported." Her grin grew wider. "Franziska told me you don't like to be separated from Hansel. It would be a shame to be shipped off to America without him, wouldn't it?"

"You can't speak to us like that!" Hansel said, stepping forward.

Frau Kleinschmidt turned on him and leaned her pretty face down close to his. "Let's get this straight right now, *Liebchen.* I can speak to you any way I damned well please. I have greater rights over you than your mother or father ever had, and you've got to obey by law. If you don't, I will beat you. If you try to run away, I will chain you. If you refuse to work, we will settle this in the courts. Now let's be reasonable. I can always sell your contracts. Working for a beautiful, *charming,* young woman in her laboratory or store front will be much easier than working alongside the clockwork men in a coal mine, or as a chimney sweep, or—" she turned back to Gretel, "in one of the local brothels. Imagine where you'll be after a few months there with your pretty golden curls?"

Her voice hardened, and she fixed a saccharine smile upon her face. "Now step forward and do as I say."

Gretel moved toward the machine and Frau Kleinschmidt handed her the idle tube. "Put this in your mouth and I'll show you how my latest beauty elixir is made," she said. The tube had a hard-rubber stopper in the end of it, bored with two holes. "Bite down on the stopper, but make a seal with your lips." Gretel took the proffered rubber tube and stuck it into her mouth.

"Breathe naturally," Frau Kleinschmidt said.

Gretel breathed into the tube. The wheels on the machine turned, the bellow contracted and the spinner on top whirled clockwise. The amber light blazed.

Frau Kleinschmidt frowned. "Breathe harder."

Gretel took a deep breath and exhaled as hard as she could into the rubber tube. Again the amber light lit.

"Once more," she said, turning the dial to *Vacuum*. Gretel took a deep breath, then put the tube to her mouth. No sooner did she seal it with her lips then she felt the tug of the machine pulling the breath from her lungs. Pain burst forth in her chest.

"What?" she cried, fighting for breath. The tube fell out of her open mouth and she caught the end of it in her hand. The bellows contracted with a *whoosh* and the green light on top of the machine lit.

"We got a good sample that time, despite your idiocy," Frau Kleinschmidt said, rubbing her hands together. "Watch the glass coils above the beaker."

As they watched, water vapor appeared, then condensed in the coils and dripped into the second beaker.

"I mix your breath with a secret ingredient already in the flask and condense it into my beauty elixir," she said. "It's amazingly potent. I use it myself quite regularly.

"Your job, my dear, will be to take a similar machine — one without the condensing apparatus — to the hospitals and collect the breath of the poor dying souls pent up there. You'll probably wind up helping a few on their way."

"Wouldn't that be murder, then?" asked Hansel.

"No one will protest," said Frau Kleinsschmidt. "Everyone knows a hospital is merely a *gateway to death*. If you want to survive any illness you have, you'd best call a doctor and be treated at home."

Gretel fingered the breathing tube. "But most people can't afford to have a doctor call at home. That's what the hospital charities are for."

"Don't worry, *liebling*," said Frau Kleinschmidt. "I donate generously to the hospitals. They won't mind you being there at all once you tell them you work for me. And if anyone tells you how pretty you are, be certain to let them know you use *Frau Kleinschmidt's Youth and Beauty Elixir*. You're a walking advertisement."

Gretel picked up the breath machine and walked the ten blocks to the hospital. December wind tore at her face, even through the new scarf Frau Kleinschmidt had given her. Though demanding, she provided for her and Hansel, giving them both new clothes and coats. And, *Gott*, she had mittens and a scarf this winter — something she hadn't had in a long time. If Frau Kleinschmidt wanted her to go to the hospital and collect the exhalations of a few dying souls, who was she to complain?

Still, Gretel hated hospitals; her mother had died in one when they couldn't afford to send for a doctor to treat her at home. She could do this for someone who treated her far more decently than her stepmother. *As long as I follow all the rules*, she thought.

She lumbered up the steps with the machinery and waved to the nurse at the front desk. They were well-accustomed to her comings and goings at the hospital now. She turned right toward the injured ward. She tried to pick someone who looked hale and strong, and might only be here for the nursing care of a broken bone: someone she knew wouldn't die on the machine.

She'd had that happen once in the dying ward where Frau Kleinschmidt instructed her to go. She couldn't bear it if that happened again.

"Hallo, *süssling*!" Kurt Bauer waved from the middle of the room. A chorus went up from the nineteen other beds in the ward. Several men waved as she made her way to Kurt's bed. She smiled and waved, then sat down on the chair beside Kurt's bed. His broken left leg was splinted from ankle to thigh and propped on pillows.

"Hello, Kurt. How are you today?" She unwrapped her scarf and took off her gloves. The whole ward seemed to settle down and pay attention to their conversation.

"Bored to tears. And me stuck here another month at least. Are you here to see who can blow green again?"

She smiled. "You gentlemen did so well last time, Frau Kleinschmidt sent me back for more. Do you feel up to it?"

"Anything for a pretty lass like yourself," Kurt said.

"I suspect you mean, 'Anything to relieve the boredom!'" She clouted him gently on the shoulder.

"Never!" he said. "What about the rest of you boys?"

A chorus of whoops went up around the room, except for, "Not me!" It came from the bed nearest the door. Gretel didn't recognize him.

"That's Heinz," said Kurt softly. "Just got here yesterday. Still cranky from having his leg set. Broke his thigh in two places and he howled like a baby when they straightened his leg. Took three of Herr Doktor's assistants to hold him down."

Gretel turned to him. "It's just a machine to catch your breath, Mr. Heinz, but it's not a requirement."

Kurt spoke up. "You should help Gretel out. Just blow into the tube and then she'll stay and visit for a while. It's easy. I'll show you."

Gretel set the machinery up on a borrowed trolley and handed the breathing tube to Kurt. He blew a green light on the first try. "See? I told you it was easy."

Then she was off, pushing the machine from bed to bed, visiting with each man, then handing the tube over if they decided to help. Most did, but Heinz declined.

She started to pack her things when Kurt said, "I'll do it again, *süssling*. Bring the machine over."

"But that's not necessary. I'm sure I've got plenty of samples for Frau Kleinschmidt."

"But I want to." He waved her over. "Come on. It means I get to visit with a pretty girl for a few more minutes. You wouldn't deprive me of that, would you?"

She smiled, then pushed the trolley over.

"You never did tell me what this dial does," he said, pointing at the side of the machine when she'd reached his bed again.

"It's for people who have trouble blowing green," Gretel said. "It helps them."

He nodded, then took up the breathing tube and exhaled into it. The spinner whirled clockwise, and the green light came on. "Guess I won't be needing that, then," he said chuckling. He turned to the cranky man in the front of the ward. "Come on, Heinz, give the girl a minute of your time."

"If it will get you to quit harping on me," he said. In a kinder voice he said, "Bring the machine. I'll give you a breath."

"Thank you, Mr. Heinz." She bent and whispered to Kurt. "And thank you, too. You've helped me out immensely."

She pushed the trolley to the front of the room and showed Heinz how to blow. The light lit amber.

There was a sudden commotion outside the ward and a shrieking woman was wheeled by the door in an invalid's chair. Gretel recognized her at once. "Stepmother! What are you doing here?" She hadn't seen her stepmother since she'd delivered Hansel and herself to Frau Kleinschmidt months ago. *Of all the places to run into her,* she thought.

The shrieking stopped, and the woman froze Gretel with a look of suspicion. "What am I doing here? Isn't it obvious?" She pulled up her skirt to show the barest edge of a presumably broken ankle, wrapped in plaster. "What are *you* doing here? You're supposed to be working for Frau Kleinschmidt."

"I *am* working for Frau Kleinschmidt, *Franziska*. I'm collecting breath from these invalids for one of her products."

"Franziska?" her step-mother screeched. "I am your step-mama and will be addressed as such."

Gretel stepped toward Franziska and lowered her voice. "Once you sold me into indenture, that relationship ceased, Franziska, and I am glad for it. I've been much better off in her service than I ever was with you—"

"Help! Fräulein Gretel! Heinz needs help!" Kurt yelled.

Gretel turned back to the invalid's ward. Heinz lay on the bed, eyes wide open, blue lips locked around the red, rubber intake tube of the machine. He didn't appear to be breathing. The bellows pumped furiously and the spinneret on top whirled in wild abandon. The green light blazed.

"Who pushed the dial to *Vacuum*?" she cried, twisting it back to *Normal*.

"He did," said Kurt, looking distraught. "I told him to try it when he couldn't blow more than amber."

"Doktor!" she yelled.

A moment later, a doctor pronounced Heinz dead. He looked at Gretel.

"This is your fault," he said. A spate of agreeing grumbles rose from just outside the door of the ward where a crowd of volunteers and ambulatory patients gathered. "Frau Kleinschmidt's experiments on the sick and injured must be stopped," he continued. "There must be no more killing."

Nods and agreeing murmurs followed his statement. The hospital administrator stepped through the crowd. "I'm going to have to ask you to leave," he said to Gretel.

Gretel sighed. Frau Kleinschmidt would not be happy about this.

"The news got here before you did," Frau Kleinschmidt said as Gretel walked in the door. Gretel's shoulders slumped. Somehow, she thought if she hurried, she could make it back to the house and break the news to Frau Kleinschmidt gently.

"What are we going to do now?" Gretel asked.

"Since we can't obtain what we need from the hospital anymore—"

"You don't know that," Gretel said. "It's just one voice. You're a respected apothecary. They can't make you stop."

"They can, and they will," Frau Kleinschmidt said. "Hospitals and sanitariums rely on the donations of benefactors to keep their doors open. No one will want to donate if they continue to allow my machines inside. And I can't give enough to keep the doors open. That avenue is dried up. We can create a paying clinic here at the shop, but that will take some time to set up and advertise. In the meantime, I've put in place some measures to keep us going."

"Come with me," she said, heading in the direction of Hansel's room. Frau Kleinschmidt threw open the door. Hansel lay restrained upon the bed, his wrists and ankles fastened to the bedposts. A breath-collecting mask covered his nose and mouth, the small machine pumping away on the floor.

"What are you doing to him?" Gretel cried. "How did you do this? He would have never agreed."

"A simple sleeping draught in his tea, and a suggestion to take a nap when it overcame him was all it took. Trusting soul." She *tsked*. "Once he was fully asleep, it was nothing to bind him to the bed and start the machine working. This will be an interesting experiment," she said. "I'm going to keep his breath separate from the rest. I have a feeling that children might provide a better product than the breath of the dying...which brings me to your new task."

She pushed Gretel out of the room, pulled the door shut and locked it with a key she kept around her neck. "You will find me a stray little boy or girl by the morning, who will take Hansel's place, or I'm afraid that Hansel won't last very long."

"You can't ask me to do that. Not after what happened today..."

"Then Hansel will die."

"Here," Gretel said, leading a small girl into Frau Kleinschmidt's sitting room early the next morning. The apothecary's back was to Gretel. She sat at a large, mirrored table, brushing back dark, wiry hair, which she normally kept tamed into the bun at her neck.

"Get out of here this instant!" Frau Kleinshmidt snapped, but not before Gretel caught a glimpse of her haggard face reflected in the mirror. No, not just haggard, but old and wrinkled. Sallow skin hung lank beneath her eyes and jaw. She looked to be ninety-years old or more!

Frau Kleinschmidt's voice mellowed. "I'm not decent. Just give me a moment to get a wrapper on."

Gretel backed out of the room with the little girl, still watching the mirror. Crippled, age-spotted hands moved to a smaller version of the breath machine sitting on an occasional table nearby. She lifted a tube to her mouth and turned the dial from Reverse to Propel and turned the machine on.

The machine pumped rapidly, the spinneret rotating wildly counter-clockwise. Frau Kleinschmidt jerked upright from the sudden rush of air and elixir into her lungs. She turned the machine off and held her breath.

In a moment, Gretel saw the wrinkles on her face smooth, the sagging jaw sculpt into a more pleasing line and the bushy, tangled hair relax into the smooth curls Gretel had seen on many mornings since she'd been indentured. No wonder Frau Kleinschmidt required her to continue the breath collecting!

The small, bony hand in her own tightened almost painfully. "She's a witch!" the girl whispered.

Gretel nodded. "I think so. Will you help me get rid of her?"

The girl chewed on her lip for a moment. "Will you still feed me? Can I have enough for my brother, too?"

"Most certainly," said Gretel. "Here's what I need for you to do." Gretel told her the plan as they walked to the kitchen and cut bread and butter for both the girl and her brother. "Come back as quickly as you can. Tell your friends I'll feed them all today if they promise to help."

The children started arriving before Frau Kleinschmidt completed dressing. Six children sat around the small kitchen table, chewing on hunks of bread and butter and slices of cold ham and cheese.

"What's going on here?" she asked in her most imperious voice.

"This is Britta," Gretel said, indicating the girl who'd agreed to help. A tattered dress and holes in her shoes marked her as coming from one of the poorer families on the street. "She's willing to breathe into your machine for a meal, as is her brother, Fritz. The prospect so excited them, their friends decided they would help as well." Four other dirty and tattered children, bird-thin and with mouths full, looked up at Frau Kleinschmidt and nodded.

Frau Kleinschmidtt looked at the laden table, and tilted her head as though she were calculating something. "There's some merit in that," she finally said. "Okay, *Fräulein*: bring them in, as many as you can. A free meal to any child willing to breathe six times into the machine. For now, let's get to the laboratory and start collecting."

She ushered the children through a side door into the store front, and then down the stairs behind the counter. Gretel followed.

Frau Kleinschmidt paused at the top of the stairs to say softly, "You and I will discuss my privacy later. I'll have to think about your punishment."

"Yes, ma'am," Gretel said, and curtsied.

"Over here," Frau Kleinschmidt said, drawing the children toward the counter and the breath machine. She flicked the switch to start the pump. "Who's first?"

"I'll go," said Fritz, stepping forward. "What do I do?"

Frau Kleinschmidt held out the rubber tube for him to take. "Put this in your mouth and blow. Six times."

"Can you show me how, please?"

An annoyed look crossed Frau Kleinschmidt's face. "Gretel, you show him."

Gretel frowned and stepped forward.

"If you please," said Fritz, stepping in front of Gretel. "You're the expert, Frau Kleinschmidt. I'm sure your showing me would be better than your assistant. You created this machine, after all."

Frau Kleinschmidt preened. "All right, but just this once." Gretel flicked the switch to start the machine humming, and then Frau Kleinschmidt put the tube in her mouth.

Britta stepped forward and grabbed Frau Kleinschmidt's free hand. Gretel turned the dial to *Vacuum*. Frau Kleinschmidt's eyes got wide, and she tried to pull the tube from her mouth. Fritz wrenched her hand from the tube and another boy kicked her feet out from under her. Frau Kleinschmidt fell to the floor, the vacuum seal of the machine keeping the tube in her mouth. Her screams were sucked into the machine.

The children sat on top of her until her struggles ceased. Her face wrinkled and sagged. Age spots appeared on her hands. Her hair grew gray and wiry, then whitened and thinned. Her skin and bones sagged in upon themselves, and the children screamed and got away from the desiccating shell. The tube fell out of the mouth, but the body continued to molder. In seconds, nothing more than dust lay where Frau Kleinschmidt had fallen.

A stream of black liquid flowed into the heated beaker and boiled. Clear liquid condensed in the coils and dripped steadily into the waiting flask.

"Women smear that on their faces?" Fritz asked.

"That and other things, all for the sake of beauty and youth," Gretel said.

"Not me," said Britta.

"Nor I," said Gretel. "But we can talk about it later, if you want. Right now, I've got to rescue my brother. Frau Kleinschmidt has him locked up in one of the upstairs rooms above the store."

"What about us?" asked Fritz.

Gretel smiled. "You've earned that meal we discussed, and then some. Why don't you go back to the kitchen while I release my brother?"

As children headed up the stairs, Gretel unhooked the standing flask, corked the top of it, and placed it into her apron pocket. She stooped to the dust that was formerly Frau Kleinschmidt, and pulled the door key from her remains. Then she ran up the stairs to the storefront, and then up another to the bedrooms above.

She let herself in with the key. Hansel lay asleep on the covers, pale in the morning light. He came awake as she untied his hands.

"Gretel?" He sat up. "Why am I so tired? Have I been ill?"

"In a way," she said, loosening his ankles, and then coming to sit next to him on the edge of the bed. Deep lines surrounded his thin, haggard face. Even his hair hung limp. *Amazing*, she thought, *how such a short time hooked up to the machine could steal youth.* "Drink some of this," she said, pulling the flask from her apron pocket.

"What is it?"

"One of Frau Kleinschmidt's elixirs."

"Do you trust it?" he asked.

She nodded, and he took a small sip. His face plumped slightly, and he lost the haggard look, but he still looked thin. "Another sip."

He smiled. "Oh, I'm feeling so much better now. I wonder what she puts in this one."

"You don't want to know," she said, taking his hand and squeezing it. "Come on down to the kitchen. I've some new friends I'd like you to meet. Later, we can talk about my plans for running the apothecary in Frau Kleinschmidt's absence."

"She's gone?"

"Come along. We'll fill you in."

"Gretel," Fritz said, rising when she and Hansel entered the room. "We have an idea."

Fritz introduced the other children in the room. They filled Hansel in on the plight of Frau Kleinschmidt, and then Fritz said, "You know, there are plenty of children like us from poor families, and like my cousin Dietrich here—" Gretel recognized him as the larger boy who'd knocked Frau Kleinschmidt off her feet, "who are living on the streets the best they can since they got no relatives to take 'em in. We'd be willing to work for some food, and maybe a few *thaler* now and then, if you had it to spare."

"But the *Youth and Beauty Elixir* was the best-selling item here," Gretel said. "Without it, this shop earns only a modest income. There won't be enough to keep you all fed, let alone keep you employed."

"But what if you kept selling the elixir?" Fritz asked. "There will always be women willing to buy it."

Britta added, "And always someone willing to blow in the tube, if you give them a meal or a few *thaler*."

"They're right, Gret," Hansel said. "What does it hurt if we keep selling the elixir?"

"The people whose breath we steal?"

"It's not stealing if you pay them for it," Fritz pointed out.

Gretel sat on a stool near the stove. "What about our plans to return to Prussia?" she asked.

"Gramma won't miss us. If we stay, we can make our own way, and help some of the families in the neighborhood."

"I'm willing to stay," Gretel said. "But we can't use the machine." She thought of the pain of the machine pulling the breath from her. "I won't let anyone use that machine again."

There were protests from the children, but Hansel said, "If that's what it takes to stay, I agree. Where's the machine?"

Fritz retrieved it from the laboratory, and at Hansel's direction he took it outside to the small courtyard in the rear. Gretel brought the portable machine as well. And while all the children watched, Hansel beat both devices to pieces with the handle of the broom Frau Kleinschmidt made him use so often.

Hansel smiled. "I don't even have to clean up. The clockwork birds will eat the pieces."

In the morning, Gretel found a marvelous clockwork egg in a copper mesh nest on the windowsill at the back of the house. Once wound by the dial on its side and sat upright on its larger end, the copper and steel oval lifted up on two metal bird feet and paced forward a few steps. It turned, and then opened—the top half falling over to reveal a tin chickadee, small wings beating against the egg as if to break out. Amber and green eyes blinked at Gretel in confusion.

She ran to show Hansel.

From that day forward, Hansel and Gretel paid the children to scavenge parts for them which they sprinkled in the small courtyard. Daily, flocks of clockwork birds came to feast.

Every few days they found another small clockwork object in the nest on the sill.

As the birds feasted and fattened, the collection of clockwork objects grew, filling the shelves of what once had been Frau Kleinschmidt's Apothecary. Collectors from all over the German States, and as far away as London and America, flocked to the shop to purchase them. And Hansel and Gretel and their new friends never went hungry, or wanted for anything, ever again.

The Giant Killer

based on Jack the Giant Killer

JONAH KNIGHT

XCUSE ME," SAID HANNA LEE. SHE LEANED IN, JOINING THE PORTER to look out the train window. "I could not help but notice that these people seem to be, what is the proper description? Fleeing in terror?"

The porter nodded and turned from the window to face the sixteen-year-old woman before him. "It's one of the giants, I expect."

"I thought that the giants were inactive?"

The porter shook his head and his cap wiggled. "They been getting ornery after their maker died. Confederates never got to Boston, of course, but three of the steam-work giants patrol, same as before the war. I seen Cormorgan marching around the train yards plenty of times. Looking for an army to fight."

"I see," said Hanna, watching the people scatter beside the tracks as her train slowly approached North Union Station. "It would appear his behavior has changed."

Grinding steel brakes rattled the car, bringing them to a sudden stop amidst the screaming Bostonians. *Typical*, thought Hanna. Every mission she had been sent on to recover artifacts from the War Between the States had found her diverted and sidetracked. And now giants. "Nothing to do about it, I suppose," she said to herself.

Hanna put her hand on the porter's shoulder and firmly turned his nose from the window. "Perhaps you could see us safely from the train?" She held the little smile on her lips, and motioned to the car full of near-panicking passengers. The porter nodded, straightened his vest, and began calling out orders, ushering the people toward the exit in a calm fashion.

Hanna secured her bonnet and scarf, and carrying her reticule, a sizable handbag, descended onto the dusting of Boston snow. She turned away from the rest of the fleeing passengers and went to see the spectacle.

Three train cars ahead of her stood Cormorgan. The steam-work man was only about eight feet tall, but he was as wide as three men and round like a barrel. He had torn open the side of the coal car and was shoveling the fuel into his furnace through a door in his chest. Flames spilled out, blackening his iron hide. Hardly a giant, really.

Hanna watched a pair of police officers creeping up behind the giant. One held a long iron rod like a spear and the other aimed a rifle. The rifleman fired and hit, but the bullet ricocheted harmlessly away.

Cormorgan's head rotated around in its socket, his three eyeholes focusing on the officers. His body turned about, rotating at the waist, squaring off with the police. The fire exhaled from his chest as he spread his arms out wide and lurched forward.

His thick legs reminded Hanna of Greek columns. They were not steady, but the giant moved with surprising speed above the waist. He clamped his hands around the chest of the rifleman. The man screeched as Cormorgan lifted him, crushing his bones. As the man flopped lifelessly, the giant pulled him in, cramming the broken body into the gaping furnace as well.

Hanna could smell flesh burning even at this distance. She held her scarf up to her nose to block the stench and looked about the train yard for a few moments before a plan came together. She began to jog alongside a neighboring track that housed a train loaded with lumber. She loosened her scarf, positioning herself behind the remaining officer.

The officer, with the red whiskers and wild eyes, yelled to her, gesturing with his spear. "Go! Get away!"

"Keep your eyes on the task before you," Hanna replied, calmly looking about for a safe place to set her reticule, before spying a mostly dry spot under the train. *Now then*, she thought, as she pulled the scarf from her neck and rubbed its ends together.

Hanna lived on trains much of these last few years and, when she had the good fortune to procure a private car, she would spend her hours building useful devices to assist in her non-traditional occupation. She was particularly proud of this scarf and its magnetic properties although, she had to admit, it was truly her aunt's design.

The blood splattered across Cormorgan's body smoldered as the giant advanced. He clumped awkwardly, one step at a time, arms quickly lashing out. The remaining officer ducked and scrambled to stay out of his reach.

"Excellent," Hanna said. "Lure him this way if you could." She felt the magnetism within the scarf begin to activate. *Just a few more moments, then*, she thought, and counted down from ten.

She twirled the scarf in front of her and walked in front of the officer. "What are you..." began Red Whiskers.

Cormorgan stepped onto the track as Hanna counted three. She pulled her arm back on two, and threw the scarf on one.

The scarf stiffened, attaching itself in part to Cormorgan's left leg and in part to the train track. Hanna began to count down again. The giant lunged forward, but finding himself anchored, tipped over crashing into the ground.

"You trapped it," Red Whiskers said in awe, as Cormorgan spun his arms in the dirt.

"Not for long," said Hanna, pulling the spear from his hands. *Eight*, she counted. She jumped up onto the nearest lumber flatbed, perched on a log, and with the spear began prying at the latches holding down the pile of wood.

"What are you doing?" asked Red Whiskers.

"Attempting to bury the giant," she said, straining in a most un-ladylike manner. *Six*, she counted. The first latch popped off and the logs shifted. The officer scrambled out of the way as Hanna dug the spear into the second latch.

Fire spilled out of Cormorgan's chest as he lay face down, pounding at the earth. *Three*, counted Hanna as the second latch popped. She jumped aside and watched as the logs stayed exactly as they were. *One.* The scarf lost its magnetic charge and Cormorgan began to push himself back to his feet. Hanna took a breath, wedged the spear into the pile of logs, and threw her weight behind it.

The timber spilled, flowing over the side of the flatbed, raining down on the giant. His back dented, his arms cracked, his head split. When the deluge ended, all that could be seen of the giant were the bottoms of his feet sticking out from the pile of wood.

"Ah," said Hanna to herself, brushing her gloved hands together lightly to remove the dust. "That seemed to turn out just fine. Would you mind," she held out her hand toward Red Whiskers, "helping me down?" The officer shut his slack-jawed mouth and rushed around the logs to offer his assistance as the porter ran up beside them.

"You killed Cormorgan," the porter said in a soft voice, picking up her scarf.

"In my defense," said Hanna, draping her arm around the officer's neck as he lifted her to the ground, "he didn't leave me many options. Thank you," she said, accepting the burned scarf. "It does look a bit damaged, doesn't it? Out of commission for the time being. I trust we are still on schedule to depart for Bangor this evening?"

Red Whiskers cleared his throat. "I'm afraid not, miss. The mayor has put a halt to all trains until the giant situation is resolved."

"Are they all revolting?" asked the porter.

"Only two others," said Red Whiskers. "Two-headed Thunderdel in the Public Gardens and Galigantus in the harbor."

"And no one can stop them?" asked Hanna.

Red Whiskers shrugged. "The maker built them in a secret laboratory. Seemed a fine idea until he died and no one knew how to turn them off."

Hanna pouted. True, her schedule did have flexibility, but she did not want to set a precedent of attending to every local crisis she encountered in her travels. However, she considered, these were the famous giants of Boston. Incredible machines that had not yet seen their equal.

"Well," she said, turning toward the porter. "If the trains will not depart before the matter of the giants is resolved, perhaps you would care to escort me?"

"To your hotel?"

"To slay the giants."

It was mid-afternoon when the streetcar Hanna and the porter had boarded arrived at the southern gate to the Public Gardens. Hanna felt a mild pleasure at the quality of the transport as they disembarked. *If only they could do something about this soot*, she thought, brushing at her pale dress.

"Should I go in with you?" asked the porter, looking very much as though he would prefer not to enter the gardens.

Hanna watched the car slowly rumble away down the street before turning her attention to the large swath of nature in the middle of the city. "I suppose I could go in alone," she said, preparing a look that would encourage him to accompany her, but was interrupted by a violent cacophony from within the park.

A giant rose up from a grove of trees two blocks down. In a cloud of black steam he stepped over the wrought-iron fence beside the streetcar. This giant was much bigger than Cormorgan, at least twenty feet tall, perhaps more, with two heads and three arms. (Hanna assumed the third appendage was an arm, as no dignified maker would have constructed it to be... Well, she preferred not to consider what else it might represent.)

"Two-headed Thunderdel," said the porter under his breath. "He's a mean one."

"He is an automaton," said Hanna, as she walked quickly toward the giant, rummaging through her reticule. "How would his personality differ significantly from the others?"

Two-headed Thunderdel wrapped two of his arms around the streetcar and lifted it from the tracks. He shook it violently, knocking the passengers loose. Once they were on the ground he stomped them into pudding, one by one. His left head seemed to laugh with each squelch. Hanna slowed in the street, almost in shock, and watched the giant crush the last of the passengers beneath his now gore-covered foot. Hoisting the streetcar onto his shoulder, Two-headed Thunderdel clamored back over the fence and began to stomp away through the trees.

She pointed back toward the park gate. "I will return for you there," she said to the porter, and shoved her reticule into his hands before breaking into a full run. She jumped over the broken bodies and scooped up a parasol that had been discarded by its recently deceased owner. She tucked it under her arm, vaulted the fence, and pushed on through the trees after the giant.

It was an easy trail to track. Two-headed Thunderdel was certainly big and strong, but much like his brother Cormorgan, he was slow. In no time at all Hanna grew close enough to see, but not to be seen.

They came to a break in the trees and Hanna held back to watch. Two-headed Thunderdel stomped out to the edge of a lagoon, stopping before a pile of streetcars. Hanna counted six of them, piled up from the shore out into the water. The giant ripped the roof from his new acquisition and shook the coal out onto a pile beside the trees. Satisfied that he had all of the dark treasure, he took the carcass of the streetcar and carefully placed it beside the others in the lagoon.

Two-headed Thunderdel stomped back to his hoard of coal and slowly, awkwardly, knelt before it. He reached up with two hands, sliding fingers between his heads, and pulled. His heads swung up and apart, each on a hinge. He guided them, turning his heads upside-down, stopping beside each shoulder. From his neck, fire rose up from his furnace. With his third arm, Two-headed Thunderdel shoveled coal up and into his gaping hole. The heads continued to swivel about, on alert.

Hanna stooped behind the tree and mapped out her course of action in the air with a finger. She nodded in agreement with her plan and set down the parasol to hike up her dress. She connected the tops of her boots to her leggings and then to her knee braces. Opening the panels on each boot heel, she wound the cranks, feeling the springs tighten and cables growing taut.

She stood and stretched, feeling the ticking running up each leg. It was immodest to do this series of squats with her knees showing, but with such temperamental devices, warm-ups were necessary, if embarrassing. She secured the parasol and readied herself before sprinting toward the giant.

The left head saw her coming and roared a grinding, metallic call. Hanna jumped, propelled high into the air by her boots. The giant's left arm was still holding his left head upside-down when she landed on the massive metal bicep and grabbed onto his earhole to steady herself. The head gnashed his jaw and she felt the heat from the furnace as coal continued to be shoveled in.

Hanna skewered his left eye with the parasol. The glass within shattered and gears began to grind. She jerked the parasol back and struck the right eye as well, wiggling the parasol around within before opening it as best she could, wedging it tight.

Two-headed Thunderdel shook and bellowed again, from both mouths this time. Hanna felt herself begin to slip from the arm and jumped off. She revolved in the air and landed smartly in the mud, splattering her hem with dirt.

The giant lurched to his feet and turned toward her. His heads were still upside-down, the left damaged and spinning madly while the right fixated upon her. Fire spat up out of his neck and he reached out with his third arm.

Hanna trotted backward, eyes focused on the advancing giant. She dodged as he lashed out and then jumped when he struck again. She changed course, running toward the streetcar graveyard. Kicking off of the first car, she soared through the air, and landed on the one farthest out from shore, then waited as it bobbed in the water.

Two-headed Thunderdel stomped onto that first car and it sank into the mud. Hanna crouched. The giant stepped out on the next car and it lurched forward, sinking. His third arm grabbed out at her as he advanced, and she sprang at him straight toward the blinded left head.

Already off-balance, Two-headed Thunderdel twisted so the right head could track her. Hanna landed on top of the left head and jumped again. The streetcar beneath him collapsed and the giant tumbled into the lagoon. As Hanna hit the ground, she felt something in her right boot snap. *Oh, for goodness sake*, she thought, feeling the sudden unwinding of the cables along her leg.

Hanna shook out her right leg and watched Two-headed Thunderdel thrash wildly as icy water flooded into his furnace. Steam and smoke billowed into the air, and the burning hot metal began to crack. He jerked with hurdy-gurdy motions before coming to rest mostly submerged in the water, his fire extinguished.

Across the lake a small crowd had gathered. She watched them pointing at her, scrambling about on the bank until one of them, an officer, she thought, lost his footing and tumbled into the mud near the shore.

Hanna sighed and trudged back toward the porter, unsuccessfully brushing the mud from her pale dress. One more giant to deal with and she could get her journey back on track.

The sun had begun to set when Hanna finally caught sight of Boston Harbor and the massive bulk that was the giant king, Galigantus. He rose up at least thirty feet above the water while standing submerged up past his knees. Even as Hanna and the porter walked quickly through the crowd toward the wharf, Hanna heard the roaring of the giant's steam-powered furnace and the grinding of his joints.

As she grew closer, Galigantus picked a small fishing boat from the water. The captain screamed and jumped, trusting to a swim in the icy bay as a better chance for survival. The giant lifted the boat to his furnace, a massive hole where his mouth should be, spewing blackest steam. Galigantus swallowed the ship whole, and flames spit out across the harbor.

"Perhaps I can tip him under like the last one," said Hanna, biting at her lip.

"Not Galigantus," said the porter. He was sucking air, his chest heaving and legs aching from this unwanted exertion. "He was made. To patrol. The harbor. They say. He can. Stay. Under water. Hours."

Hanna harumphed, trying to construct a strategy. Her boots and scarf were broken. She did have the gloves, but suspected they would not be enough and so began to rummage through her reticule looking for ideas. A line of officers stood blocking the way as she reached the wharf.

"This int ya best time for a stroll," one of the men said, holding up his hand.

Hanna looked up from her bag. "I appreciate the concern, gentlemen—"

"Sergeant McCue," interrupted the officer.

"Pardon me, Sergeant. But unless you can provide me with a way to get closer to…" she turned back to the porter. "What is he called?"

"Galigantus," he wheezed.

"Of course." She turned back to the sergeant. "I cannot very well defeat Galigantus from the shore, so I will be going down the pier."

"Wharf," gasped the porter.

"Excuse me," she said. "I will be going down the wharf."

"Oh, will ya?" Sergeant McCue crossed his arms and scowled. "I have enough to do here without some lass pushing her nose around."

"That's her! That's the giant killer!"

Hanna turned to the officer who had spoken. It took her a moment to recognize Red Whiskers from the train yard. "She's the one that put down Cormorgan!"

"Cormorgan's put down?" said the sergeant, his eyebrows furrowing.

"I was there," said Red Whiskers.

Sergeant McCue turned back to Hanna, taking stock of her slight frame and soiled pale dress. "This little thing has slain a giant?"

"Sergeant!" They all turned as another officer ran from the crowd. He was covered in mud, waving his arms over his head.

"Sergeant. Two-headed Thunderdel has been slain in the lagoon. I think it was a woman in a pale dress that done it. Drown him, she did." He came to a stop and leaned forward, resting his hands on his knees. He was heaving, trying to catch his breath, when his eyes came to rest on a pair of woman's boots caked in mud. He followed them to a pale dress and up to Hanna's cheeks, flushed with embarrassment. "Oh," he said. "She's already here."

"Well," said Hanna. She shrugged slightly and turned back to her reticule, pushing her components around with growing frustration. "Someone had to do it," she mumbled.

Sergeant McCue gaped at Hanna, unblinking, until his eyes were cold and dry.

"So," said Red Whiskers. "You're going to slay Galigantus, as well?"

Hanna looked up, her lips pressed together and her eyes flittering around, staring out at the giant in the harbor. She shrugged slightly. "This one is quite big," she said quietly.

"Biggest of them all," agreed the porter.

"Built to sink ships, he is," said the Muddy Man.

"I can't seem to..." Hanna trailed off and bit her lip. "Does he ever come on land?"

Everyone shook their heads except for the sergeant, who was still staring at her.

"Has anyone, I don't know, run a ship into him?"

Everyone nodded their heads a bit sadly.

Hanna sighed and looked back down into her bag. "I don't suppose any of you has a weapon capable of slaying a creature the like of Galigantus?"

The police exchanged glances. "Well," the Muddy Man said. "There's Paul Revere's sword."

Inside the Paul Revere Museum, the curator lifted the sword out of the glass case with gentle fingers. All of the officers were silent and bowed their heads reverently.

"I didn't know Paul Revere had a sword," said Hanna.

"Oh, yes," said the curator. "As legend has it, with the War for Independence on the horizon, Boston's favorite son forged this weapon from silver and steel. He carried it into every battle, and it was always the difference between victory and defeat. They say it could cut through armor as easily as bone, but its secrets have been lost to time."

"I don't recall learning this in my history lessons," Hanna said. "May I?" The curator looked to the officers. They nodded and, swallowing, he held out the sword, resting it in Hanna's open hands. It had a wide blade with a thick handle. And it was heavy. The inlay on the scabbard was greatly detailed, stars and stripes with red, white, and blue silver. As she drew the weapon from its sheath, all of the men took in a breath. In the museum lamplight, the blade glistened as though made of ice.

"Ah," said Hanna. She rested the sword on top of the display case and dove back into her reticule, coming out with a set of tools.

"Please, no," said the curator, with a horrified look on his face, as she withdrew a screwdriver and calipers.

"There seems to be a panel here," said Hanna, leaning over the pommel. After a few nervous moments, a small compartment opened in the grip. "I do believe," said Hanna softly, "That Mr. Revere has not been given adequate credit for his craftsmanship."

She took up additional tools and looked around the room at the men. "I shall just need a few more moments," she said.

"It's not too heavy?" asked the porter, nervously eyeing the sword strapped to Hanna's back.

Hanna shook her head and continued to tie her hair up in a pile. There were times when she enjoyed fantastic daydreams of cutting all of her hair as short as her bangs but, standing by the wharf, she was quite aware of the setting sun and knew that this was not a moment for unreasonable thoughts. Galigantus was coming back into view after patrolling the harbor.

With her hair secured, she held out her hand to the porter. "My bonnet, please." As she tied it in place, Hanna joined Red Whiskers and Muddy Man as they, along with a horse, struggled to move a cannon down the wharf.

"He will be in range soon," said Muddy Man, urging the horse onward.

From her reticule, Hanna withdrew a pair of modified opera glasses. She strapped them over her eyes and focused on Galigantus. The leviathan's mouth took up most of his massive head and neck, steaming and groaning. His torso was constructed with long swaths of steel, leaving vertical seams running from his shoulders to his waist. Hanna nodded to herself, connecting pieces of a plan, before returning the glasses to her reticule.

At the end of the wharf, they turned the horse. The porter held the reins as the officers detached the cannon.

"You should go back," said Hanna.

"Someone needs to fire the cannon," said Muddy Man, aiming the cannon.

"Takes two to do that," said Red Whiskers, loading in a cannonball.

"Perhaps I'll take the horse back," said the porter, with more than a touch of anxiety in his voice. "That sword's not too heavy?"

Hanna smiled at him. "Thank you very much for your help. I am quite grateful. If you would, hold this for me?"

The porter took her reticule but couldn't turn his eyes from the giant looming closer. "I'll just go now," he said and led the horse quickly away.

Hanna turned toward Galigantus and said to the officers, "When you are ready."

The ball exploded from the cannon with such force that Hanna could scarcely track its trajectory. It slammed into the giant's right shoulder, rocking it slightly.

"Oh, quite good," said Hanna as the giant turned toward them. She pushed up her sleeves and began turning gears on her right armband. A sheet of molded iron slid up over the outer side of her hand by the pinky. She folded over the top and fit each finger into the slots and repeated the process on her other arm. She flexed and readied herself.

"Ready now?" Red Whiskers loaded the harpoon and wrapped the end of the cable around the wheels of the cannon. "Go," she called, and Muddy Man lit the fuse. The harpoon slammed into Galigantus' chest.

"Be off now," said Hanna, and the officers began to run. *Well, now,* she thought as the giant grew even closer. *I can't imagine that this will take very long, one way or another.* She grunted most unfeminine embarrassing noises as she rolled the cannon off the end of the wharf. As the iron weapon fell, the cable pulled tight and jerked the giant forward. He righted himself, maintaining his balance, leaning toward the wharf.

Hanna jumped up, gripping the cable tight in her iron gloves, and began to pull herself, hand over hand, toward the giant. She moved quickly and smoothly, just like in her training drills, as Galigantus regained his balance and began to grab for her.

Hanna took her right hand off of the cable and reached back for the sword. She twisted the peen block on the end of the pommel and activated the extraordinary weapon. As she drew the blade free she felt the vibrations running through her arm as the grip begin to warm. She swung backhanded and sliced through the cable just before the giant could grasp her.

Released from the pressure of the cannon, Galigantus stumbled back and held his arms out to steady himself. As she swung through the air, Hanna lifted up her feet. When she collided with the nether regions of Galigantus, it was with the soles of her boots.

She slid the sword back into its sheath and began to climb up the cable. She was nearly to the harpoon when the giant regained his footing and looked down upon her.

In the cold, damp breeze, sweat beaded up beneath Hanna's undergarments and she vowed again to find a solution to such discomfort. Grasping the harpoon, she pulled herself up and rested a knee upon it, steadying herself with a hand on the giant's chest.

She looked up into the eyestalks of Galigantus, which poked out from his iron head and flopped about in a quite unnatural way. The giant opened his mouth hole, exhaling steam and smoke. His hands came in toward his chest to snatch her up.

Hanna stood up on the harpoon and drew the sword again, flipping it in her grip, aiming the blade downward. She bent her knees and leapt just as the giant's hands came clutching where she stood.

Landing on the top of the fists, one foot on each of his hands, she pulled the sword up over her head with both hands on the hilt. The giant pulled his hands away and Hanna stabbed. The sword vibrated, bleeding heat, and her aim was true. The sword slid into the seam between iron plates just below the giant's fire-breathing mouth. Hanna held on, jerking down on the sword, slicing the giant down the middle.

Above her, as his chest split open, Hanna felt the heat from the furnace. She bent her head down, hoping the bonnet would deflect the fire as it was designed to do.

The iron chest plates spread open. The wound, peeling, oozed fire. Galigantus' arms grew farther apart as the hole spread wider.

As Hanna slid further down, she watched her feet sinking closer and closer to the frigid water. Not pleased about the prospect of a early winter soaking, she took her left hand off of the grip, flexed her iron gloves, and grabbed tight onto a seam in the giant's waist, stopping her descent.

The great machinery inside Galigantus broke apart. Iron beams and great gears snapped like twigs. His arms flailed, slowing, grinding down. As the great heat in his furnace cooled, his joints locked into place and came to rest, leaving the giant machine a statue, to rust in Boston Harbor.

Hanna held on, kicking out for footholds. She craned her neck, looking toward shore, and could see the officers piled in a boat, steaming toward her as fast as they could. She sighed.

I suppose, she thought, *it will be at least another day before the trains are running. I wonder whether I can convince them to let me keep the sword.*

The Hair Ladder

based on Rapunzel

DIANA BASTINE

"WE DON'T HAVE THE MONEY."

Julia wrapped her arms around her husband, snuggling close. "But think how nice it would be for the baby." She patted her growing belly, pulling his hand to do the same. He tried to resist, but he could deny his wife nothing.

"The old woman only comes once every season," Julia almost whined. "Besides, we've been saving…."

"We've been saving for the baby," her long-suffering spouse replied, with every attempt at firmness.

"Oh, Thomas, please?" Julia batted her eyelashes at him, before burying her face in his chest. "I really must have one of her clockwork toys. I think I might die if you don't bring me one." She widened her innocent blue eyes in horror. "Or it might even affect the baby. You wouldn't want anything to happen to the baby, would you?"

Thomas knew it was nothing short of blackmail, but he also knew it would work. They had been trying for quite some time to have a child, and were finally on the verge of a successful birth. He would do nothing that might risk a safe and healthy delivery. He gathered his coat, for even though the winter had turned to spring, it was still a chilly morning, and he had a long walk to the town square.

Thomas didn't need to read the sign outside of the old woman's tent: Clara's Clockwork Creations. He knew he was close when he started hearing the steady drone of gears. Most of the clockwork creatures were small and intricately detailed, but the combined sound was still powerful enough to carry on a still, clear day. He gathered his ragged coat closer with a sigh, then strode closer to the tent, being careful where he placed his somewhat large feet. He certainly had no desire to step on one of the delicate creations — he wanted to choose carefully, not be forced to buy whatever he crushed!

The old woman, Clara, greeted him politely. He had seen her many times before; she came to town four times a year, and Julia always begged him to stop so she could watch the beautiful clockwork toys that she knew they couldn't afford to waste their hard-earned money on. Thomas wasn't expecting the old woman to recognize him however. She didn't know his name, but she clearly recognized his face.

"How is your lovely wife?" she asked him, as he carefully picked up an exquisite mechanical peacock. As he turned it from side to side, its tail feathers slowly spread out in a broad fan, each metal "feather" painted in bright blue-green. Its head bobbed slightly, before the tail feathers contracted back again. He could barely hear the faint whir as the gears turned inside its body. Thomas knew the peacock was going to be far too expensive, and he quickly put it down before Clara started to convince him to purchase it.

"Julia is well," he answered. "She would have come today, but she is expecting our first child and sometimes feels a bit unwell in the mornings. She is looking forward to the summer, when we will have our new addition." Thomas didn't normally babble like this, especially not to total strangers, but he was still flush with pride at the thought of being a first-time papa.

"Oh, a child!" Clara said, clapping her hands in delight. "I adore children. They are so appreciative of my work." She spread her hands to encompass her clockwork creations. "Many craftsmen scorn my beauties; they find them to be frivolous, and a waste of resources, but children appreciate the fine work and detail, more so than you might think. They are often more careful of my work than their parents are." She smiled, having clearly observed Thomas' delicate approach.

He shook his head in disbelief. "I cannot imagine anyone looking down on your skills, Miss Clara," he said sincerely and emphatically. He picked up a charmingly detailed little field mouse, admiring its "fur" and long tail. The tiniest metal threads were visible as its whiskers, and he could have sworn its tiny nose twitched just a bit.

The old woman closed his hand — gently — over the mouse. "You must have it," she said. She held up a hand when he opened his mouth to protest. "No, I insist," she said. "It is for the child." When he finally nodded in acceptance of the generous gift, she loosened his hand again, just long enough to take the mouse and carefully wrap it before returning it to him. He thanked her most sincerely, and headed home, certain that his wife would be satisfied.

"A *mouse*?" Julia shrilled. "That's what you bought for m– for our son or daughter?"

"Julia, please, listen to me. The woman, Clara, gave this to us as a gift specifically for our child! It would have been churlish for me to tell her that it wasn't good enough. Besides, look at the workmanship—it is incredibly skillful. I've never seen this degree of detail in any metalwork before."

Julia swatted away his hand, which he had held out to her so she could see the mouse more closely. The tiny clockwork creature fell to the floor. Thomas cried out, fearing the delicate mechanisms inside the metal shell might break.

Julia stamped her foot, barely missing the mouse's tail. Thomas knelt, picking the toy up carefully, so as not to cause any further damage than might have already occurred. "You don't love me," she sniffed. "And you don't care about the happiness of our child." Her eyes were filling with tears.

"Julia, her prices are very high. As they should be," he said. "She deserves a fair payment for her work. It was most generous of her to give us this little marvel as a gift. Please, I beg you to be satisfied."

"I want something better," Julia said with a sniffle. She moaned. "I must go and rest now. The child is restless, and pains me." She knew her husband well, and knew that even if the tears didn't get to him, any threat to their child would have the desired effect.

Thomas spent the majority of the evening walking around the streets of their small village. He was restless, and didn't know what to do. He knew he couldn't afford one of Clara's bigger and better pieces, even if he spent every penny they had, and he didn't wish to offend her after her act of generosity. But he also knew that his wife would make his life hell—and possibly endanger the health of their child—if he didn't satisfy her whim.

He slowly walked to the town square. The vendors were packing up their tents and wares, returning to their tethered airships. He saw that Clara had already gathered most of her creations, and must have been taking some of them to her 'ship, as he did not see her near her tent.

When he heard a faint sound, he looked down at his feet and saw a tabby cat. He crouched down, and reached out to pet it. It was only then that he noticed that there was a faint whirring sound beneath the louder purr. Sure enough, when he began to stroke its ears, he realized that the fur was actually painted metal. Again, he marveled at the old woman's talent. The "cat" started butting its metal head into his hand, and when he stood up, it wound between his legs. He smiled sadly. If only he could afford it....

Thomas suddenly became aware that nobody had noticed him standing there. He looked around. People were busily occupied with taking down their booths, and saying good-bye to their friends and comrades. Clara was still nowhere to be seen. Surely she would never miss one clockwork creature among so many. And it had wandered over to him. After all, it might have wandered away completely if he hadn't been standing there. Trying mightily to squelch his growing guilt, he carefully picked up the cat and tucked it inside his coat, furtively checking to make sure no one saw him.

Later that spring, Thomas and Julia became the proud parents of a beautiful baby girl whom they christened Ramona. Julia had been delighted with the charming tabby cat, and had remained in good health and good spirits throughout the remainder of her pregnancy. Admittedly, she had been more taken with the cat than the child was, but that was all right with Thomas. Just so long as she was happy. Although it did bother him just a little that Julia seemed almost more taken with the cat than she was with her own child. Still he doted on mother and baby alike, and was relieved that the clockwork cat had done the trick. Not to mention the fact that he hadn't gotten caught....

Thomas was playing with Ramona on the floor of their small house after work one evening in early autumn, when there was a knock at the door. Julia had wound up the clockwork cat, to watch it stalk the miraculously undamaged mouse. The cat's tail twitched back and forth, with not even the slightest jerking motion. Only the whirring of its gears gave away the movement of its feet as it readied itself to pounce.

Thomas picked up his daughter, carrying her to the front door, since his wife was obviously too occupied with the "child's" toy. When he opened it, he nearly dropped Ramona onto the floor. There stood Clara, and he was certain she had brought the authorities with her. He swallowed.

But Clara smiled brightly. "Why, hello, you lovely child!" she said to the infant, before turning her attention to Thomas. "When I saw neither you nor your wife in the town square today, I asked around to discover if all was well. I wasn't surprised not to see you this summer, with the arrival of the new baby. Someone told me where I could find you, so I thought I would come and congratulate you and see if you were still enjoying the mouse."

Thomas was still unable to speak. At first it had been fear and guilt holding his tongue (the same emotions which had kept him away from the town square that very day, as he had been certain they would show on his face), then relief. It was short-lived however, as the cat abandoned both mouse and mistress to approach the front door. It sat down, gears whirring, and purred loudly, drawing the old woman's attention. When she looked down, her face froze.

Clara slowly raised her face to look at Thomas. He didn't see accusation there, but the hurt and betrayal in her eyes were worse. When he looked away, because he could stand her pain no longer, she turned her attention back to the cat. "I looked all over for you before I left last time," she whispered, her voice hoarse. "I was afraid some larger animal took you, mistaking you for a real feline. I thought I had left you in danger, through my own carelessness." She looked up at Thomas again. "But you had stolen her, hadn't you?"

Thomas couldn't meet her gaze. He nodded miserably. Ramona, sensing his distress, began to whimper.

"What's all of the fuss about?" Julia interrupted. When Thomas had confessed to her that he had taken the cat, she hadn't cared. The old woman had plenty of clockwork company, she'd told him, and shouldn't miss one cat. Thomas had carried the burden of guilt for both of them.

"I don't understand," Clara said. "Wasn't the mouse good enough? I thought it was one of my most skilled creations." She tried to get Thomas to meet her eyes. "I thought you felt that way too. Didn't it please your wife? Why didn't you simply bring it back? Perhaps we could have come to an agreement. But instead you stole from me."

"Well, you can't have the cat back," Julia said imperiously. "I refuse to part with it!"

Thomas set Ramona down in her cradle, where she continued to whimper, irritating Julia even more. She slapped the child, shouting at her to be quiet, which of course had the opposite effect.

"I know I must pay you for the cat," Thomas said finally, his voice heavy with shame and guilt. "But I have no money for it. All of our money goes to our daughter's needs. Perhaps I could do some sort of work for you in exchange?"

"I have no need for that sort of thing. I think I would prefer it if you simply returned my property."

As Thomas reached for the cat, to return it to Clara, Julia snatched it from his hands. "No! The cat is mine!"

Ramona's whimpering had now turned into howls. Her face was red and twisted, and she was starting to gasp for breath. Instead of comforting her daughter, Julia clutched the clockwork cat. Clara looked from mother to father, then nodded briskly.

"Fine. I shall take the child in exchange."

"What?" choked out Thomas. "No! You can't take our daughter! Julia, give her the cat. I beg you. Miss Clara is giving us a chance to right the wrong I've done to her. Please, give her the cat."

Julia stubbornly clutched the cat. "No." She turned her back on all of them. "Let her take the child instead. I won't give up my cat." The cat, not knowing any better, simply added its clockwork purr to the other noise. Thomas realized his wife was not going to change her mind.

Clara walked to the cradle, and gathered the hiccupping infant into her arms, patting her back and making soothing sounds. The howls started to revert back to whimpers, and the deep red color began to fade from her tear-stained cheeks. Clara turned to Thomas, who was still staring at his wife in disbelief. "I will give her a good life, young man; I promise you that. She will want for nothing."

Clara was true to her word. Under her tutelage and care, Ramona blossomed into a bright and happy child, eager to learn the secrets of Clara's mechanical creations. Clara remembered how, when she was a curious young girl, she had been discouraged by the men in her village from learning metal-crafting skills. When she wished to go to the local university, she had earned nothing but laughter and scorn, so she tracked down every book she could find in the library or from visiting booksellers (who were much less disparaging of a young woman's scientific curiosity) and taught herself the craft, starting with the basics. She had also absorbed enough knowledge of mechanical workings to tend to her own airship, which was more than could be said by many of the men she saw in her travels. Clara had a gift, and a love, for the work she did, and it was easy to pass these along to Ramona, as the child had no preconceptions. Her unconventional upbringing left her open to whatever possibilities Providence brought her way.

As Ramona grew older, Clara became more reclusive and less welcoming of visitors to the airship. Her time in public was almost exclusively limited to the fairs and markets to which they traveled to sell their clockwork wares, or to purchase or trade for supplies. The two women spent most of their time in each other's company, which suited them both, as they spent most of their waking hours absorbed in the minutiae of assembling their creations. Ramona was uncomfortable in the crowds that attended the markets where they sold their wares, and preferred the solitude of the airship. Clara never had to worry that Ramona's parents might try to reclaim their child—Julia clearly didn't want her, and Thomas apparently had no more desire to attend the seasonal markets, whether from shame or grief the old woman didn't know. Clara hadn't seen him in all the years since she took Ramona as "payment" for the stolen clockwork cat. She had seen Julia on occasion, but Julia always passed her tent and moved on to the next vendor. Which was just fine with Clara.

During this time, the two of them discovered that Ramona's hair had a very unusual quality: not only was it extremely difficult to cut, but when they succeeded once during Ramona's early childhood, it grew back overnight. It grew to a quite remarkable length, and remained there. It also became tougher as Ramona grew older; by the time she reached adolescence, it was as strong as the metal filament thread they used in their craft work. This was the main reason it was virtually impossible to cut. The two women agreed that they would probably need a blowtorch to get the job done, and neither of them wished to risk that! But it did come in handy. One time, the rope tethering the airship to a tree slipped its knot and Ramona used her hair to anchor them. Sometimes the coils of hair drove her to despair, but after that incident, she grew to appreciate her strange and unusual gift, or at least to be less exasperated with it. She encouraged Clara to use her mane as a ladder from the ground to the deck of the airship, instead of depending on the far less sturdy rope one. Rope strands could fray, knots could come

undone—but Ramona's hair was as tough as steel. All Clara had to do when she returned from any absence from the airship was to call out, "Ramona, Ramona! Lower the hair ladder!" And Ramona would step to the railing of the gondola's deck, sit down, lean against the railing and lower her hair over the side. Clara would nimbly climb up, and arrive safely aboard. Even though the strands were as strong as metal, they weren't slick in any way, so Clara never had any difficulty maintaining a good, firm grip.

One day, when they were again in Ramona's hometown, and Clara was away selling their clockwork creatures, Ramona heard a voice calling out: "Ramona, Ramona! Please lower your hair ladder." She stepped to the deck of the airship's gondola and saw a woman she didn't recognize. She did, however, feel a strange twinge in her heart. The woman held out her hands in pleading. "Please, Ramona! I must speak with you!"

"How do you know my name?" Ramona asked her in suspicion.

"How do I know your name? I'm the one who named you, you silly child! You didn't think that old hag was your true birth mother, did you? Now stop being foolish, and let me come up there!"

Ramona was confused. She had certainly picked up over the years that Clara was not her true mother, but the old woman had been a mother to her in every other sense of the word. She had never thought much about her parents, and Clara was never comfortable speaking of how Ramona came to be in her care, but the young woman had on a few scattered occasions wondered if they were still alive and, if they were, what had happened to them.

Julia was pacing below the airship, glancing nervously over her shoulder. Clara may have believed that Julia no longer had any interest in her daughter's welfare, but that didn't mean that Julia had no interest in any other part of Clara and Ramona's business. Julia had certainly publicly snubbed Clara at the town square market, but that didn't mean she wasn't aware of the old woman's comings and goings. She'd followed her during one visit, and overheard Clara's catchphrase for boarding the airship.

Ramona's curiosity got the better of her, and she lowered her hair over the side of the gondola. Julia climbed up, as quickly as she was able, though far more awkwardly than the nimble Clara. When she was standing firmly on the gondola's deck, she turned to catch Ramona's curious gaze.

Ramona tentatively reached out her arms to welcome her birth mother with a friendly hug, but Julia pushed past her.

"Where do you keep the toys?" she asked brusquely.

"Wh-what?" Ramona asked, confused.

Julia had found her way to the stairs leading below-deck. She quickly clattered down them, Ramona on her heels. Julia began picking up pieces, works-in-progress, dropping them back unceremoniously on the worktables.

"What are you looking for?" Ramona asked her, trying to keep Julia from damaging anything delicate.

"The cat and mouse don't work anymore. I need something new," Julia whined.

Ramona put a restraining hand on Julia's arm, turning the older woman to face her. "You're not here to see me," she stated.

Julia strove desperately to adopt a concerned, maternal expression, failing miserably. "Oh sweetie, of course I am." She patted Ramona's arm condescendingly. "But you want your poor old mother to be happy, don't you?" she wheedled. "I thought surely you wouldn't mind parting with one of your silly little toys for my sake." She pulled out of Ramona's grasp to continue rummaging through the partly-finished creatures.

"All of the completed creations are at the market," Ramona said with a frustrated sigh. "There's nothing here except for partially built ones, or ones that didn't come out well enough to sell. If that's the only reason you're here...." This mother-daughter reunion wasn't working out quite the way Ramona had expected. But then, she was beginning to suspect that maybe she shouldn't have had any expectations at all. She sighed.

Julia was still fingering the works on the table, growing increasingly disappointed. She picked up the blowtorch Ramona had been using to cut a large metal sheet into workable pieces before her work was interrupted by her mother's calls.

"Please put that down," Ramona said sternly. "That's a dangerous tool if you're not trained in its use."

"And you are, I suppose," Julia sneered. "Is that what that old woman has taught you? How to be a freakish outcast like herself?"

Just then they were interrupted by the sound of Clara calling from below. "Ramona, Ramona! Please lower the hair ladder!"

Ramona hurried to the stairs to the deck, throwing over her shoulder: "Just put the torch down, please. I think you should go as soon as Miss Clara is back on the airship."

As soon as she got to the gondola railing, Clara waved up at her. "I'm sorry, honey; I know I'm interrupting your work. But I forgot to bring my midday meal, and I'm beginning to feel a headache coming on. One of my 'neighbors' is watching the tent for me, so I'll be as quick as I can."

Ramona had already assumed her usual position, and dropped her hair over the side. Clara quickly began her climb. Suddenly Ramona heard a man's voice call out, "Julia, don't!"

At the same time, Ramona heard the sound of the blowtorch firing. She twisted back toward her mother and saw Julia approach, lit torch in hand. Ramona kicked out, trying to force the woman away, but Julia easily avoided the blow. She dropped to her knees on the gondola's deck and set the torch to Ramona's hair. Julia didn't have any idea how tough the filaments of hair were, and was expecting the strands to part with ease from the intense heat. Instead, the flame barely scorched the thick strands.

Ramona desperately tried to shove Julia away, terrified of moving too forcefully lest she cause Clara's grip to loosen. Julia merely shifted a bit to pin her down. Ramona tried to twist away from the flame, barely noticing increased noise below: Clara calling out at the sudden sway of the hair ladder and the unknown man continuing to plead with Julia to stop.

By this time, several of Ramona's coils of hair had begun to succumb to the heat of the torch and Ramona summoned her strength to shove Julia off of her. Julia half sprawled on the deck, and lost her grip on the torch. Ramona, fearing for Clara's safety above all else, didn't know what to do. Leaping to her feet to seize the blowtorch was unthinkable with Clara's weight hanging from her hair, and Ramona was afraid even kicking it out of Julia's reach would require too much movement which would dislodge the old woman's grip for sure. But did she have any other choice? As Julia reached once more for the torch, Ramona knew she had to do something. She tried to shift her body as carefully as possible, mindful of Clara dangling somewhere between the airship and the ground, literally hanging on by a thread, or at most several of them. Julia knocked her off balance, having no need to be as careful as Ramona, and set torch to hair yet again. Ramona felt more and more of the damaged coils starting to separate. She shoved at Julia again, harder this time, mindless of the heat from the blowtorch.

At the same moment Julia fell back, Ramona's hair gave way completely. The sudden release sent Ramona's prone body crashing into her mother. Julia cried out as she lost her balance, tipping backward over the gondola railing. Her scream blended with Clara's as they both plunged toward the ground. Ramona's anguished cry rose in counterpoint as the other two women's fell away. Somewhere below, the man cried out as well, until the sound abruptly cut off. Gripping the railing, Ramona stared down in horror, sick with grief and the stench of burned hair.

On the ground below the airship, both women lay in a tangle of golden hair, their bodies at unnatural angles. Beneath the coils Ramona could make out a few extra limbs, which she assumed belonged to the male stranger. From the deck of the airship, it appeared as though Julia's neck was broken, but Clara's fall had been partially broken by the stranger and cushioned by the thick coils of hair. Even so, several of Clara's limbs were twisted. On wobbly legs, Ramona staggered to the controls of the airship, and with shaking hands she opened the ballonets to allow the heavier air into the gas envelope above, lowering the 'ship as slowly as she was able. She found one of the old ropes they always kept on hand—"just in case," as Clara always said—and tethered the airship. Her hands shook so badly that it took her several tries, but she finally managed.

When she was finally on the ground, the first thing she noticed was that Clara was moaning and starting to stir. The impact had knocked the breath out of her, but she didn't seem to have suffered any mortal injuries. Ignoring Julia's motionless form, Ramona hurried to the old woman's side. The man buried beneath the mound of golden hair appeared unconscious, but otherwise unharmed. Ramona breathed a word of thanks, then knelt beside Clara and took her hand.

"I'm going to get some help, and then I'll be right back," she whispered to Clara. Clara nodded, still trying to catch her breath. "Just lie still."

By the time Ramona had risen to her feet, the man had regained consciousness and taken in the situation around him. "Please, let me help," he said, quickly getting to his feet. He winced from his bruises, but remained steady.

Ramona's overwhelmed brain had finally made the obvious connection. "You're my father, aren't you?" She ended on a slight note of hesitation, in case her inference was incorrect after all.

"I am." He crouched beside Clara, then rose, cradling her gently in his arms. Ramona guided him to the airship, where he set the old woman carefully upon her bed. Clara moaned again, and opened her eyes. It took her a moment to recognize Thomas. "Thank you," she murmured before he could avert his eyes.

After helping Ramona pack up their merchandise and transport it back to the airship, Thomas remained with them, proving indispensable during Clara's convalescence. The old woman recovered quickly from her mild concussion, although her badly broken left leg never healed properly. But Ramona was able to cobble together a piston-powered brace which enabled the other woman to walk with relative ease. The three of them constructed a proper ladder, made of metal and wood, and lived happily ever after.

The Perfect Shoes

based on The Red Shoes

JODY LYNN NYE

THE BALLET COMPANY STOOD POISED ON THE STAGE THAT SMELLED OF chalk and sweat, awaiting the ballet master's command to dance. Monique Dortmond hovered on tiptoe in her taped pink toe shoes, her hands above her head in fifth position, her body stretched into the perfect attitude of ethereal majesty. Her wavy, dark hair had been scraped fiercely back into a tight bun to show off the slenderness of her neck and the scalloped hollows underneath her cheekbones. Her slim but muscular body displayed utter grace, unlike Kerry, to her left. The blonde dancer's heavy hips and thick ankles made her look more like a tree trunk than a sylph. Then, the twitching began. Monique felt her left foot wobble ever so slightly. She had exercised her arches again and again. Her legs were as strong as steel cables. Her stamina was excellent. Why, then, the trembling?

Because she was not concentrating on her performance. All the ballerinas of the Paris Opera Ballet had their eyes not on the middle distance, but on Mademoiselle Henriette Malinois, the prima ballerina of the company, who was dancing the part of *Giselle*. Her posture was ideal. Her arms seemed as though they were two reeds swaying in the wind. Her long, slender neck suggested the blossom of an arum lily. But her body, however it may have seemed to come from the very sketches of the artists and sculptors who sat in the darkened theater, did not excite the jealousy of the rest of the company. No, Monique and the others coveted her shoes.

Ballet dancers wore out pair after pair of toe shoes, almost one a week, rehearsing and performing. It was the greatest single expense that the Ballet de Paris had. The slippers on Monique's feet were on their fifth day. As such, the wooden toe-boxes had begun to rub hard against her skin as their meager padding wore away. She wouldn't be surprised when she took them off later to discover blood covering her toes. No dancer showed her unshod feet in polite company. Their toes became misshapen, and the scarred, ridged flesh seemed at odds with the beauty and grace of the dancer above. But Henriette's perfect shoes of bright red silk never hurt her. They never wore out. She could depend upon them to bear her up through the longest and most complicated recitals. While the others sat in the wings and importuned the shoemakers to hurry and fit them next, Henriette was able to continue flitting, leaping, and spinning.

As the principal female *danseuse*, naturally Henriette would be given the most beautiful costumes, shimmering silk sewn with priceless Bruges lace and studded with jewels, crystals, pearls, and gold. Her partner, Jean-Marie, with his sweep of dark, wavy hair and deep-set dark blue eyes, was so handsome that Monique's breath caught in her chest whenever she saw him. But those shoes! Monique knew that if she had them, she could dance across the very stars.

It was almost impossible to concentrate with those beautiful shoes twinkling before her. As the tallest of the junior dancers, she performed in the center of the tableau behind Henriette, so it was unavoidable that the principal ballerina would not constantly be in her eyeline. Monique did her best to ignore the shoes, pretending that they were made of hot coals or burning pitch, or a network of poisonous red spiders, and that every step Henriette took brought her closer and closer to a painful death. The brilliant smile Henriette wore wasn't a smile at all, but a rictus, a grimace, a stifled scream. But, no. It was a smile of supreme satisfaction in her work, and not a little because of the knowledge that the rest of the company envied her so much they would bleed pea green if poked with a pin.

In contrast to the illusion of perfection that it appeared to be from the audience, the ethereal images of Fairyland were no thicker than a piece of wood. Only Henriette was the untouchable fairy princess she seemed to be. People from across Paris and beyond came to sit in the darkness and watch her spin and soar. The music died away and the company came to a halt. Monique could hardly contain her jealousy as the watchers in the darkness were moved to applause. The ballet master dismissed the company with a sharp clap of his hands.

"Return at three, without fail!" he commanded.

The dancers didn't hesitate, lest they be called back individually for criticism. Monique and the others retreated down the stairs into the crowded dressing room and sat down to undo their shoes. Monique, Kerry, and their friends gossiped among themselves. They giggled together about the pianist, whose mistakes seemed to be the results of an excess of wine the night before, and discussed plans for lunch. The cafés to the north and south of the theater awaited, with meals that were nourishing but not too heavy, nor too expensive for a junior dancer's purse. The cobblers and costumiers rushed to the benches to measure the dancers for new shoes and costumes. Monique was at the far end of the line nearest the door. The cobblers would not reach her for an hour. She watched out of the door as a cluster of reporters and admirers surrounded Henriette, standing before her solo dressing room. The prima ballerina nodded and smiled, responding to their compliments and accepting bouquets of red and pink roses.

"I saw the way you stared at Mlle. Henriette's shoes," a low and raspy voice said. "What would you give for them?"

Monique looked up in alarm. Before her stood a gray man. His suit was gray, as was his hair. Holding fast to the bridge of his pale nose was a pair of pince nez with silver rims. His upright collar of pure white was tied with a silver ribbon. His boots, too, were silver gray, and shimmered as though no speck of dust or mud would dare to adhere to them. He looked like a ghost in the backstage shadows.

"Who are you to care?" Monique asked, tossing her head in defiance.

"I am one who might be able to grant your wish," the man said. He pursed his thin, pale lips in a tiny smile. She noticed then that behind his spectacles, his eyes were of two different colors. One was as gray as his hair. The other was almost golden bronze. "If you will permit me to introduce myself, mademoiselle, I am Monsieur Thierry de Raymond." He handed her a small square of pristine white pasteboard. On it was the single word, "Inventor."

Monique regarded it curiously.

"What do you invent, monsieur?" she asked.

"Wonders. I have been commissioned to create a dancing doll after the image of Mademoiselle Henriette. One cannot doubt the marvel that she is, but I have been more captivated by you."

"Why?"

"Answer my first question, then I will answer some of yours, perhaps. Those shoes. What would you do for them?"

Monique stared as Henriette's feet clad in the exquisite red silk pumps disappeared behind her dressing room door, and it felt as though a part of her heart was torn away.

"Anything!" she burst out.

"What would you give for them?" the gray man asked.

"Anything!"

"Your soul?"

Monique glared up at him. He regarded her with curiosity and a hint of worry.

"What is my soul worth compared with those shoes?" she demanded. "They will make me the perfect dancer!"

"But that is in the wrong order, mademoiselle," he said gently. "You will never have those shoes until you can outdance Henriette, and that will never happen in your lifetime. Her every move is already perfection." The man's eyes widened behind his curious glasses. "But I can assist you. If you will become my mistress, I will ensure that you will become the principal ballerina of the company. Your dancing will be flawless, and the red shoes will be yours."

Monique peered at him. Men of means, and women, too, often sought lovers from among the ballet company. The dancers' bodies provoked great interest from the public, who sometimes saw them as goods on display for purchase. Bargains had been struck, to good results on both sides, but she had also heard of dreams that were shattered the morning after. Still, she had risen as high as she could in her present circumstances. What harm could it do? He was far from her ideal, being too old and too homely, with his narrow shoulders, protuberant front teeth, weak chin, and receding hairline, but if he could help her to achieve her dream, he was good enough. The kindness in his eyes appealed to her. But she held her head high.

"I will not trade myself for an illusion," she said. "I'll agree to your terms, but you may only have me once I have become the principal ballerina of this company."

The man's small mouth pursed again, and his mismatched eyes twinkled.

"Agreed, Mademoiselle Monique. I will not fail you. After tonight's performance, then?"

She emerged from the theater late that night in her best dress, a tightly-corseted russet gown with a bustle under a cream lace jacket with a peplum that emphasized her small waist, and high-buttoned shoes that were more comfortable but no less constricting than her dancing slippers. The high, closed black-sided carriage into which M. de Raymond helped her on the street behind the theater that night had no horses or driver. He flicked a bronze switch that brought the steam-driven engine at its rear rumbling to life, and climbed into the box with her. It glided off over the cobblestoned streets, whirring and clicking as if it was talking to itself.

"How does it know where to go?" she asked, marveling at the smoothness of the ride.

He smiled.

"I have instructed its mechanism to follow the same roads that we took coming here," he said. "It knows when to turn, when to slow down and stop, and how to recognize an obstruction in the road, even one as small as a cat. That is the genius, if you will permit me, of my inventions. It will repeat known motions perfectly each time I require it."

"I must be back in my residence by eleven, or they will cast me out and I will lose my position in the company," she said, a trifle nervous. She wished she could see out, but appreciated the privacy. If she was to make an utter fool of herself that night, the fewer witnesses the better. Small bronze lamps glimmered on each wall of the car. M. de Raymond kept a respectful distance from her on the padded, oxblood leather seat.

"Do not fear. I will not destroy your dreams. Only you can give up on them. Are you certain you wish to do this?" He peered at her. There was a weird cast to his left eye. Then she realized it was not a real eye. The iris opened and closed with the tiniest of bronze metal gears. A frisson of fear chilled her belly, but she refused to show the dread she felt.

"I am," she declared.

The carriage came to a halt. She looked around curiously as he assisted her out of the car. They were in the circular drive of a chateau, a handsome edifice with a high tiled roof and gables. Warm light gleamed from sparklingly clean windows. As they approached the door, it opened soundlessly. No servant leaned out, but a chime pinged in the darkness. Ensconced lights illuminated themselves one after another, shedding warm yellow light on paintings in gold frames, alabaster sculptures, and numerous machines whose use she could not begin to guess. A huge double staircase rose up toward a carved wooden gallery of surpassing beauty. Monique inhaled scents of honeyed wax and lavender.

A voice erupted from a black, cloth-covered speaker near the entry hall.

"M. de Raymond, do you require anything?"

"Brandy and tea, Mme. Gruber. In my workroom, if you please."

"At once, sir."

Instead of leading her up the grand stairs, he opened a green baize door and escorted her down a set of narrow stone steps to a cellar. It, too, was different than what she expected. Instead of the earthy smells of roots and the mold that encrusted port bottles set down to mature, the room reeked of machine oil and hot metal. Lights went on here, too, as they approached, shedding their gleam upon huge standing devices made of blackened steel with vicious-looking silver saw blades and drill bits. The most lights stood around a huge worktable scattered with hand tools, curls of copper wire and bronze gears. In the corner, enclosed by panes of glass three inches thick, was a steam generator. Curled tubes of metal spiraled out of the top of the enclosure and branched out to the various pieces of equipment. M. de Raymond opened the bottom of the enclosure and fed logs into the small furnace at its base.

Monique felt hemmed in by all of the equipment. It seemed such an impersonal space, but M. de Raymond clucked and puttered about as though it was a garden. She felt for a moment as though someone watched her. She looked up into a pair of staring blue eyes. She jumped, then realized it was a half-constructed human figure about two feet tall. To her shock, the china face looked exactly like Henriette. This was his commissioned invention.

Another chime sounded, this one much closer by, and a hatch in the wall slid upward. Behind it was a brass tray. Upon it were a Sevigny tea service, two cups, two balloon glasses, and a cut-crystal decanter. M. de Raymond did not move to take it. Instead, it emerged from the hatch on rows of small brass wheels. When it reached the edge of the counter, it extended those wheels until it touched the worktable, then glided over the intervening gap like a boy stepping neatly over a puddle. She half expected the tray to serve them, but M. de Raymond did the honors, giving her a generous snifter of brandy as well as a cup of steaming tea.

"To our mutual pleasure," he said, with his strange, pursed little smile. They drank, then he set the tray aside. "I must take all your measurements, now. Take off your dress and your shoes." When she hesitated, he shook his head. "Come, come, Mademoiselle Monique. You wear less for costume fittings. Please. I will not hurt you. I admire you and want to grant your wish. Stand still, please."

He put on a massive magnifying lens that made his golden eye the size of her head. Working with the tiniest of tools, he had her stand up and strike poses. In her underthings, Monique felt awkward, like the clockwork doll that regarded her glassily from the other side of the room.

"Your arms are good," he said, exercising her elbow and raising it up and down. His hands were gentle but very strong. "I shall not have to manipulate them. Your legs, on the other hand, will require plenty of guidance to learn to work properly."

Monique snorted at the insult.

"What would you know of a dancer's skills?" she asked, in an icy tone. He peered at her through the immense magnifying glass, and his golden eye's pupil widened into a gaping chasm that seemed as if it would swallow her.

"I am the maker of the greatest clockworks in the entire world," he said. "I was educated in China and Switzerland. I surpassed all my masters, and the cost of my education was one of my eyes. I didn't mind, because the one I have now is perfection itself. I know, because my eye calculates the niceties of what is an ideal angle or an ideal range of motion. I watch movement, and I can reproduce it in every detail. Now, hold still."

He ran his hands up and down her legs. She was afraid that he would break his promise and attempt to seduce her there and then, but he treated her as though she was another clockwork doll. She lifted her feet on his command, turned, held one leg out, then the other. He measured and clucked and hummed to himself, absorbed in his task. After a time, she relaxed. He was very kind, if a little strange. Every so often, the unfinished mannequin would catch her eye, and she shuddered.

Yet a third chime came, this one pinging ten times. M. de Raymond took off his magnifying lens and stood up.

"Hurry and dress," he said. "I must take you home now."

Instead of allowing the carriage to run by itself, he had Monique guide him through the streets of Paris to the humble boarding house where she lived with twenty of the other girls from the company. The clock in the hallway lacked ten minutes of the dangerous hour. Monique almost collapsed with relief. He had kept his promise to get her home safe. M. de Raymond was an honorable man.

The other three girls who shared her room demanded details of her late-night rendezvous, but she put them off with an enigmatic little smile. What could she say? That a strange little man had offered to fulfill her dreams?

Three days went by before she saw him again, sitting in the audience during afternoon rehearsal. He had a sketch pad on which he jotted quick notes as the company went through its paces. Once in a while, Monique caught the glint of his golden eye. He was not watching her, but Henriette, with her perfect choreography, in those perfect shoes. For the next week, he appeared in the same seat in the middle of Row Six. Monique was jealous and curious, but he never approached her. The most acknowledgement she got from him was the occasional preoccupied nod, as he sketched and made notes. When on the seventh night he beckoned to her outside the stage door, she all but ran to him.

"Where have you been?" she demanded.

"Granting your wish," he said. He smiled and guided her to his carriage. "Please. I am eager to have you see."

In the middle of his cellar workroom, the oddest objects awaited her. A pair of shoes made of bronze, with what looked like the ghost of a pair of legs extending upward from them, a web work of thin golden wires, stood upon a pedestal. The soles of the gleaming shoes were made of smooth suede, which would not slip on the stage. They looked strange but also of surpassing beauty, like the designs on the Palais des Artes. At his direction, she took off her shoes and outer garments. He helped her to slide the contraption onto her legs. Instead of having to lace the shoes around her ankles, the shoes seemed to clamp against her skin. The wires themselves wound underneath her bloomers almost all the way to her bottom. She thought at first the wires would be pliable, but they stiffened on contact with her flesh. At her ankles, knees, and hips, there were clockwork joints, gears, and flywheels, but as tiny as those in a fine watch. They would be invisible under her tights. Strangely, the shoes and their attendant gadgetry felt perfectly comfortable, as though they were a part of her body.

"They are strong enough to steer your legs in the directions that they need to go," he explained. "The gears operate on a perpetual-motion cycle. As you move, you power the engine in each toe, giving them the energy to follow the choreography in which they have been instructed." He opened a large phonograph, wound it up, and engaged the needle on the revolving wax cylinder. The thin strains that issued from the horn were of Adolphe Adam's immortal composition, Giselle's solo to free her lover from the evil Willis. "Now, dance!"

Feeling a little embarrassed in the stark workroom, Monique set herself into the first position, and launched herself into the footwork. She jeted and pirouetted, achieved leaps and arabesques, all in perfect time to the music. When she came a little short on a leap, or did not stretch far enough, the wires around her legs pulled her farther. She stumbled, but the shoes set her right again, smoothly carrying her into the next step.

"What are they doing?" she demanded, her feet turning on their toes in tiny fluttering steps. "I am doing the steps correctly."

"But without inspiration," M. de Raymond said. His golden eye narrowed, but his expression was kindly.

"Inspiration?"

"This is the difference between you and Henriette," he said, shaking his head. "She immerses herself fully in the dance. I have instructed the shoes in the way she takes her steps. She is a genius of motion." He lifted the phonograph needle and reapplied it to the end of the cylinder. "Again. This time, you will see."

And Monique did see. Where she fell short, the shoes urged her on, steering her this way and that, as if she was M. de Raymond's horseless carriage. The shoes were not made as ordinary toe shoes. Instead, they appeared to be of hundreds of small segments, lifting her to the heights or flexing to help her spin and leap. It was a revelation. She felt uplifted by the perfection of their movements.

"They are amazing, monsieur!" she exclaimed, and threw herself into the dance.

The tiredness of the day fell away, and she felt energized and inspired. The shoes taught her as no dance master had ever been able to. Every little motion was measured and corrected. He watched her, his eyes bright.

When she finished her third run-through of the solo, M. de Raymond stopped the phonograph.

"That is enough for this evening," he said. "The mechanisms need time to rebuild their charge. Are you satisfied?"

"Oh, yes!" she exclaimed. "They are a marvel! You have my utmost admiration. I am so grateful to you, monsieur."

It was the wrong thing to say, for when he bent to help her off with the shoes, he began to fondle her legs with gentle hands. His eyes, the silver and the gold, were full of hope.

"No," she said, pushing him away with one palm on his shoulder. "I have not yet achieved my dream."

He looked disappointed, but he drew back. "You shall achieve it. I will wait."

With the help of the clockwork shoes, Monique's technique at the next rehearsal was better than any of her previous performances. From the curious eyes upon her, the others were trying to determine what the indefinable something was that made her different than just the day before. Their curiosity lifted her spirits so much that she held her back straighter and her motions became more dramatic than ever, so much so that during the second act, the assistant choreographer disappeared and returned with the director of the company. They watched her intently from the wings, then from the dress circle in the audience. Monique noticed, but her eyes were upon Henriette.

With the shoes' help, once she observed Henriette taking a step, she could duplicate the motion, tweaking a little at a time until she was doing it as well as the prima ballerina herself. That wasn't her opinion alone. During the break, when she was rubbing rosin into the leather soles of the bronze shoes, she began to hear talk from the other dancers.

"She has made a deal with the devil," Kerry whispered, then looked apologetic when Monique glanced her way. Monique felt hurt that her friend would say such a thing, but it had a kernel of truth.

She had made a deal, not with a devil, in truth, but a lowly gremlin. The ugly little man who so desired her favor that he made improvements nightly in the mechanism. The gold wires now rose under her tights up to her waist and pressed against the small of her back.

"Your motions will power the motors endlessly now, without need to recharge," M. de Raymond said. "You need never stop dancing."

With the shoes' help, even the endless repetition with the line of junior dancers felt like a joy. Her body grew more knowledgeable in the subtleties of the dance, and her confidence grew in its wake. Monique wanted to dance all of the time. Even after the nightly performances ended, she was energized enough to skip and pirouette out of the theater. She still slept alone, waiting for the day she would step out of Henriette's shadow.

And then it came.

On Saturday morning, Henriette tried to project her usual *joie de vivre*, but her forehead wrinkled as she executed complicated steps as though she suffered some hidden discomfort. When she sprang across the stage in a tour jete that she had done thousands of times before, she came down on her right foot, and collapsed to the stage. The rest of the company gasped in disbelief.

The assistant ballet master rushed to Henriette's side. The other dancers gathered around. Blood, the same scarlet as its silk, poured from her left shoe. The assistant unwound the silken tapes and revealed the young woman's foot. On the ball beneath her toes was an oozing dark spot the size of a coin.

"A blood blister," he said, in alarm. "Call for the doctor! We must prevent infection."

"It's nothing," Henriette protested, though Monique saw the strain in her forehead and the cords in her neck. "I can go on."

"You must not," the doctor confirmed. The plump man sat back, adjusting his pince nez. "It's a blood blister, probably caused by these infernal shoes." He shook the guilty slippers at her. "You ought to get rid of them."

Monique, close by, almost reached out to take them, but Henriette seized them from his hand and cradled them.

"Oh, no, no, monsieur," the diva protested. "I swear to you, that injury did not come from these. It was my own folly. Last night, I attended three parties in the 8th arrondissement, all with splendid orchestras and irresistible dance floors." She blushed. "I danced with a royal prince—I dare not tell you his name. He would not let me stop."

"Well, I am stopping you, mademoiselle," said the doctor. "You must be off that foot for at least a week, perhaps two."

"Oh, no! But who will go on in my place?" Henriette protested. Monique's heart filled with hope. She met the company director's eye. He smiled at her and put his hand on her shoulder.

"Mlle. Dortmond will. Only until you have recovered."

The staff bustled around Monique, hiding Henriette from her view.

Just like that, she became the understudy. She acquired a private dresser. Within a few days, the management assigned an assistant to escort her to and from her performances. Young girls and handsome young men brought her bouquets of flowers. She was so busy signing autographs and posing for photographs at the stage door every night that she had no time for M. de Raymond. He waited hopefully at the edge of the crowd. At first, she did her best to get free to join him. He took her away to small, exclusive restaurants, where they toasted her success with the finest wines, or to his chateau, where the invisible Mme. Gruber provided excellent food. Monique began to feel pleasantly at home there with him and his strange inventions. He bustled around her, becoming ever more solicitous and generous. But as the throng grew, she found she preferred the adulation of others. She began to ignore his quiet presence in favor of more fashionable and influential visitors. After a time, he didn't come back to the stage door at all. If he was in the audience beyond the footlights, she could not see him there. She had to admit that she was relieved.

The two weeks whirled by in a rush of excitement. The run of *Giselle* finished, and they began rehearsals for a new ballet for the autumn, *La*

Fille de Marbre. With the help of her wonderful shoes, she was able to reproduce the moves set by the choreographer flawlessly on the first or second try.

"I did not know we had such a phoenix among the geese," the choreographer said, very pleased. The other dancers were not so delighted by Monique's advancement. She was hurt that they couldn't share her joy, but put it down to jealousy. Heaven knew she had felt the same.

Because Monique had begun rehearsing as the diva in the new tableaux, Henriette had no place when she returned. The former prima ballerina refused to be relegated to the line of dancers, and disappeared a few days later. The red silk shoes disappeared with her, but Monique didn't care. She had her own unique footgear that was becoming the envy of Paris.

"I heard a rumor that Henriette has gone to the Commedia del'Arte in Milan," Kerry giggled to a circle of confidants in the main dressing room. "She will have to start out as a junior dancer once again. It will be so humiliating!"

Hearing the companionable laughter, Monique attempted to join the gossip, but the others fell silent. They regarded her—not coldly, but at a distance. She backed away, stung, but tried to keep her head high. What did it matter? She was the greatest dancer in the company, undoubtedly in all of Paris!

"Oh, Mademoiselle Monique, a reporter from *Le Monde* is here to interview you!" her assistant chirped, taking her by the arm and escorting her back to her dressing room. Everyone wanted to hear about Monique, the girl who had stepped forward from the line to become the star. She never revealed the filigree of wires around her legs, and her dresser was bribed heavily and sworn to secrecy as to the *Art Nouveau* contraption Monique wore under her costume.

La Fille premiered to a glorious reception. Flashbulbs went off whenever she stepped out of the stage door, and followed her to her horse-drawn taxi. On the warm summer nights, she went to reception after ball after private dinner with handsome aristocrats, and enjoyed every minute of her celebrity. She even performed at a grand gala thrown by Lady Catie Tandy, the celebrated British beauty. What did it matter that Monique's former friends scarcely spoke to her? She was the prima ballerina of the Ballet de Paris. Artists sketched her; sculptors begged her to pose for them. Noblemen brought her flowers and expensive gifts.

They whispered in her ear, begging for her favors, to put her into an *apartment mueble,* to carry her off to a chateau in the countryside for a lifetime of passion. Their attention was titillating, but Monique was no fool. She put them all off, waiting for just the right offer.

But one night, her taxi was not waiting. Instead, the closed carriage awaited her. M. de Raymond stood beside it, his thin, pale face beaming. Monique felt cold shock, as if water had been thrown in her face. She had not expected to see him. He presented her with an armload of red roses.

"Congratulations, mademoiselle," he said, kissing her hand. "You have achieved your dream. Now, lovely lady, keep your promise and allow me to achieve mine."

Their agreement came back to her in a rush. She felt color mount to her cheeks. She had made a bargain, but it was a bad bargain.

"I'm sorry, M. de Raymond," Monique said, holding her head high on her slender neck. "I regret, but I value myself too highly to become a mere mistress. That is out of the question."

"You are quite right," M. de Raymond said, with a definite nod. "Such an arrangement would demean you, and that is far from my intentions. We have spent pleasant hours together, and I have come to care deeply for you. Dear Mademoiselle Monique, I want you to marry me. Will you?"

Monique was even more taken aback at that thought. She felt a wave of revulsion overwhelm her.

"Marry you! You're a toad. I could have a marquis! Men are throwing themselves at my feet! Men far richer and far more handsome than you."

"What about your part of the bargain? You promised me your love in exchange for success," he said, a trifle of color creeping into his pale cheeks.

She tossed her head. "I do not sell myself. You have my gratitude."

"But without me, you would not have this triumph," M. de Raymond protested. Both his eyes, the silver and the gold, widened. For the first time since she had known him, he looked angry.

"But I have earned it. I no longer need your help," she said, denying the small voice at the back of her mind that agreed with him. "I have become the dancer I always knew I could be." She thrust the roses back into his arms. "Please, monsieur. Do not contact me again. I will see to it that you receive adequate remuneration for your device. But it is not worth my body and my love."

His eyes flashed. He dropped the roses on the pavement, and drove away, leaving her on her own.

After much private consideration, she made a very private sale of superfluous jewelry and other gifts from her many admirers. From its proceeds, she sent M. de Raymond two thousand francs, a princely sum. He ought to be satisfied with that. Monique was relieved not to have his strange golden eye upon her night after night. She had enough to concern her.

Her new position excited jealousy among her former colleagues. They whispered about black magic and deals with the devil behind her back. Her scented dusting powder on her dressing room table was substituted with chalk, and messages for her began to go awry.

Dancers she thought were her friends began to lay traps for her, such as spilling liquid in the wings just where she would step off and bound onto the stage. If it was not for the suede soles and the clever gears of her shoes, she would have fallen flat on her face in the beginning of the second act. No doubt some of them, Kerry in particular, intended to trip her up so one of them could go on in her place. But the shoes would not let Monique fail. She stumbled, but the framework around her lower body controlled her movements and brought her back into line almost before the eye could blink.

Kerry gawked in astonishment at her recovery, and made the sign against the evil eye with her fingers. The others saw it and copied it, some with glee on their faces.

It had been a perfect performance. The audience had erupted with deafening applause, but no one came to celebrate it with her. The whispers spread to the crowd of gentlemen admirers, who began to eye her askance. All the invitations that she anticipated went unoffered. On a Friday night in summertime Paris, she was left in the theater all by herself.

Monique was hurt by her isolation, and returned home to the boarding house to sit alone in her room. The shoes were her only true companions. The little gears in the framework seemed to wink at her, inviting her to touch the curves of the wires, the brilliant pliability of the bronze clockwork shoes.

As there was no one around, she put the dancing shoes back on. When the wires fastened against her skin, the toes began to tap. All by herself, in the small room, the shoes took her on a new dance, whirling and leaping. How clever they were! They could choreograph all by themselves. Monique danced until she was exhausted, then climbed into bed before her roommates returned. She did not care what they thought.

Monique's foes glared at her as she returned to the stage the next morning. Kerry could not conceal her disgust that the oil had not sent her flying. No, her performance had been so perfect and evocative that it had garnered headlines in the press. The assistant dance master came to have her autograph a copy of the day's paper to place in the box office, so all could see the new prima ballerina's fame. Monique enjoyed the surge of pride it evoked in her heart. She had become famous across Paris, perhaps the world! The rest of the company all saw it there. The jealousy felt like a miasma in the theater, as much a part of the odor as the sweat and chalk.

The management treated her as though she was a precious jewel.

"We should have M. de Raymond create a clockwork doll in your likeness," the company director said, as she took refreshment during the afternoon break. "One that dances with your spectacular precision."

So he did not know of her former connection to the inventor. Monique smiled, her pleasure increased by the look of disgust on the faces of her fellow colleagues through the door of her dressing room.

But as she made her way up the stairs to the stage to resume rehearsal, a body hurtled down toward her. It struck Monique and knocked her head over heels. She fell the rest of the way to the basement floor. Her dresser and two of the stage hands helped her up.

"Oh, how clumsy of me!" Kerry said, moving in as if to help her. She stepped heavily on Monique's foot with the wooden toe of her shoe, evoking a cry of pain from Monique as her instep was crushed. The shoe let out a weird screech, as if it was also hurt. "I am an oaf, an elephant! Are you all right?"

Monique refused to show weakness, even though her right foot throbbed with pain.

"Yes, thank you for your solicitousness," Monique said, keeping her face sweet and composed. "All is well."

All was not well, however. The dance master called the company to order. Monique took her position in the center of the stage, waiting for instruction, but her right foot began to twitch. She thought it was only the bruise, but her foot moved by itself. The mechanism encasing her right leg lifted it into the air and pointed it out to the rear in an arabesque. Giggles erupted from behind her.

"Stand still, please!" the master called. "Wait for the music!"

"Yes, monsieur," Monique said, and composed herself again. But her feet refused to cooperate. They twitched again, then rose to their toes and did a little pirouette. No matter how many times she was admonished, she could not hold her feet still. The master fell into a terrible rage.

"Do you think that because you are the principal *danseuse* you are permitted to make a mockery of this company?" he bellowed.

"No, monsieur," Monique said, then executed a full turn and a jete. "I am so sorry. I didn't mean to do that." The master pointed furiously to the wings.

"Leave the stage! You are dismissed for the day!"

Monique tried to keep her dignity as she left, but her feet continued to leap and spin, all with utter perfection, all the way off the stage. Laughter pursued her down the stairs and out of the theater. No one looked sympathetic or rueful at her disgrace. She had no friends left.

As she flitted from foot to foot, kicking and stepping, her dresser summoned a taxi. Monique's feet drummed impatiently against the carriage's floor all the way back to her rooms. They kicked and turned, making it almost impossible to climb the stairs and enter the house. As soon as she was in private, she stripped off the mechanism and threw it against the wall. What had Kerry done to it? The bronze shoes flipped and flopped where she had flung them like a pair of fish.

She was so upset that she stayed barricaded in her room, hoping that none of her roommates would return until she had regained her composure. Still, toward evening, a tapping came at the door.

"Mlle. Monique?" her landlady's voice said. "A messenger from the Baron du Lacplessis sent an envelope. He requests an immediate reply."

"Tell him to go away!" Monique cried. She leaped up and shut the twitching shoes in her trunk. "I am unwell."

She took to her bed and pulled the covers over her head. The landlady was a kindly woman. She brought a tray of soup laced with brandy. The shoes kicked at the walls of their prison.

"What is that noise?" the old woman asked.

"I don't know, Madame," Monique said, affecting an air of puzzlement. "Perhaps a rat?"

The landlady left, shaking her head.

What could she do? Monique stared at the vibrating case. She should bring them back to M. de Raymond, but she was too ashamed to face him. How could she return to the theater the next day? She had learned so much from the repetition and adjustments that the shoes had put her through, but they were the perfect dancer, not she.

Her roommates were careful not to talk of her disgrace in front of her, but they shot humorous glances in her direction. Monique pulled her covers up over her head and pretended to sleep.

She dreamed of dancing on the stage, with all eyes upon her. They called her back again and again for more curtain calls. Bouquets were thrown onto the stage. Instead of picking them up, she leaped over each one. How strange! Then frigid air gusted into the theater, blowing her out into the street. Monique hugged herself against the cold.

Then she woke up. To her horror, she realized she was in the middle of the Rue de Boudreau in the dark in her night dress! The shoes were on her feet, pulling her along. They twirled and leaped, and she had no choice but to go along with them. She stumbled toward a bench, but they kept her upright, inexorably trotting and pirouetting down the street.

In vain Monique attempted to steer the shoes. She knew the way to M. de Raymond's fine home, to the northwest of the city, but the shoes seemed intent on flying southward. They took her down the Place d'le Opera, through the garden of the Tuileries, and toward the Pont des Artes. Horses pulling late-night carriages screamed as she dipped under their noses and up onto the opposite pavement. From the waist down, Monique's body did not belong to her.

How had the shoes been put back on her feet? Had one of her roommates found them and dressed her in the metal harness as a joke?

Or, more likely the shoes themselves crept out of the box and fastened themselves upon her. With their design corrupted by damage, they wanted to keep on dancing and dancing. M. de Raymond told her that her body supplied their power. They would not let her go until she died!

Monique twirled and whirled through Paris, unable to stop even when she was exhausted. The framework resisted every effort to dislodge it from her flesh, and the flywheels turned as she breathed.

The sun rose over the tiled roofs and black wrought iron balconies. Dogs barked at her and chased her through the cobblestoned streets. Children laughed and threw rubbish at her. All this was because she had lost sight of her vision of a bright future in the spotlight. She wept, pleading for help from passersby. Some men tried to catch her and bring her to a halt, but her legs kicked out, catching them in the face or the crotch. They let her go, with curses. There was no curse greater than the one that already made her suffer. Her feet began to bleed. Soon all the flesh would have been worn away from her bones.

How could she not have been kinder to Kerry and the others on her rise to the top? They could have remained her allies. And poor M. de Raymond! How cruel she had been to him. Even as her legs took her into a series of leaps and jetes, she put her hands together in prayer.

"God, if you have any mercy for a poor sinner, hear my plea!" she cried. "I am sorry for my arrogance! I should have been happy to keep my place in the line, behind the diva. Spare me, and I will be a humble servant to You hereafter."

The shoes took her toward the bridge leading toward the Lyons road, past delivery vans and tourists entering the city. They gawked and laughed at her. A photographer from *Le Monde* came up beside her on a two-passenger, steam-driven tricycle. Instead of responding to her cries for help, he leaned out from behind the driver and took a photograph of her with a huge box camera. The flashbulb blinded her. After that, she did not care where the shoes carried her. Her humiliation was complete. That photograph would be in the evening paper. No one would ever see her as the prima ballerina again, but as a laughingstock. The shame made her want to die.

Hour after hour on the country roads soaked by summer rains left her covered with mud neck to toe. She was hungry and thirsty, but could not stop for food or water. Night approached. She had been dancing for nearly twenty-four hours, and her numb legs were caked with dried blood. At last, she had red shoes like Henriette. Monique laughed bitterly at the irony.

Ahead, she spotted the span of a bridge. If she grabbed the handrail as she passed over it, she could pull herself up on it and fling herself into the water. She and the shoes would sink into the fast-flowing stream, never to be seen again. The timing would be tricky, but she was used to counting beats and preparing for the moment. This would be her last dance, and thank God for it!

Thirty yards. The shoes still leaped and tiptoed, in their own choreography. Twenty. Monique held her hands ready. The rail was painted blue. It was odd how she focused upon that. Ten. Eternity waited.

Hoot-hoot!

A sound from behind distracted her from self-destruction. The shoes made her spin in place. As an angel descending from heaven, she saw M. de Raymond's carriage approaching. It pulled up alongside her, then blocked her. Two arms made of bronze reached out from the front of the box and held her fast. M. de Raymond leaped out.

"I have been looking for you," he cried. "It was only because I saw your picture in the paper that I knew where you had gone."

"Thank God for you!" Monique exclaimed. Her legs kicked fiercely. M. de Raymond took one of his small tools. Trapping her right foot under his arm, he plunged the tine into the toe mechanism. The gears stopped turning, and the framework around her body fell away.

"I am sorry," Monique said, her heart in her eyes, then collapsed.

When she awoke, she was in a bed covered with clean white sheets. M. de Raymond stood on one side, and a learned-looking doctor with a stern expression was on the other. Her legs throbbed with pain. They felt as heavy as lead weights.

"Your feet are very badly injured, mademoiselle," he told her. "You will never dance again."

"I do not want to," she said. The doctor retired, shaking his head. M. de Raymond took her hand in both of his. The golden eye looked sympathetic.

"You were kind to come all that way for me," Monique said, her heart full of regret and appreciation. "Never in all these months did I say thank you. Thank you. Thank you for the gift, and thank you for taking it away again. It doesn't matter who wears the shoes. Such beauty can corrupt the wearer and make her forget how to be grateful."

"It doesn't matter," M. de Raymond said, pursing his lips in his tiny smile. She realized how she had missed that strange little expression. "You enjoyed them, for a while."

"Give me time to recover, then I will depart," Monique said. His kindness made her feel uncomfortable. She had been so cruel. Now she felt worthless. "Surely there will be some small job I can do now that I can't dance."

"But why leave?" he asked.

"Well, you won't want me, now that I'm no longer the prima ballerina," Monique said.

"Ah," he said, taking both her hands. The golden eye glinted. "That was your condition, not mine. I do still want you. If you will have me."

As soon as her feet were healed, they were married. M. de Raymond remade the shoes so they would carry her up the aisle, clad in a long white silk dress with a veil studded with more pearls and gems than any costume she had ever worn. She had never felt prouder to wear any garment.

That night, after the wedding feast, they went to see the ballet. They sat in a booth next to the President of the Republic. The shoes went on at the center of the stage of the Paris Opera Ballet company. They performed by themselves, like disembodied, golden ghost legs, without a person in them. They did everything perfectly, and Monique applauded with all the others of the audience, content to admire them from afar.

About the Authors

Danny Birt has been a contributing author to several sci-fi, fantasy, and professional magazines, anthologies, and journals, as well as a writer for an app. Formerly, he was an editor for Flashing Swords Magazine and Ancient Tomes Press, and is now a freelance editor. Most recently, Danny's 2014 short story *To Thy Sylph Be True* was recognized by Tangent Online as a Two-Starred Recommended Read. In addition to literary publication, he composes classical and filk music, such as his nonstop hour-long piano solo "Piano Petrissage," and the ever-peculiar album "Warped Children's Songs." Danny's humorous music has been featured on radio and internet programs such as The Dr. Demento Show and The Funny Music Project. He's also performed in ensemble at Carnegie Hall.

Career hats Danny has worn other than author, editor, and composer include being a music therapist, a massage therapist, a college instructor and program director, and an on-screen actor.

Currently he lives in the Shenandoah Valley in Virginia with his wife and kiddo, where he owns and operates an integrative therapy business.

James Chambers writes tales of horror, crime, fantasy, and science fiction. He is the author of *The Engines of Sacrifice*, a collection of four Lovecraftian-inspired novellas published by Dark Regions Press which Publisher's Weekly described in a starred-review as "...chillingly evocative...." He is also the author of the short fiction collections *Resurrection House* (Dark Regions Press) and *The Midnight Hour: Saint Lawn Hill and Other Tales*, in collaboration with illustrator Jason Whitley as well as the dark, urban fantasy novella, *Three Chords of Chaos* and *The Dead Bear Witness* and *Tears of Blood*, volume one and two in his Corpse Fauna novella series. His short stories have been published in the anthologies *The Avenger: Roaring Heart of the Crucible*, *Bad-Ass Faeries*, *Bad-Ass Faeries 2: Just Plain Bad*, *Bad-Ass Faeries 3: In All Their Glory*, *Bad-Ass Faeries 4: It's Elemental*, *Bad Cop No Donut*, *Barbarians at the Jumpgate*, *Breach the Hull*, *By Other Means*, *Chiral Mad 2*, *Clockwork Chaos*, *Crypto-Critters (Volume 1 and 2)*, *Dark Furies*, *The Dead Walk*, *The Dead Walk Again*, *Deep Cuts*, *The Domino Lady: Sex as a Weapon*, *Dragon's Lure*, *Fantastic Futures 13*, *The Green Hornet Chronicles*, *Hardboiled Cthulhu*, *Hear Them Roar*, *Hellfire Lounge*, *In An Iron Cage*, *Lost Worlds of Space and Time (Volume 1)*, *Mermaids 13*, *New Blood*, *No Longer Dreams*, *Shadows Over Main Street*, *Sick: An Anthology of Illness*, *So It Begins*, *The Spider: Extreme Prejudice*, *Qualia*

Nous, To Hell in a Fast Car, Truth or Dare, TV Gods, Walrus Tales, Weird Trails, Warfear, and With Great Power; the chapbook *Mooncat Jack;* and the magazines *Bare Bone, Cthulhu Sex,* and *Allen K's Inhuman.*

His tale "A Wandering Blackness," one of two published in Lin Carter's Doctor Anton Zarnak, Occult Detective, received an honorable mention in The Year's Best Fantasy and Horror, Sixteenth Annual Collection. He has also edited and written numerous comic books including Leonard Nimoy's Primortals, the critically acclaimed "The Revenant" in Shadow House, and "The Midnight Hour" in the anthology Negative Burn. He is a member of the Horror Writers Association, the current chair of its membership committee, and recipient of the 2012 Richard Laymon Award. He lives in New York.

Elaine Corvidae has worked as an office assistant, archaeologist, and raptor rehabilitator, but she always wanted to be a writer. Her fantasy novels have been praised by reviewers and readers alike, and have won the Dream Realm and Eppie awards. She lives near Charlotte, NC, with her husband and several cats.

Kelly A. Harmon used to write truthful, honest stories about authors and thespians, senators and statesmen, movie stars and murderers. Now she writes lies, which is infinitely more satisfying, but lacks the convenience of doorstep delivery. She is an award-winning journalist and author, and a member of the Science Fiction & Fantasy Writers of America. A Baltimore native, she writes the Charm City Darkness series, which includes the novels *Stoned in Charm City, A Favor for a Fiend,* and the soon to be published, *A Blue Collar Proposition.* Her science fiction and fantasy stories can be found in *Triangulation: Dark Glass, Hellebore and Rue,* and *Deep Cuts: Mayhem, Menace and Misery.*

Ms. Harmon is a former newspaper reporter and editor, and now edits for Pole to Pole Publishing, a small Baltimore publisher. She is co-editor of *Hides the Dark Tower* along with Vonnie Winslow Crist.

For more information, visit her blog at http://kellyaharmon.com, or, find her on Facebook and Twitter: http://facebook.com/Kelly-A-Harmon1, https://twitter.com/kellyaharmon.

Jonah Knight is a multiple time musical guest of honor at various SF/F conventions up and down the east coast, from The Steampunk World's Fair to his home base at MarsCon. The songs on his six (soon to be seven) albums range from supernatural steampunk to creepy

Christmas to paranormal modern folk. Although primarily known for his music these days, he spent three seasons in the Kennedy Center's playwright training program and had a number of his plays produced around the country as well as an official performance at the Faust International Theatre Festival in Hong Kong. He occasionally takes a break from writing music to work on a script or short story. His music can be heard all over the internet including www.jonahknight.com. He lives in Frederick, MD, though not for too much longer.

Gail Z. Martin is the author of *Vendetta: A Deadly Curiosities Novel* in her urban fantasy series set in Charleston, SC (Solaris Books); *Shadow and Flame* the fourth and final book in the Ascendant Kingdoms Saga (Orbit Books); *The Shadowed Path* (Solaris Books) and *Iron and Blood* co-authored with Larry N. Martin.

She is also author of *Ice Forged, Reign of Ash* and *War of Shadows* in The Ascendant Kingdoms Saga, The Chronicles of The Necromancer series (*The Summoner, The Blood King, Dark Haven, Dark Lady's Chosen*); The Fallen Kings Cycle (*The Sworn, The Dread*) and the urban fantasy novel *Deadly Curiosities*. Gail writes three ebook series: *The Jonmarc Vahanian Adventures, The Deadly Curiosities Adventures* and *The Blaine McFadden Adventures. The Storm & Fury Adventures*, steampunk stories, are co-authored with Larry N. Martin.

Larry N. Martin is the co-author of the new Steampunk series *Iron and Blood: The Jake Desmet Adventures* and a series of short stories: *The Storm & Fury Adventures* set in the Jake Desmet universe. These short stories also appear in the anthologies *Clockwork Universe: Steampunk vs. Aliens, The Weird Wild West, The Side of Good/The Side of Evil, Alien Artifacts,* and *Cinched: Imagination Unbound* with more to come. Larry and Gail also have science fiction short stories in the *Space, Contact Light* and *Robots* anthologies and a new Steampunk novella, *Grave Voices*.

Much to his embarrassment, **Bernie Mojzes** has outlived Lord Byron, Percy Shelley, Janice Joplin and the Red Baron, without even once having been shot down over Morlancourt Ridge. Having failed to achieve a glorious martyrdom, he has instead turned his hand to the penning of prose, in the pathetic hope that he shall here find the notoriety that has thus far proven elusive. In his copious free time, he co-edits and publishes *Unlikely Story* (www.unlikely-story.com).

Christine Norris is the author of several YA works, including *A Curse of Ash and Iron* and the *Library of Athena* series. She is overeducated; however, she has never flown an airship. She has a complete weakness for British television, as well as an addiction to movies, re-told fairy tales, and police procedural shows. She also believes in fairies.

Jody Lynn Nye lists her main career activity as 'spoiling cats.' When not engaged upon this worthy occupation, she writes fantasy and science fiction books and short stories.

Since 1987 she has published over 45 books and more than 140 short stories. Her newest books are *Rhythm of the Imperium*, third in the Lord Thomas Kinago series; an e-collection of cat stories, *Cats Triumphant!* (Event Horizon); *Wishing on a Star*, part of the Stellar Guild series, with Angelina Adams (Arc Manor Press); a collection of holiday stories, *A Circle of Celebrations* (WordFire Press); and her novella in the second in the Clan of the Claw series, *Tooth and Claw*.

Coming next in the pipeline is the next Myth-Adventures novel, *Myth-Fits*, scheduled for June 2016.

Over the last twenty or so years, Jody has taught in numerous writing workshops and participated on hundreds of panels covering the subjects of writing and being published at science-fiction conventions. She has also spoken in schools and libraries around the north and north-west suburbs. In 2007 she taught fantasy writing at Columbia College Chicago. She also runs the two-day writers workshop at DragonCon.

Jody lives in the northwest suburbs of Chicago, with her husband Bill Fawcett, a writer, game designer, military historian and book packager, and a black cat, Jeremy.

Check out her websites at www.jodynye.com and mythadventures.net. She is on Facebook as Jody Lynn Nye and Twitter @JodyLynnNye.

David Lee Summers is the author of ten novels and numerous short stories and poems. His novels include *Owl Dance*, a wild west steampunk adventure which tells the story of a microscopic alien swarm manipulating events in 1877 New Mexico, and *The Solar Sea*, which imagines the first voyage to the outer planets aboard a solar sail spacecraft. His short stories and poems have appeared in such magazines and anthologies as *Realms of Fantasy*, *Cemetery Dance*, and *Human Tales*. In addition to writing, David edited the quarterly science fiction and fantasy magazine *Tales of the Talisman* for ten years and has edited three science fiction anthologies: *A Kepler's Dozen, Space Pirates* and *Space Horrors*. When not working with the written word, David operates telescopes at Kitt Peak National Observatory. Learn more about David at davidleesummers.com

Jean Marie Ward writes fiction, nonfiction and everything in between, including novels (2008 Indie Book double-finalist *With Nine You Get Vanyr*) and art books. Her stories appear in numerous anthologies, such as *Athena's Daughters, The Clockwork Universe: Steampunk vs. Aliens*, and *Tales from the Vatican Vaults*. The former editor of *Crescent Blues*, she is a frequent contributor of video interviews and short subjects to BuzzyMag.com. Her website is JeanMarieWard.com.

Jeff Young is a bookseller first and a writer second—although he wouldn't mind a reversal of fortune. He received a Writers of the Future award for "Written in Light" which appears in the *26th L.Ron Hubbard's Writers of the Future* anthology. Jeff has contributed to the anthologies *By Any Means, Best Laid Plans, Dogs of War, In an Iron Cage: The Magic of Steampunk, Clockwork Chaos* and *Fantastic Futures 13*, as well as the upcoming anthologies *Gaslight and Grimm* and *The Ministry of Extraordinary Weapons*. He is the editor for the Drunken Comic Book Monkey line for Fortress Publishing as well as the anthology *TV Gods*. He has led the Watch the Skies SF&F Discussion Group of Camp Hill and Harrisburg for thirteen years.

About the Editors

Award-winning author and editor **Danielle Ackley-McPhail** has worked both sides of the publishing industry for longer than she cares to admit. Currently, she is a project editor and promotions manager for Dark Quest Books and has recently started her own press, eSpec Books.

She is the senior editor of the *Bad-Ass Faeries* anthology series, *Dragon's Lure, In an Iron Cage, The Society for the Preservation of CJ Henderson*, and *The Side of Good / The Side of Evil*.

Danielle lives in New Jersey with husband and fellow writer, Mike McPhail, and two extremely spoiled cats. She can be found on Facebook (Danielle Ackley-McPhail) and Twitter (DMcPhail). To learn more about her work, visit www.sidhenadaire.com.

Diana Bastine is presently a free-lance author and editor living in the mountains of NC. She is the author of the YA fantasy series consisting of *The Source, Shapeshifter,* and *Selkie*. These novels, and the final, previously unpublished volume, *Gabriel's Secret*, will be released by Double Dragon e-books in 2016.

Diana is known to her friends and family as the "Fairy CatMother" and sells t-shirts and tote bags with this logo. She is a certified Reiki Master/Teacher as well, and practices other forms of energy healing, including Crystal Energy Therapy and Energetic Cord Cutting. Diana loves to read, knit and improve her brain! She loves puzzles of all sorts, including jigsaws, math and logic puzzles, and word puzzles of every variety. She enjoys exercising first thing in the morning, eating healthy foods and swears her only vice is 85% and up dark chocolate...

About the Artist

Dustin Blottenberger learned his love of carving from his father, a woodworker. Dustin works in various media, but focuses on print-making, painting, and blacksmithing. In 2014, he and Brigitte Winter co-founded No Discipline Arts Collective (NDAC), an informal collective of artists, writers, and art-lovers. He also writes short-form fiction and is at work on a fantasy novel that features hairless dog-people and man-eating forests. He was most recently published in the December Issue of 101Fiction (101fiction.com).

You can find him on Twitter, Tumblr and Wordpress: @NeverSay-Dustin.